NOTES FROM SMALL PLANETS

Nate Crowley is the author of a slowly increasing pile of books, and is an editor for PC gaming website Rock Paper Shotgun. He lives in Walsall with his partner Ashleigh, his daughter, and a bunch of crabs and lizards and stuff, plus a cat he insists on calling Turkey Boy. He likes cooking stews, having baths, thinking about the sea, and getting way too into strategy games. You can find him on twitter as @frogcroakley, where he'll talk to you about all sorts of interesting things, or maybe even tell you a joke.

🐦 @frogcroakley
www.nate-crowley.com

NOTES
from
SMALL
PLANETS

Nate Crowley

HARPER
Voyager

Harper*Voyager*
An imprint of HarperCollins*Publishers* Ltd
1 London Bridge Street
London SE1 9GF

www.harpercollins.co.uk

First published by HarperCollins*Publishers* Ltd 2020
1

A catalogue record for this book is available
from the British Library

ISBN: 978-0-00-830686-1

Printed and bound in the UK by CPI Group (UK) Ltd,
Croydon CR0 4YY

For Thalassa
I hope you find magic wherever you look.

CONTENTS

KEY TO SYMBOLS

KEY TO SYMBOLS IN THIS BOOK

 Why?

 'Can't Miss' Experiences

 Region by Region

 A Brief History

 Today

 Climate and Terrain

 Wildlife

 People

 When To Visit

 Getting Around

 Eating and Drinking

 Currency

 Don't Forget to Pack

 Manners and Etiquette

 Itinerary

8

PUBLISHER'S NOTE

As you will know, for a short period some years ago, hundreds of new planets became accessible to mankind. The Worlds, as they were called, were places where magic appeared to be real; where humans lived alongside strange creatures, and where the impossible was commonplace. Until last year, it was thought that not a single piece of travel writing about the Worlds had survived. And then, in a filing cabinet acquired from the bankruptcy of a small London vanity press, we found *Notes From Small Planets*. It was the work of one Floyd Watt, a former diplomat, journalist and television personality, who had hoped to rekindle his fame with this extraordinary travel guide. But Floyd fell into a bitter dispute with his editor, Eliza Salt, and just eight chapters into his work, he went missing. Eliza herself disappeared two weeks later, and shortly after, the Worlds themselves vanished. Floyd, Eliza and *Notes* were all forgotten.

At least now, incomplete though it is, this work has finally seen the light of day. For fidelity's sake, we have reproduced Floyd and Eliza's marginalia as footnotes; their robust exchange of views only add colour to an already vivid account, of lands at once exotic and strangely familiar. In the pages that follow, you will learn about the cultures, the landscapes and the histories of eight worlds we shall never visit again. We've even taken the liberty of including excerpts from Floyd's own notebooks, and commissioned maps and illustrations based on his own . . . spirited sketches. Floyd might not be the chronicler we would have chosen for these lands, but he's what we've got. And though we can't follow physically in his footsteps, we have done all we can to make the journey as easy as possible for the mind's eye. So, *bon voyage*: and as Floyd himself was so fond of saying, 'Don't think about any of it too hard.'

— Happy travels

INTRODUCTION
by Floyd Watt

Hail traveller, and well met!

I wanted to start by telling you a little about myself and my career. However, I can't, since my esteemed editor Ms Eliza Salt has cut the lot, on the basis that this was 'a guidebook, not [my] fucking autobiography'. Charming.[1] It was only sixteen pages – barely touching on my diplomatic work, let alone my time in the national press – but there we go. No point in crying over spilt life lessons, eh?

No indeed, reader. Why dawdle in what's gone before, when there's so much ahead of you? And gosh, there is a *lot* ahead. The Worlds are . . . well. People say a lot of things about the Worlds, but as with so many things in life, the best way to find out is to jump in without really listening to what anyone says, and learn by getting your hands well and truly dirty.

That's been my *modus operandi* ever since my school days at Saint Beef's Academy for the Brave (ah, halcyon youth . . .), and it's always seen me land on my feet, no matter how dicey the situation. Whether by my charm, wits or wealth of 'street smarts',[2] I've made my way safely through every one of my globe-trotting adventures. And now, intrepid reader, all of that hard-fought experience is yours to draw on, via this handy little volume.

Before you do dive head-first into the Worlds, however, I will offer you one stern word of warning. While you'll find much in the Worlds to delight, tantalise and inspire, you'll also find plenty of unsavoury elements: dirty places, nasty people and repulsive customs. If you've any sense, you'll know to pluck the best from what's on offer and ignore

---

1 *Well, that's a professional way to start the book off, Floyd. – ES*

2 *Not to mention your vast inherited wealth and sprawling old boys' network, hey? – ES*

the muck. Luckily, I've walked the path before you, so you can rely on me to separate the baddies from the goodies, and steer you away from less-pleasant locales.

Even if much about the Worlds remains a mystery, I like to think they show us just what we could achieve as a species if anything were possible. And indeed, with the sheer amount of resources and open space the Worlds offer, perhaps anything *is* possible now. It all starts with curious travellers.

So what are you waiting for? Get out there and leave some boot prints – and don't forget to bring home some good souvenirs!

— Floyd Watt

EDITORIAL NOTE
by Eliza Salt

I had once hoped to produce travel writing of my own. But we can't always choose our fortunes, so instead I've had the pleasure of editing Floyd's. I suppose he's the man for the job. Indeed, who better than a disgraced diplomat with a drinking problem and a habit of appearing on game shows whenever he runs out of money, to pen the first ever travel guide to other worlds?[1]

I shall do my level best to help him – or at least to provide damage limitation. Because although Floyd would have you believe it's my job to stop him having any 'fun' (which is rubbish, since he does what he likes no matter what I say), it really *is* my pleasure to bring you this guide. To open the door to a whole suite of other realities, both for seasoned travellers and first-timers, is one hell of a privilege. Well, a purgatory of a privilege. Exploration has not been easy, especially when you're teamed up with a man who wants to sell bootleg cigarettes to line his own pocket and starts civil wars like other people open bags of crisps.[2] But despite all of it, I feel like I've learned something important.

Like Floyd, I think the Worlds outlined here really *do* show what we could achieve as a species; both good *and* bad. Many of them, indeed, are brimming with hope, excitement and frivolity. But even the cheeriest among them still reflect our own history, whether through their propensity toward war, their glorification of colonial endeavour, or their harsh enforcement of gender 'ideals'. They've taught me that, even in places where magic is real and resources are virtually limitless, people will still find reasons to be complete shits to one another. It's a good

---

1 I'm a retired diplomat, thanks. And I'll thank you to remember that I appeared on *Noel's Dog Food Challenge* for charity.

2 Entirely unfair. Those pirates were desperate for smokes, and there has only been the one civil war – which I thought we had agreed not to mention???

reminder that sometimes, you have to stop finding excuses to explain away the things that aren't right - either with yourself or the society you live in - and start to just *make things better*.

In your journey through the Worlds, maybe you'll find the same, and see not just the wonders, but the places where we can learn from reflections of our own mistakes. You'll also, no doubt, have plenty of opportunities to learn from Floyd's mistakes as well. The man's a disaster.[1]

Good luck.

— Eliza Salt

---

1 Cheers for that.

CHAPTER ONE
Mittelvelde

1. WELCOME TO MITTELVELDE

Mittelvelde is fantasy. Packed with folk just human enough to socialise with, but not quite too human to stab, it's the quintessential escapist destination. Its mountains are vast and icy, its woods deep and dark, and its Orcs intimidating yet reassuringly defeated. It's a place both strange and familiar: no matter where you wander in this myth-clogged land, you won't feel lost.

? Why Mittelvelde?

Mittelvelde was one of the first of the Worlds to be discovered, and to many it still can't be beaten. Its enduring popularity is thanks in part to its unique cultures, and in part to its mind-shattering landscapes: from the sun-dappled lowlands of Rannewicke to the forbidding caverns of Kranagar, this land leaks grandeur like the back end of a poorly cat leaks shit.

There are critics who say the place has lost its shine already, becoming the epitome of the 'beaten track'. And there's some truth in this: especially with the Elves gone, the place has taken on a definite 'death of magic' vibe. Mythical creatures – once so common they would beg for food at campsites – are getting thin on the ground, and genuine Wizards are now outnumbered by bedraggled con men looking to string people along for drug money.

But the wonder is still there, if you know where to look. With the possible exception of the region known as Fysteros[1] – where magic is dead but the body's still being kicked – Mittelvelde is still rife with hidden

---

1 Fysteros has – in my view – become little more than a cheesy, blood-soaked parody of itself at this point. I mean, honestly, there's just no need for that much violence, even if it brings the cash in. How do they keep finding new pretenders to the throne at this point? What's in it for these people?

gems.[1] And it's only becoming easier to see the best of this world. The infrastructure projects being pushed by the Bison King of Tharn have fostered a burgeoning tourist economy, while his victory in the War of the Haunted Mace – and the consequent signing of the Pact of Grimlakk – has opened up the 'exotic'[2] Orcish culture to travellers.

Mittelvelde remains a timeless destination, and a perennial classic: if you want to travel in fantastic worlds, you owe it to yourself to see this one first.

WHY I LOVE MITTELVELDE
by Keith Swiftblade, tour guide & ranger

I've spent three years in Mittelvelde, and it already feels like home. I used to be a recruitment consultant, but these days I'm more at home tracking Ettins across the plains of Syrillar than cajoling people into office jobs. There's just nothing like watching a sunrise over the shattered stones of an Elven beacon for lifting the spirits, and there's no better night out than mead and roast venison in the halls of the Bison King. But most of all, I love the proud and traditional nature of the Mittelvelder people themselves. This is a land so tangled in myth you can't walk ten feet without meeting someone whose great grandfather kicked the guts out of an Orc warlord, and who has a twelve-verse drinking song to commemorate the occasion. If you've ever felt burdened with the sensation that your life is a bit empty, Mittelvelde will rejuvenate you: here, even getting up in the middle of the night to piss feels faintly epic. My friend, this destination bows to no other.

---

1 Often literally, if you take the opportunity to stay with Dwarves. They're obsessed with hiding gems.

2 *Floyd, you realise putting this in quotation marks just makes you look like a bigot? – ES*

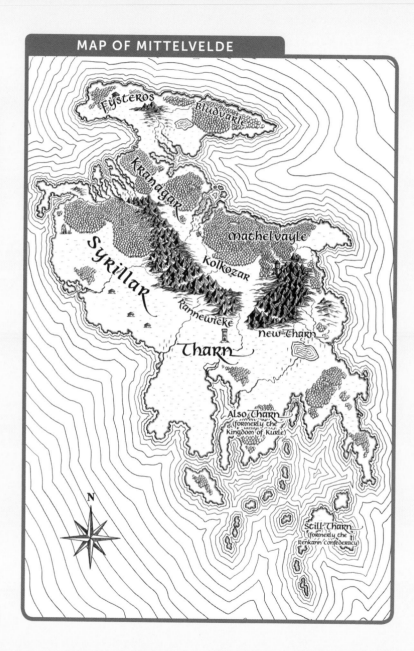

1 Duel a dragon

Nothing typifies the fantasy experience more than going toe to toe with a ten-ton reptile that *absolutely loves money*. And while dragons might be scarcer than they used to be,[1] a decent guide can still track one down for you. It's not the safest pursuit, but with mercenary bands growing more affordable and fire-resistance charms widely available, it's an increasingly survivable business.[2] Advanced excursionists may even wish to attempt the latest trend in adventure travel: pretending to be a Wizard and bullying a group of hapless nobodies into a harrowing cross-continental odyssey, before making them fight a dragon while you basically just watch.

2 Meet a long-forgotten heir to a throne

Mittelvelde is a land bristling with ancient kingdoms, and each one has an impossibly convoluted line of succession. Add to that the absolute spaghetti nest of prophecies about great leaders, and a crowded tavern on any given night has about a 30 per cent chance of containing a secret monarch, complete with a tattered cloak and an air of smouldering nobility. Desperate for followers, these types make excellent – and cheap – tour guides, and at the very least are always good for a photo opportunity.

3 Witness an epic battle between good and evil

The best time for witnessing giant battles was a while back, during the War of the Haunted Mace. Still, even with the Duke of Night dead and most of her Orcs rehabilitated, plenty of copycat warlords have sprung up in recent years, raiding the edges of the noble Bison King's

---

1 And their hoards increasingly comprise cheap watches looted from other unfortunate tourists.

2 Please, though, forget the cheap Fysterosi 'slayer ranches': a chance to fight a dragon for the price of a mid-range meal may sound enticing, but when you're handed a length of chain by a jaded knight smoking a roll-up and given two minutes to go mental on a heavily sedated alligator, you will feel nothing but shame. Believe me.

EPOCHAL STRUGGLE

The sixth, seventh, eighth and ninth ages of Mittelvelde have been defined by conflicts in which humans, Elves and Dwarves have banded together to defend their lands from a series of increasingly large maniacs in spiky armour. These Orc warlords always have a similar MO:

1: Forge an enchanted weapon.

2: Scrape together a legion of Orcs and Goblins, garnished with whatever monsters they can scare up from the badlands.

3: Take a big swing at decent civilisation.

The last of these conflicts – the War of the Haunted Mace – was the fault of Yattan-Gur, the Duke of Night,[1] an Orcish sorceress who raised an army a hundred-thousand strong to carry out her will. However, despite the Duke's dreaded machinery at Gollimmar, and the ghostly bludgeon she wielded (which gave the war its name), the Forces of Good prevailed in the end. Thanks to the Bison King's bravery,[2] the Haunted Mace was shattered, robbing the Orcs of its hideous strength, and the Duke's generals – led by the repentant Orc chieftain Grimlakk – turned on their dark mistress, boiling her alive.[3] It was a great day for Good.

---

1 They say Yattan-Gur means 'final liberator' in Orcish, but by 'they' I mean Orcs, so do take it with a pinch of salt.

2 With the Elves slowly vanishing from the world, and the Dwarves increasingly focused on digging holes, the Forces of Good pretty much boiled down to the Bison King and his vassals this time round.

3 Again, the Orcs say the mace was a piece of powerful healing technology and call Grimlakk 'the traitor general' – it's a sobering indictment of just how badly brainwashed they were by the Duke.

realm.[1] Reprisals are common, and tour operators can arrange viewings at a safe distance, with a chance to loot the battlefield for souvenirs afterwards. In Fysteros, of course, battles are virtually a daily occurrence – although since both sides are almost always made up of complete bastards, there's rarely any sense of 'good versus evil' to them.

4 Find a cursed trinket

Mittelvelde's history isn't all on parchment – it's written in the soil and the rock, with layers of dungeons and catacombs that date back to the earliest ages of the world. And as any connoisseur of fantasy travel knows, dungeons mean treasure: just half an hour's rummaging through cobwebbed bones will likely win you a mysterious heirloom, with a grim enchantment to boot.[2] It's all luck of the draw – you might find a crown that turns the wearer into a ghost or an amulet that whispers playground insults at night. Who knows? Maybe you'll lose your mind, run off to live in a cave and spend decades crooning obsessively to an enchanted hair clip. It's all part of the fun.

Region by Region

Of Mittelvelde's landmasses, the largest by far is the continent of Tinnethaine. While another major continent far to the west is also rumoured to exist – the Elvish homeland of Larathainne – its viability as a destination is complicated by the fact that it's partially a metaphor. Tinnethaine, which is much easier to understand, is split up into the following regions:

---

1 Of course, there are plenty of dullards in exile who question whether the Bison King was ever truly 'good' in the first place. However, since his troops wore silver armour and fought Orcs in obsidian mail, (*and especially since he was kind enough to offer you use of a summer villa in New Tharn, right? – ES*) the ethics of the situation seem pretty bloody clear to me.

2 *Just for the record, Floyd, this is not even the first time in this, the first chapter of your guidebook, that you've given the thumbs up to the looting of dead bodies as a leisure activity. – ES*

1 Tharn

Tharn's lush grasslands are the original territory of the famed Bison King, the most powerful human ruler in Mittelvelde. His new capital at Bannahirr might be controversial to some,[1] but it's first-class for luxury, thanks to wealth liberated from the former territories of the Duke of Night.

2 Rannewicke

Tharnish vassal state: very rural. Think pigs, wheelbarrows and old men roaring in dank pubs. All forests guaranteed non-haunted, except for mysterious roadmen who sing nearly incessantly. Ideal for those who want fantasy without even the mildest of peril.[2]

3 Kolkozar

Kolkozar, the queendom of the Dwarves, sprawls beneath the mighty Wyrmryggrad mountains, and can be about as fun to holiday in as a working mine. Because that's what it is. But for those in the know, it's also got a reputation as Mittelvelde's ultimate nightlife destination.[3]

4 New Tharn

New Tharn is where most Orcs and Goblins live, and it was the Duke of Night's capital during the war. Even under the Bison King's generous rule,[4] it hasn't quite recovered: the liberated Orcs still live in gargantuan slums, while the sky is dark with smog from the Duke's reclaimed war forges, built on the volcanic highlands of Gollimmar. There's no doubt, though: New Tharn is on the up and up, and could be next year's hottest destination.

5 Mathelvayle

Once the great garden of the Elves, Mathelvayle has become overgrown by a vast, dense forest since their departure, and is now home to giant talking centipedes, renegade Orcs and all manner of beasts. It's rough, tough country, but it's the last word in gloomy fantasy forests.

---

1 *Given that it's basically a big theme park built by what amounts to slave labour, perhaps? – ES*

2 They also grow an awful lot of weed here, so it's a popular hangout for Wizards.

3 This is partially because it's always night underground and partially because the Dwarven metabolism runs on ethanol, meaning that keeping up with them requires a teenager's enthusiasm for getting piss-yourself drunk.

4 And he is generous: just last month he set aside a new fund to put up statues of himself all over New Tharn, to replace all the smashed ones of the Duke.

6 Syrillar

On the coastal plain of Syrillar sits Alethiar, the long-deserted capital of the Elves. And while the weird immortals who built it are still sighted there from time to time, the savannah beyond its walls is blissfully empty.

7 Kranagar

After the collapse of the Dwarven queendom that flourished there, this underground metropolis is now hopelessly tangled with Tinnethaine's dungeonsphere. Once, only die-hard adventure tourists would consider plundering its depths, but these days – especially since the establishment of Descensus as an adventure-sports capital – it's overrun by group bookings.

8 Fysteros

Fysteros is a grim, dark land isolated from the rest of Mittelvelde, comprising seven human-only kingdoms, whose inhabitants spend all their time squabbling over a metal chair. And with the coffers of the ruling houses so exhausted by constant war, you can be *sure* it's packed with tourist-traps.

9 Bludvarle

If Fysteros is bad, Bludvarle is worse. A dismal arse-beard of tundra trailing out into the arctic sea, it is peopled by frostbitten hulks who seem to exist only to constantly invade Fysteros. Unless you are desperately into ice fishing or starvation, there's little reason to visit Bludvarle.

2. UNDERSTANDING MITTELVELDE

A Brief History

There's no way to give a brief history of Mittelvelde. That's not hyperbole – it's genuinely impossible. The world's past is divided up into (probably) nine ages, each of which have their own sets of gods, cultures and languages. Nonetheless, it's worth knowing the very basics.

Mittelvelde Today

As a new tenth age blossoms following the war, Mittelvelde is on the up and up. As part of the peace treaty known as the Pact of Grimlakk, the Orc territory of Takkna's Land has been liberated and ceded to the Bison King, who has renamed it New Tharn. Under his benevolent hand, the Duke's war forges are being put to good use making consumer goods, providing honest work for the region's Orcs and Goblins. Also, as a stipulation of the pact, the Bison King has secured a guarantee of safety for all tourists in Mittelvelde, and so communities that would have ripped tourists limb from limb just ten years ago are now hugely welcoming. Thanks to the Bison King, it's a great time to visit Mittelvelde.[1]

Climate and Terrain

None of Mittelvelde's landscapes do things in half measures. Its forests are ancient and gnarled, its mountains stately and eagle-haunted. Even the humming swamplands down south are majestic in a way, if

---

1 *Floyd – I know we've discussed, but . . . don't you think your coverage of the King seems just a little biased? Does all this have anything to do with that villa? And just why has the Bison King been inclined to do so many favours for you? – ES*

you find the reek of wet guffs awe-inspiring. Geographers say Mittelvelde's layout makes no sense whatsoever from a theoretical standpoint, with mountains arranged contrary to all understanding of geology and rivers chucked onto the map like a bunch of tired blue worms. But who cares? It looks absolutely smashing on a map, doesn't it?[1] A warmer, drier climate prevails in the western plains of Syrillar, cooling to temperate as one enters the southern lands of the Bison King, while subarctic conditions can be found in the far south, as well as in the highlands and mountains of Kolkozar and Kranagar. The northern subcontinent of Fysteros has its own, peculiarly volatile climate that pays little heed to conditions in the rest of Tinnethaine. Summer can last years, before taking a hard swerve into a decades-long winter virtually overnight.[2] And, of course, in Bludvarle it's shit all the time.

🔆 Floyd's Tip

One big weather issue to flag is Wizards: when these fellows get into a barney over something, their mountain-top shouting matches can result in unseasonal blizzards and plagues of crows for miles around, which can absolutely destroy your picnic plans.

Wildlife

Mittelvelde's wildlife falls into two broad categories: noble beasts and monsters. The former, which range through Tinnethaine's overland, tend to be slightly more majestic versions of normal animals, while the latter dwell either in the deep woods or in the world's sprawling underlayer of dungeons. In some cases, they're just bigger versions of 'nasty' animals such as spiders or rats – but go deep enough,

---

1 And frankly, I'd only ask for a geographer's opinion if I wanted to know which brand of colouring pencil to use.

2 At the time of writing, the region is perfectly clement, but that won't stop every single inhabitant of the place offering you their own grim weather forecast at the drop of a hat. It's very repetitive.

THE AGES OF MITTELVELDE

[As summarised by Floyd, from orientation materials at the 'Welcome to Mittelvelde!' exhibition in Bannahirr's tourist information centre.]

Y0–1320: THE FIRST AGE – An incomprehensible block of mythology in which the world was created. Some Wizards claim to have been there at the time, but Wizards say a lot of things, and are usually just trying to trick you into buying them a drink.

Y1321–2419: THE SECOND AGE – Probably Dwarves?

Y2420–4068: THE THIRD AGE – Elves arrive in Tinnethaine by boats from Larathainne. Initiating trade with the Dwarves, Queen Elaheime founds the Elven capital of Alethiar, and begins working on salad recipes, or whatever it is that Elves do to pass the time.

Y4069–4849: THE FOURTH AGE – More Elf stuff, most likely. Dragons, Ettins and many other spectacular creatures start to appear in Mittelvelde.

Y4850–5400: THE FIFTH AGE – Humans arrive in Tinnethaine, led by the Bison King's ancestors, and a golden age begins. Late in the age, Fysteros is founded; the Fysterosi Civil War begins immediately.

Y5401–5832: THE SIXTH AGE – Darkness is brought into the world by Orcs and Goblins, who come out of a hole or something.[1] The first War of Inhuman Aggression is begun by Deepdark Baron

and you'll encounter creatures that feel as if a team of anxious drunks were given a long weekend to fill a bestiary. Of course, many of Mittelvelde's animal species are said to possess high intelligence, the ability to use tools, and advanced languages, leading to a growing movement to reclassify them as 'people' – but this seems a little far-fetched.[1] Dragons are a particular grey area (it's hard to dismiss

---

1 *At least, it does to people who enjoy betting on fights in the Bison King's Super Monster Arena, right Floyd? – ES*

Taschnak, whom Orcs call 'the Defiant'.[2] The Fysterosi Civil War continues.

Y5833–6712: THE SEVENTH AGE – The Bison Kingdom is founded from a collection of war-weary principalities that defended against Taschnak. This happens just in the nick of time, as the first Bison King immediately has to defend against Bloodlord Shettkro, 'the Protector', in a second great war. Elves make less of an effort to help during this one. The Fysterosi Civil War continues.

Y6713–7004: THE EIGHTH AGE – Elves begin to depart Tinnethaine, ceding land to human communities settled by the Bison King. The Dwarven kingdom of Kranagar falls to the hoard of Bugnakk 'the Avenger'. The Fysterosi Civil War continues.

Y7005–7221: THE NINTH AGE – Only a few Elvish communities remain; Dwarven culture consolidates around the ancient capital of Kolkozar. Late in the age, Mittelvelde shakes under the boots of Yattan-Gur, the Duke of Night, and the War of the Haunted Mace commences. At the last minute, the tactical genius of the Bison King turns the tide, and darkness is defeated. The Fysterosi Civil War continues.

---

1 Some Orcish scholars claim that Orcs were the original inhabitants of Mittelvelde, and that their land was subsequently carved up by successive waves of invaders – a tragic hangover of the propaganda inflicted by the Duke of Night on her once-noble subjects. Also, without wanting to sound rude, how scholarly can one really expect Orcs to be?

2 This is almost certainly a spelling mistake, and they mean 'Defiler'.

something as a big flying crocodile when it's posing you a riddle, after all), but it's only a matter of time before they're all slain anyway, putting a neat end to the question.

✳ The **Serendipiteagle** (*Aquilafelix Gigas*) is a vast bird of prey, beloved by Wizards for its ability to show up and rescue people when their lives depend on it. They're completely unreliable the rest of the time, but still worth their weight in gold in a clutch.

MITTELVELDE

✳ The noble **Glowboar** (*Sus Luminosus*) is – along with the **Elderstag** (*Cervidus Venerabilis*) and the **Dire Rabbit** (*Oryctolagus Chungus*) – one of the many regal game animals at large in the forests of Tinnethaine. It's basically a pig with glowing tusks.

✳ The **Royal Bison** (*Bison Mittelveldi Rex*) was a brilliant silver bison, standing nine-feet tall at the shoulder, which roamed the plains of Tharn in herds ten-thousand strong. They were the favoured quarry of the Bison King's ancestors. Unfortunately, they recently became extinct due to . . . cancer or something.[1]

✳ The legendary **Hörse** (*Equus Perfectus*) is identical to a normal horse, but somehow better in every way. Hörses have complex genealogies, intricate manners, and are utter snobs, refusing to allow anyone outside of royalty to ride them.[2]

✳ The **Bigwolf** (*Lupus Bastardis*) is a wolf the size of a rhino, native to the tundra of Bludvarle but kept by many nobles and knights across Fysteros. Foul tempered and prone to dropping massive, meaty turds, they're a perfect emblem for their realm.

✳ Pity the **Sparrilla** (*Gorilla Passerinus*), one of the midrange monsters commonly found in Tinnethaine's dungeons: it has the robust body of a gorilla, but the head and mind of a common domestic sparrow. Whatever Wizard created it must have been a real git.

✳ The **Eavesdropper** (*Sphaera Multiaures*) is a feared deep-dungeon monster resembling a hovering meaty sphere, with a toothy maw and hundreds of human ears arranged across its surface. It is said to particularly despise bards.

---

1 *Really. That's the best cover-up for overhunting you could come up with?*
– ES

2 Endlessly correcting people's language too. I spent the best part of an hour arguing with one about the definition of the word 'haste'.

People

Until consensus is reached on the animals/people issue, the civilised folk of Mittelvelde have been defined as those being roughly humanoid, and these are split into seven peoples.[1]

Humans

It should be pretty clear what humans are, because you probably are one.

Orcs

Big, muscular folk with grey skin and heavy jaws, the Orcs are the second-most common people in Mittelvelde. The vast majority live in huge, semi-buried hives in New Tharn, while some outlaw settlements, still loyal to the Duke, persist in the forests of Mathelvayle and the hills of Kranagar. Orcish society is largely matriarchal, and probably based around hunting and sports, I would imagine.

Goblins

These horrid things are like small, skinny Orcs, and tend to show up wherever Orcs do. They've never really been great warriors, tending instead to loiter around Orcish settlements, cooking and playing nonsensical games.[2]

Dwarves

A people of short, intensely broad stature resembling tiny, bearded wrestlers, the Dwarves are a diminished but still significant presence in the world. All female, they live in vast fortresses beneath the world's mountains, in colonies led by a handful of egg-laying queens. Completely obsessed with digging holes.

Elves

The few Elves left in the world live deep in Mathelvayle, and in ruins on the coasts of Syrillar. They are an extremely unnerving people, with clammy milk-white skin, eyes with horizontal-slit pupils, and ornate platinum antlers sprouting from their hairless heads.[1]

---

1 There used to be an eighth classification – Halblets – for the people of Rannewicke, before it was determined that they were in fact just Humans who were a bit short.

2 *Floyd, I'm not sure Goblins are what you think they are. – ES*

Needless to say, they also have pointy ears.

Wizards

Although it's hard to tell the real thing from imitations these days, Wizards are definitely . . . something. They tend to look human, although spend more than a few hours in the company of one and you will see they are anything but. Capricious and scheming, Wizards have their own weird agenda for the world, and will take extraordinary measures to see it play out. Trust them at your own risk.

IF MITTELVELDE WERE 100 PEOPLE

47 would be humans

27 would be Orcs

10 would be Goblins

8 would be Dwarves

5 would be 'the Big Lads'

2 would be Elves of various kinds

1 would inevitably be a Wizard, or at least someone pretending to be one

---

1 Frankly, I won't miss them when they're gone. Creepy bastards.

The Big Lads

There are dozens of giant humanoid species roaming Tinnethaine, from the tree-like Gargelms of Mathelvayle to the Ettins of Syrillar, and the Trolls, Ogres and Frost Giants of the mountain regions. They all maintain simple, tool-using cultures, and are generally respectful of the Pact of Grimlakk. For ease of classification, these are all lumped together under the category of 'the Big Lads'. They are mostly reasonable, with disastrous exceptions.

Some time after stopping for lunch, I caught my first glance of a fantastic humanoid. We were crawling up yet another scree-choked pass, when the cart's donkey grew agitated. Sniffing the wind, my guide sat bolt upright with alarm, and brought the cart to a dead stop. I tried to ask what was happening, but he clamped a filthy hand over my mouth and extended a wobbling finger into the blizzard ahead.

It was an Ogre – or potentially a Troll? It was hard to tell through the flurries of snow, but it was definitely that sort of thing: huge and grey and horribly muscular, like an elephant forced into the shape of a man and made to subsist on a diet of raw steak. I am fairly sure it had tusks, and it carried what appeared to be a club of some kind (possibly a big bone?) over its shoulder. Even though it must have been eighty yards away, its footfalls caused pebbles to rattle down the mountainside beside us and bounce against the cart's wheels.

For a moment I thought it was coming straight for us, and my bowels grew loose – the bloody thing would polish off our donkey like a braying kebab, then knock us back as a ghastly amuse-bouche – but then it wandered off into a side branch of the pass and disappeared. A long while after the rumble of its footsteps had subsided, my guide offered me a bleak nod, and we continued on our way.

— FROM THE TRAVEL JOURNAL OF FLOYD WATT

3. PLANNING YOUR TRIP

 ## When to Visit

Making an exception for the frankly bizarre climate of Fysteros, Mittelvelde is good to visit all year round, with no particularly punishing extremes of weather. More martially inclined travellers should take note that campaign season is in early spring, when Tharnish expeditions and Dwarven Grudging parties tend to head out into Mathelvayle to disperse camps of rogue Orcs. There are also a number of festivals that are worth catching if you can:

Larathariarien

This Elvish festival, held on the Spring Equinox, is meant to celebrate rebirth. Or death. Or boiled eggs, for all we know. Mainly it involves the last remaining Elves parading slowly through the woods, keening an eerie song and waving lanterns about. Which is all right, if you like that sort of thing.

BLAZGAN!!!!

Named after the famous Dwarven battle cry,[1] this midwinter extravaganza – also known as 'opposites week' – totally transforms Dwarven society. After a year of backbreaking labour, the Dwarves blow off steam by spending a week acting in the most undwarvenly manner possible. They are idle, overly polite, and eat and drink completely reasonably, giving them a rare respite from the thundering hangovers that otherwise accompany a life of hard liquor and heavy industry.

Bisontide

Bisontide, an event celebrating the defeat of the Duke of Night, is held four times each year, and participation is mandatory for all citizens of Tharn and its vassal kingdoms. Bisontide customs include the smashing by children of large paper-mâché Orc effigies and the bellowing of incredibly

---

1 It roughly translates as 'Party Time'

aggressive 'carols' in pubs. All in all, a great family day out.[1]

The Grand Old Duke of Orcs,
She had ten-thousand Orcs
She marched them up to the top of
  the hill
And we slaughtered them for the
  glory of the Bison King
All hail the Bison King.
— **Popular Bisontide Carol**

Blood of the Children

For many years, it was presumed that the Orcish summer festival of *Bruhz-nur*, or Blood of the Children, was some kind of monstrous carnival of infanticide. Now that visitors are finally being allowed in to witness the ceremony, however, it turns out to be a weird contest in which Goblins gather to show off their talents before elder Orcs. Apparently, to the Orcs, *Bruhz* means blood in the sense of vim and vigour when used in the genitive case, rather than actual, y'know, violence juice.[2] Still, it's odd that the event's name references children when there's none to be seen at the festival itself – just Goblins. Where do the Orcs keep their kids, anyway?[3]

 # Getting Around

Most of Mittelvelde is best experienced at walking pace, although cart services run between most of the major destinations, especially south of Kolkozar.[4] Horses and other steeds are available for daily hire, though it's worth noting that the small woolly rhinoceroses favoured by the Dwarves are famously intolerant of male riders.[5]

---

1 *Apart from Orc families, I presume? – ES*

2 *A likely story.*

3 *Oh for fuck's sake, Floyd. You have to be kidding, right? You can't seriously think . . . OK, never mind, it's almost funny how much you've missed the obvious here. – ES*

4 Whatever you say about the Bison King, you can't deny he's made the carts run on time. I respect that.

5 Please don't learn this the hard way, like I did.

RULES AND REGULATIONS

At the start of any trip to Mittelvelde you'll need to report to the Bison King's capital of Bannahirr in order to procure the right travel documentation. On arrival, you'll head to the Visitor Orientation Meadhall for a quick briefing and security check by the Bison King's special knights[1] – mainly, they'll be no bother at all and will just want to check you're not planning on bringing contraband to any Orcish settlements. After that you'll be free to party the night away at any one of the city's sanctioned Revelry Areas, before tucking yourself in for bed at the brand new Grand Bisonia Hotel, a . . . marvellous edifice, which stands as testament to the King's burgeoning love affair with concrete. While you're there, why not take in one of the astonishing military parades held by the King's men at arms, visit the city's Monster Zoo[2] or watch one of the Wizard Shows? They are all excellent value.

---

1 *That'll be his secret police, then. – Eliza*

2 It's only half a groat to throw rocks at an Ogre stooped in a muddy cage, but you'll feel a bit bad afterwards.

 ## Eating and Drinking

Being largely a medieval-ish world, you'd be forgiven for assuming Mittelvelde's food was nothing to write home about. But due in part to the superbly fertile landscape and in part to the prevalence of hearth magic in even the humblest kitchens, the bog-standard peasant kibble here is sublime. And if you've got the gold to splash out on fresh food, fine drinks and exotic meats, you can eat like the Bison King himself.

MITTELVELDE'S
BEST BARS and RESTAURANTS

The Bisonhall: *For a reasonable pre-arranged donation, travellers can dine in the style of the Bison King himself, sampling vintage meads and meaty delights from across the realm, at the heart of the capital. Although the signature dish of silver bison is no longer available, and you can no longer eat in the King's actual hall (the new venue is a larger replica with more table space, and has a rotating cast of bards playing the man himself), it's still a must-see.*

💡 Floyd's Tip

Keep your diet carnivorous around Gargelms, the gigantic tree people of the forest, or eat nothing at all. Chomping an apple in front of one of these folks is the equivalent of sitting down for lunch with a human and taking a big, cheerful bite out of a bollock. Massive party foul; they'll flatten you.

Nourishment Depot Seven: *Meat's not been on the menu for some time at this austere cafeteria for the working Orcs of New Tharn, but if you want a genuine taste of greyskin food, this is the place. The portions of fried bogworm and bloddtuber mash are truly warrior-sized, designed to sustain an Orc's burly frame during an eighteen-hour shift at the forges. And, of course, it's all washed down with gallons of the potent local liquor, Grak. Joyously authentic, especially when the locals sing their welcome song.*[1]

Illeiythan: *Named after the Elvish word for 'enjoy yourself,' this luxury game ranch at the heart of Syrillar – part of a new chain based in Bannahirr – offers a smorgasbord of BBQ big game*[2] *served up by quaint Orc serving staff in traditional 'warrior's' garb. Of course, there are no*

---

1 *It's a protest song, Floyd. – ES*
2 And I really mean big – the elephants out there are preposterously large.

actual Elves here, but the decor is inspired by their spires of living silver, and there's a good selection of wines looted from the cellars of Alethiar.

The Authentic Lord Bleakheart's Death Nuptuals Experience: *The Fysterosi capital of Calthang's Keep is perhaps most famous for the infamous Death Nuptuals of Lord Bleakheart, a wedding feast at which fully half the guests were massacred in a culmination of years of brutal realpolitik. Now, after unprecedented demand from tourists, the Death Nuptuals are re-enacted twice a month: the feasts can run in excess of seventy courses, and inevitably end with the revelation that one of the dishes contained human meat, at which point the murders usually start. Guests are always guaranteed safety amid the massacre – but even so, it's not for those with weak stomachs.*

Currency

While all of Mittelvelde's peoples have their own currencies, travellers can cover themselves by converting their money into gold or one of the standard Dwarven alloys such as dwarronium. As part of his modernisation agenda, the Bison King has recently standardised currency across the many vassal kingdoms of Tharn, and Bison Groats are now accepted in all human territories.

DAILY SAMPLE COSTS

BUDGET: Less than 50 Bison Groats
Overnight stay in a peasant's hog shed: **12 BG**
Evening meal of potato stew and ale: **8 BG**
Guide for an afternoon in Rannewicke (songs included): **18 BG**
Ticket to jeer at a captured Goblin in the stocks: **4 BG**

MIDRANGE: 50–120 Bison Groats
Dwarven guest cell and oil lighting: **35 BG**
Roast cave salamander and Dwarven wine: **18 BG**
Guards for a delve into the deep: **42 BG**
Decent seat at the bat fights: **15 BG**

TOP END: More than 120 Bison Groats

Bison-class suite at the Grand Bisonia Hotel in Bannahirr:
100 BG

Dragon loin sautéed with semi-illegal Gargelm fronds: **80 BG**

Company of mercenaries to lead into battle: **240 BG**

Raven flight from Bannahirr to Alethiar: **94 BG**

 # Don't Forget to Pack . . .

Old-school clothes

In terms of gear, any travellers in Mittelvelde should wear medieval garments, if only to avoid funny looks,[1] so it's worth investing in a couple of tunics at least, and maybe some chainmail if you're planning on starting trouble.

Basic medicines

Mittelvelde is actually a fairly great place to get seriously ill or injured, as the magical healing offered by Wizards is, while pricey, nothing short of miraculous.[2] Nevertheless, basic medical needs are either not met at all or are covered by ludicrous local practices, such as the horrific Orcish custom of 'healing ants'.[3] Stock up.

Orc treats

If you're one of the increasing number of people embarking on homestay trips with traditional Orc communities, make sure you bring gifts, as it is customary for Orcs to exchange favours before and after being hosted. Without knowing exactly what Orcs like, you're probably safe packing some manky blood, a dead scorpion or something equally horrible.[4]

---

1 Except in Fysteros, where of course anything goes. You could show up there in a tracksuit if you were gauche enough.

2 Unless you get rinsed by a fraud, that is. After the incident with the Dwarven rhino thing, I got sewn up by a local chancer posing as an Archmage, who was making up spells as he went along. I ended up with two arses for a fortnight, until a genuine Wizard charged me 80 Bison Groats to correct the work.

3 *Maybe the Orcs might have better medical technology if the Bison King hadn't taken literally everything from them? I dunno, just a thought. – ES*

4 *They're actually really keen on Turkish Delight, if you ask them. – ES*

Know your ancestry

Genealogy is a massive deal for pretty much every culture in Mittelvelde. When introducing yourself, you should be able to rattle off at least two layers of 'son of/daughter of', so make sure you're either well acquainted with your family history or a consistent bullshitter. Because make no mistake: you will be quizzed.

Remember that Elves have weird manners

Trying to interact normally with Elves is a nightmare. Eye contact is either grossly offensive or mandatory, depending on the height of the sun, and different hand gestures are required when greeting members of any one of Elven society's sixty-three castes.

Try not to notice the Dwarven accent

For some reason, any translation software you care to use will interpret Dwarven speech as a mangled parody of a Scottish accent, with every term of address translated as 'laddie'. Nobody knows why, and it can't be helped. But for pity's sake, don't laugh. As far as the Dwarves are concerned they speak like yacht-club billionaires, and they really don't like it when people giggle.[1]

Don't mention the war

It's always worth remembering that the War of the Haunted Mace didn't end too long ago and has left many cultural sore spots. Especially in mixed company, you'll want to avoid getting into political discussions about the conflict, so as to avoid any . . . *orcwardness*. Even in human-only groups, you may encounter unsavoury detractors of the Bison King, and even some who claim he wouldn't have won the war at all without the shipment of assault rifles that mysteriously appeared in Bannahirr at the last minute,[2] but these bitter agitators just aren't worth your time.

---

1 A further warning: Dwarven hugs are awkward. For a start, the height differential results in a very difficult chin-to-crotch dynamic, and then they go on for ages. Not just a moment or two too long – an entire minute or more, in total silence save for the occasional companionable grunt.

2 *Yeah, it was weird that. Wasn't anything to do with you, Floyd, was it? – ES*

4. SUGGESTED ITINERARIES

 1: A JOURNEY IN THE DARK: (1 Week)

Rannewicke to Mathelvayle, via the Underground

This trip offers a smorgasbord of Mittelveldian delights, taking travellers from the creature comforts of Rannewicke to the homely, bone-adorned chic of the Orcs, via the splendour of the Dwarven capital.

DAY 1

After arrival in Rannewicke, you'll tour a series of villages on an extremely slow pony cart, in order to endure a series of punishingly substantial rustic lunches with the stout, simple locals. The day will inevitably end with a party[1] whose nature can vary: sometimes it's a village-square spectacular with fireworks and an old geezer who vanishes during a speech, sometimes it's a load of vengeful Dwarves conducting a home invasion. Either way, you'll eat your head's weight in cake.

DAY 2

Following a famous Rannewicke breakfast, you'll enjoy a second, third and maybe even a fourth famous Rannewicke breakfast[2] until early evening, when you'll head to the famous Borked Orc Inn[3] for the night. During the war, this boarding house became notorious for cowled spectres showing up in the middle of the night to stab people, and while it's totally safe now, it's worth checking for sword-marks on the floorboards of your room. It's also the place where the party of heroes that

---

1 Which you may or may not expect.

2 It largely depends on whether you're able to wake from your feast-slumber before your hosts begin packing the next meal into your mouth.

3 So named for its sign, a graphic illustration of an Orc getting brained by an unsmiling knight, which has taken on a controversial air since the end of the war.

TROLL YOUR KIDS

Those with kids to take care of might also want to consider hiring one of Rannewicke's friendly Trolls to 'kidnap' their progeny and threaten them with a roasting over a campfire. At a signal pre-arranged with the Big Lad, the crafty parent can then spring from the darkness, 'fighting off' the Troll and becoming a hero to their child for ever. The experience also gifts any parent with a credible 'if you don't behave, the Trolls will get you again' threat that will stay good for years. Worth its weight in gold.

finally destroyed the Haunted Mace was assembled, and these days it's crowded with wild-eyed wannabes hoping for another war to break out.

DAY 3

On the third day, you'll join a goods caravan headed north to Kolkozar City – the capital of the Dwarves, beneath the Wyrmryggrad mountains. At the trading post of Zoj, you'll be loaded aboard a train of colossal bronze minecarts, which will then be dragged underground by a gang of *Blozzh*, the enormous flightless bats used as beasts of burden by the Dwarves.[1] Spend the journey learning the off-key working dirges of the train crew and marvelling at the glow-crabs on the tunnel ceiling. When you finally arrive at Kolkozar central station, experience a traditional Dwarven welcome of ceremonial headbutting, before settling down in your guest grotto, or potentially the city hospital.

DAY 4

After a traditional Dwarven breakfast of fried worldsump mushrooms and a pint of chilled owl blood, it'll be time to meet with your personal guide for a gruellingly in-depth tour of Kolkozar's forge works and smelting

---

1 It's worth bringing some air freshener, as Blozzh seem to fart constantly and the tunnels are pretty close. Nobody enjoys retching on bat guff, after all.

plants.[1] Once you're done (or you find a way to make it stop), head down the deep tunnels to the royal menagerie, where you can see troglofauna such as rockchomper grubs, albino cavern lemurs, and even the great olms in their stalagmite-choked pools. When the city begins to bustle with the evening-shift changeover, rent some ceremonial chainmail and a false beard, and head to the Grand Kolkozar Opera to see the Military Choir recite a classic folk dirge. Alternatively, book a space in the public galleries for the Queen's nightly banquet, or grab a few cans and head to the bat fights.[2] Whatever you do, you're in for a severe ale monstering.

DAY 5

Hangover.

DAY 6

Once you've recovered, you'll be mounting up with a platoon of Dwarven cavalry and heading north out the other side of the Wyrmryggrads to the forest of Mathelvayle. Your hosts will be out on a Grudging, a traditional raid in the style of the Dwarves' old Orc-hunting expeditions. These days, however, Grudgings are strictly non-lethal affairs, funded by the Bison King and tasked with dispersing unlawful camps of Orcs and Goblins in the deep woods, before resettling them in permitted townships at the forest's edge.[3] Make camp with the Dwarves for the night and shake your head in disbelief that they're drinking again.

DAY 7

After bidding farewell to the Dwarves (tourists are not permitted to

---

1 The tour is truly relentless, and guides tend to have no filter whatsoever. As far as they're concerned, it's inconceivable that anyone could not be obsessed with mining. Expect to take in hours of degree-level knowledge of techniques for ore extraction, slag disposal and heat transfer (some of it in song), as well as chillingly detailed 'fun' anecdotes about every industrial accident over the last few decades.

2 A Dwarven bookie will 100 per cent ask if you fancy 'a little flutter' on the outcome of a fight. It will be funny the first time.

3 They're much safer on the edge of the plains, where the Bison King can look after them, than in the dangerous depths of the wood.

— TESTIMONIAL —

Even though they're still living by the rugged customs of their ancestors, I'm a huge fan of the back-to-basics authenticity that comes with living at home with Orcs. There's just so much to learn from the quiet dignity of these big-hearted people, and there's no doubt as to how grateful they are to learn from offworlders in return.

In Buluk, you can stay with a real family of Orcs at a modest boarding rate, with all proceeds going to the upkeep of community property via the Bison King's Benevolent Trust (BKBT). I stayed with Benedict (his actual name was B'nak'dek'shash, but that was very hard to pronounce), a small business owner who lived in a tusk-roofed roundhouse with his husbands and three small children, and he was a delight.

You may find your host gruff and often seemingly frustrated, as I did at first, but don't be fooled; this is just the Orcish way. All too soon, you'll come to learn that what seems like a miserable grunt is in fact an indulgent chuckle, if you listen right!

Life moves at a slower pace among the Orcs, so you should take the time to relax, help yourself to home cooking (the weevil fritters are a must!), and admire the beautiful, tusk-heavy orchitecture of their community buildings. While you're there, don't miss out on the chance to play Fakhtash-Vun with the settlement's children – this cool traditional game, which translates as 'survive the raid', sees children run and hide silently for hours, until imaginary Dwarven cavalry have passed by. Very cute.

On your last night, why not participate in one of the Orcs' incredibly atmospheric religious ceremonies? I went to an awesome candlelit recital of something or other, and although I couldn't understand the words, it was deeply moving. From the raised mound they were all gathered around, I think it was some kind of agricultural thing?

— *Sid Necklace, 21, Student*

WHY NOT . . . GIANT CENTIPEDES?

If you're headed to Mathelvayle anyway, consider paying a visit to Queen Shn'Shn'Nk in her glade at the heart of the woods. Her people, the centipede-like Scolopendrakin, were thought to be little more than brutal monsters when they fought under the banner of the Duke. And to be fair, they do look completely vile. Since the Pact of Grimlakk, however, they've proven to be sound conversationalists and excellent hosts, and have taken to tourism with astonishing enthusiasm. Dinner and storytelling in one of their mud-coil burrow-yurts, lit by the arse of a giant tame firefly, is a spellbinding experience, despite the gibber-inducing looks of your hosts.

attend the official business of a Grudging), you'll be guided to Buluk, the Orcish homestay where you'll end your trip. Buluk is one of the sanctioned, protected encampments where resettled Orcs and Goblins can live in peace in their traditional style, and is apparently charming. I didn't actually do this bit of the trip, as I had business to return to in Bannahirr, but here's a testimonial from some bleeding-heart gap-year type[1] we hired as a freelancer.

2: DUNGEONS AND FLAGONS: (3 Days)

Adventure Weekend in Descensus

This long weekend break, ideal for those with more testosterone than sense, will see you thrown into the very literal deep end of Mittelvelde.

DAY 1

The trip starts in chilly Kranagar, and the fortified town of Spörn, which exists only to service Descensus with food, supplies and fresh

---

1 Eliza – can you find a nicer way for me to describe him before we go to print? Cheers.

adventurers. Before you take the magical portal down to the Descensus, you'll have to fill in a good few forms detailing your skills, characteristics and – weirdly – your attitudes towards good, evil, law and chaos.[1]

DAY 2

Almost every night out in Descensus ends with a bunch of strangers drunkenly swearing an oath of loyalty to each other, and promising they'll head out to reach the bottom of the Dungeon the next day. A group formed this way is likely to be a mixed bag: there will be someone who's not taking things seriously and just wants to steal everything, and some arsehole who wants to waste time having long conversations with monsters. Nevertheless, most teams can probably make it to the double-figure levels in a day (where rats and bats give way to walking skeletons and living slime), meaning that by the second evening you'll have the kudos to drink at slightly less horrific establishments.

DAY 3

By day three your party will probably have accrued a decent selection of magical items, a good few trophies from a day's monster hunting and a selection of memories that will haunt you all in the small hours for the rest of your lives, even as you all insist the trip has been 'a right laugh.' At this point, it's your choice as to whether you want to venture downwards again: in the levels beyond fifteen or so, you pass beyond the territory kept clear by casual visitors to Descensus, and shit starts getting *seriously dark*.[2] Unless you've got a mind – and a sword arm – made of iron, it's probably best just to spend the day idling in town, and go home with some good stories.

---

1 My advice: just write whatever you want on the paperwork to get it over with, then do what you like once you're down there. Nobody ever checks what you wrote at the start.

2 During my stay I met a woman who'd been down to Level Thirty, and the look in her eyes made my mind up against ever going past Level Five again.

The light from a patch of luminescent slime mould revealed a cramped chamber, lined with alcoves like the one in which I had woken after my ill-advised beer nap, and each marked with a time-corroded statue of a Dwarf. Everything was covered in worryingly thick cobwebs, and the air was damp and thick with the smell of rotten linen. This had 'ancient tomb' written all over it. Confirming my worst fear, I looked back into the alcove and – yes – there was the web-clogged skeleton I had clearly shoved out of the way to make room to sleep.

I didn't want to look a second time, but I couldn't resist noticing that the carcass wore a magnificent dwarronium ring on the brown bones of its left index finger. This posed a dilemma. The last thing I wanted to do, especially in my delicate state, was touch the thing again. But then, what fun is dungeoneering if you don't take souvenirs?

Cringing, and fighting back a mouthful of sick, I reached gingerly for the skeleton's hand, and began to uncurl the bony fingers. The dwarf had a grip like a vice even in death, however, so I had to get right back in the alcove and use both hands. I got tangled up in the horrible bones, and thought I was just doing a magnificently cack-handed job of looting, until I realised the skeleton was fighting back.

This was my first encounter with the Undead, and luckily for me it was as brief as it was unpleasant. By sheer good fortune, while flailing to keep the thing's grasping hand from my face, I managed to snap off the finger bearing the ring, and the whole body collapsed in a lifeless jumble. I retched again. Then, with shaking hands, I took the sword and pocketed the finger with its ring – after first making sure it wasn't wriggling.

And that's how I became Level Nine holidaymaker.

— FROM THE TRAVEL JOURNAL OF FLOYD WATT

3. SYRILLARR[1] AND ALETHIAR: (5 Days/For Ever)

High Adventure on the Elven Way

Few can resist the chance to glimpse the mysteries at the heart of the Elven exodus – but be warned: this trip can get frighteningly metaphysical.

DAYS 1–4

Starting at the ancient border town of T'lashun on Syrillar's edge, you'll set out on the old Elven Way, a straight road of seamless stone leading from Mathelvayle all the way to the old coastal capital of Alethiar. Take the trip at a sedate pace on muleback, or try your hand at the emerging extreme sport known as steppesurfing, in which a wind spirit is harnessed through basic aeromancy then ridden on a sail-equipped cart behind at bone-shaking speeds.[2] If you're big on faded grandeur, camp for the night at one of the Elven Songbeacons. Carved into isolated outcrops of stone on the plain, these eerie statues of Elves experiencing acute torture once allowed their builders to speak across vast tracts of land in an instant. While the statues have been silent for more than a century now, it is said that if you climb to the antlered brow of one in the dead of night you can still hear faint sobs and mutterings from inside.

DAY 5

Finally, you'll reach the towering white walls of Alethiar itself. There are a few other Elvish settlements along the coast, but there's frankly little point in going all that way and not seeing the big one. What you experience there will vary, however: some travellers report the place to be freshly deserted, while others say it is long abandoned. Others still, myself included, saw something else entirely. Whatever you encounter there, one thing is vital to remember: *do not accept any offer to cross the*

---

1 Eliza, you keep correcting this to "Syrillar", but I swear there are 2 "r"s? (*No, Floyd, just the one. No Pirates here. - ES*)

2 In the old days you'd need a hired Wizard to do the necessary magic, making this an expensive proposition. With the advent of cheap canned spells following the Bison King's nationalisation of the Gollimmar spellforges, however, this is now achievable on a reasonable budget.

INTRODUCING: DESCENSUS

This unique township, deep under the abandoned realm of Kranagar, has been embedded thoroughly in Mittelvelde's physics-defying dungeon strata to the extent that it's entirely out of reach of the surface, and only accessible by magical means. Above and below it, and in all directions, the Dungeon sprawls, full of weirdness and danger and wealth. With no sunlight to grow crops, the city's economy is based on forage from the depths, so it's a place of bone-and-hide tents and lean-tos among stalagmites and statues of forgotten kings. The streets stink of tallow, leather, mildew and brass, and the food is . . . memorable. It's also got what you'd call a rough clientele: adventurers, entrepreneurs and burnouts whose only common characteristic is that they think 'fighting in a hole' is a reasonable lifestyle.

It's best to come to Descensus with a working understanding of what the locals call 'levels'. Essentially, with every storey of Dungeon one travels downward from the city, the more resources are found, and the more monsters guard them. Consequently, social status is governed by how many levels deeper than the city's bottom a person has ventured, and guests are no exception. The price of goods, the level of service you'll receive, and even the type of establishment you're allowed to enter all depend on what 'level' you can boast. Since you'll be Level One by default when you arrive, you'll be limited to the very shittest drinking establishments. As such, it's definitely worth heading down to the tunnels three levels below city limits and kicking apart a few of the rats and spiders that live there. After half an hour of stomping vermin, you can simply head back to town and sell the meat and pelts for booze money in a Level Three pub.

sea. While it may seem the most compelling proposition in the world at the time, it is not what it seems: the journey west is no pleasure cruise, but a metaphor for the passing of an age, and death itself. In short, a rubbish holiday. Or the holiday of a lifetime – but not in a good way. In any case, you have been warned.

I called out for the Elves as I walked their empty chalk-white streets, but only birds called back. At one point a lizard regarded me from its basking spot atop an empty wagon, but I think it was just an ordinary lizard. In the market square, stalls were still set with trinkets and jewels (admittedly, I pocketed a few handfuls), while the tavern tables were still set with pitchers of wine. I was beginning to think the city was entirely deserted, until I saw movement at the distant harbour.

At first I took it for heat haze, but as I got closer there was no mistaking: it was something like a party. Three great silver ships were docked at the marble quay, and before them an astonishing banquet had been set out on trestles. Figures were seated all along the hundred-yard tables, sipping from china cups and nibbling at plates of dainty sweetmeats as elegant servants attended them.

At the table's centre, resplendent in silver cloth, sat a woman who must have been eight-feet tall, and from whose head branched fine platinum antlers the width of a man's reach. And yes, her ears were definitely pointy. Surely this was the Elven Queen – but hadn't she left these shores generations ago?

To either side of her sat ranks of slightly smaller Elves, while they in turn were flanked by people of all kinds – humans, Dwarves and others still whose peoples I had not encountered. All looked ancient, with white hair and wispy beards, and all wore expressions of almost eerie placidity.

They continued to eat and drink wordlessly as I approached the table, and I began to feel like I was experiencing some sort of hallucination: the whole set-up seemed dreamlike, and – to be frank – desperately creepy.

But still I plodded forward, and when I got to within twenty feet, the Queen addressed me.

'Master Floyd,' she susurrated, with a voice as cold as her smile was warm. 'You've arrived just in time to join us for our final meal. Won't you come and take a place with us before we embark?'

'Good day,' I said, trying to sound urbane, although the words came out as a sort of stifled honk as I tried to process my shock at the Queen knowing my name. 'That's dreadfully kind. Yes, I would be, ah, honoured. And . . . where might you be embarking to?' The Queen laughed musically then, and cream-white membranes slid sideways across her eyes as her face creased in amusement.

'Why, to Larathainne, dearest fool! To the land of our people beyond the sea, where you may live in splendour with us.'

'Isn't that . . . just . . . an Elf thing?' I volunteered, my voice contorting into a questioning squeak.

'Not at all, Master Floyd. All are welcome in Larathainne, and many who were born to other folk are joining the voyage. Isn't that right, friends?' At this, she glanced up and down the table, where the various decrepit warriors nodded in docile agreement.

'Now come,' she said, extending a twig-thin hand towards a silver chair at the end of her table. 'Come and dine with us before we depart, and we shall talk of what lies ahead.'

Reader, I ran a fucking mile.

— FROM THE TRAVEL JOURNAL OF FLOYD WATT

CHAPTER TWO
Eroica City

1. WELCOME TO EROICA CITY[1]

The bustling metropolis of Eroica City would be a spectacle by itself: it's the quintessential urban jungle, where steam rises from manhole covers at dawn and honking traffic flows through the skyscraper canyons like a mighty river. But it's not the daily drudgery of human life that makes Eroica special – all that might as well be the business of ants compared with the epic lives of those who fly above the streets.

 Why Eroica?

Charting a moral course through life can be a taxing business. Sometimes it's simply exhausting to tell good from bad in the wide grey ocean of the world, and you wish you had a guiding light to show the way.[2] In Eroica, there are hundreds of them, and they're easy to spot because they can usually fly and they dress mostly in bright primary colours. They are the Superheroes. They're bigger than us, they're better than us and they showcase every quality we could hope to attain in their constant fight against Crime. The Superheroes aren't just superb moral exemplars, either: they're a fucking *riot* to watch. Simply look to the sky whenever you hear the sound of fists meeting flesh at Mach 3 and you're guaranteed an experience akin to being beaten over the head with a sack of action figures after nine bong hits.

---

1 Before we get any further: it's 'Eroica City', as in the Greek for Hero, not 'Erotica City', as in, y'know, boning. This is not a 'sex place'. Honestly, you wouldn't believe the number of lascivious sods who book tickets based on what they assume is a typo.

2 *I mean, you have an editor who advised you not to actively support the near-openly fascist Bison King, but clearly that wasn't what you were looking for. – ES*

Meet Your Heroes

Roughly one in five-thousand Eroicans is born a Superhero (or a Hero, as they humbly prefer to be known), but in a city of eight million, that makes for a *lot* of Heroes. Powers tend to manifest in people during their early teens, and range from common abilities such as flight and immunity to the effects of being punched, to more esoteric things like mastery of geese or the ability to make people fall asleep by playing the bagpipes.[1]

ARE THEY MAGIC, THOUGH?

Technically, Superheroes are magical, since there's no viable scientific explanation for anything they do. But since Eroica is a technological destination, they're uncomfortable seeing things that way, and so tend to excuse their astonishing abilities away with vague alibis involving mutations, radiation or animals. It's fair enough – they're just being modest.

But budding Heroes are faced with a huge question: do they join the city's ranks of licensed defenders or renounce decent society and fight as a Baddie for the forces of Crime?

The Good Life

Each day, the forces of Crime try to steal from the decent businesses working in the name of Good,[2] and each day the city's Heroes fight

---

1 Who will ever forget the iconic duo that was Honkus and the Highland Soother?

2 *From everything I've seen, 'Good' looks a hell of a lot like 'shareholder value'.*
– ES

FRANCHISE REBOOTS

Often, when multiple companies have property in the same district, several different stables of Heroes will have overlapping turf. In these situations the different stables will *never* interact — to the point of actively ignoring the presence of another company's Heroes — out of sheer respect for their sponsor's intellectual property rights.[1] IP is everything in Eroica: when one of a company's Heroes retires, the firm will usually hire a new hopeful to take on the mantle, refreshing the costume design and livery to suit current marketing objectives in the process.

1 Interestingly, for accounting purposes, paid Heroes are counted as intellectual property assets, due to the linking of character design and branding. As such, even speaking a sentence to a Hero from another company counts as use of a copyrighted brand and is expressly forbidden.

back. It's a battle with no end, and who knows what would happen if the forces of Good were ever beaten.[1] Luckily, each company employs a stable of salaried, licensed Heroes to protect their property from Crime. These consummate professionals wear astonishing costumes corresponding to the brands of their sponsor, and constantly patrol company premises, on the lookout for wrongdoing.[2]

Most companies hire Heroes on the open market, with the most powerful individuals going to the firms with the deepest pockets. Nevertheless, some CEOs – despite having no powers themselves – insist on joining their teams in person, often wearing fancy armour of their own design. This always seems like a good idea for PR purposes,

---

1 *As far as I can tell, it would just mean less property destruction and a more reasonable distribution of wealth? – ES*

2 If they can't find any criminals, they take on their secondary role as brand ambassadors and just sort of . . . sell to people. Loudly. It can be a bit disconcerting, but it makes sense – they've got to earn their keep when they're not fighting, after all.

until an actual combat scenario occurs – at which point the executive will usually talk over all the actual experts before hammering the whole endeavour into the ground with a series of appalling tactical decisions.

Baddies

Some Heroes are too twisted or foolish to earn an honest living for Good. These lost souls inevitably turn to Crime, becoming known as Baddies in the process, and waste their lives stealing cash, food and medical supplies from Eroica's economy, before distributing it to the criminal underworld.[1] Baddies can be just as powerful as Heroes, but they're universally idiots. I mean, they'd have to be, wouldn't they? Everyone knows Crime doesn't pay – and that's not even a platitude here. It's literally the case. Baddies don't get a salary at all, and anything they steal they immediately give away. Nihilistic dunces, the lot of them.

City Environs

✳ Just outside the city is **Liz Fisticuff's Home for Muscular Children**, one of Eroica's oldest and most prestigious Hero Colleges. Taking in orphans and troubled waifs from the city's stinking tenements, it educates dozens of new Heroes every year under the watchful, beefy eyes of Liz herself.[2] As a private enterprise, the Home costs a fortune to attend, so students can only complete their studies with the help of scholarships from potential sponsors, which they pay back after graduating and getting hired. It can take decades to clear the debt.

---

1 *Floyd, they distribute it to the third of the city's population living in abysmal poverty. You know that, right? – ES*

2 *And sends hundreds back to the tenements when they prove not to be that powerful, but that's not on the prospectuses, is it? – ES*

MAP OF EROICA

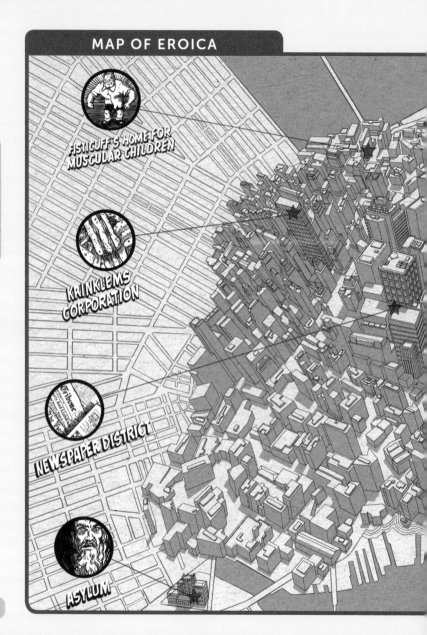

FISTICUFF'S HOME FOR MUSCULAR CHILDREN

KRINKLEMS CORPORATION

NEWSPAPER DISTRICT

ASYLUM

SPRODSLEY MOTOR CO.

PEPPLE BROS. CAT FOOD CO.

CENTRAL BANK

✳ At Eroica's heart is the financial district: a shimmering hive of smoked glass and chrome, where people in colourful braces roar into big phones all day. And at the heart of the district is the **Central Bank**, a building that has essentially been built into an unassailable bunker after long years of assault by Baddies. It's said

FACTS AND STATS

❶ Population of Eroica City 8,000,000

❶ Number of Powered 1,634

❶ Estimated % of GDP spent repairing property damage 14%

❶ Average daily caloric intake to sustain metabolism for a Hero 26,000

❶ Mean weekly income (employed citizens) .... 200 Powerdollars

❶ Mean weekly income (unemployed citizens) .... 0 Powerdollars

❶ Number of unemployed 2,530,000

❶ Annual cost of Crime ....26.3 bn Powerdollars

❶ Average IP value of a Hero with 10 years' experience ....2.3 bn Powerdollars

❶ Percentage of annual company income derived from direct posthuman marketing: 8%

THE FIVE MOST POPULOUS PROFESSIONS IN EROICA:

1. Construction
2. Newspaper journalism
3. Marketing
4. Action-figure manufacture
5. IP law

the vaults could withstand the explosion of an atomic bomb in the bank's lobby, and yet still, year after year, the Baddies find ways in. There's a fight at the bank on average three days out of five, so be sure to have your wits – and your camera – about you if you visit.

✳ With sixteen-hundred demigods constantly battling each other in the streets, all with instantly recognisable branding, the business of journalism is on permanent overdrive in Eroica. The **Newspaper District** stretches for a dozen blocks and employs more than a hundred-thousand reporters: a teeming army wearing typewriters down to smithereens in their struggle to keep up with the daily drama of the city. For tourists, nothing beats the hustle and bustle of this coffee-fuelled dynamo.

✳ All Baddies are defeated in the end, either by constant attrition or via a Showdown, and if they are captured they are given a choice: take on a sponsorship contract and become a Hero, or be sent out to the city limits and locked away in **Eroica Asylum**. There's no trial and rarely any assessment of mental health involved: it's simply assumed that you'd have to be mad to choose prison over renouncing Crime and fighting for the good of the city. Visitors can pay a small sum to tour the Asylum, jeering at the Baddies through the bars and mocking them for making poor life choices.

✳ Overlooking the sapphire waters of Eroica Bay is the shining, monolithic headquarters of the Sprodsley Motor Company, the largest corporation in Eroica. On its roof, complete with outdoor pool, full bar and private helicopter, is the clubhouse of the **Sprodsley Champions**, the most glamorous, high-profile and well-funded Hero outfit in the city. They would probably be the most successful team in the city, too, if it wasn't for the leadership of Mike Sprodsley, the company chairman's halfwit son, who insists on leading the Champions into battle despite having no powers beyond an infinitely extending budget.

✳ One of the great curiosities of Eroica City is its only Crime-free neighbourhood, surrounding the headquarters of the **Pepple Bros**

Cat Food Company. Uniquely, Pepple doesn't hire any Heroes – instead, it earmarks a quarter of what a normal firm would pay for posthuman muscle, and uses it to provide healthcare, amenities and foodstuffs for the inhabitants of surrounding blocks, whether they are employees or not. Strangely, Baddies don't touch Pepple territory, and what the company loses in revenue from advertising on Hero costumes it more than makes up for in savings on property repair.

Famous Heroes and Baddies

✳ The enormous **Kaptain Krinklems** is head of the Finesnax Five, the beloved superteam charged with protecting the Finesnax Food Conglomerate. Clad in bright green armour, she is emblazoned all over with the logo for Krinklems, Eroica City's premier baked corn snack. And with her telekinetic rending powers, not to mention her full-throated battle roar of "Enjoy baked corn snacks!", she's beloved by children across the city.

✳ As headline guardian for the Eroica Petroleum Corp, **Petrolyna** has had a bit of an image change in recent years. After her sponsor was vilified for a disastrous oil spill upcoast, her previous incarnation – a menacing, masked creature in heavy black industrial gear – was quietly retired and replaced with a cheerful oil worker in overalls, who takes a day each week to clean the muck off seabirds.

✳ A few years ago, **Skeleton Key** was one of the most popular Heroes in the city, with his eerie skull face and his ability to make his fingers change shape at will.[1] But when he was caught using his powers for inappropriate purposes – in the intimate company

---

1 As a power, this isn't in the same league as flight or energy blasts, but Skeleton Key is a creative man, and you'd be amazed by how many crises he solved with wiggly fingers.

of a competitor Hero, no less – he was stripped of his sponsorship. Inevitably, Key turned to Crime, where his grim visage and lockpicking ability has made an even bigger name for him as a Baddie.

✳ The **Crab Sherpa** is a man of very advanced years, who combats Crime by patiently and methodically guiding a large number of crabs to the scene. He can't control the crabs directly, but he certainly knows how to chivvy them along. Unfortunately he's not much good as a Hero, as by the time he arrives at a trouble spot the Baddie is either long gone or immediately begins stamping on the Sherpa's charges, while he stands to one side weeping and mouthing, 'my crabs.' Nevertheless, he is seen as a delightful underdog by millions, and so the Nebsworth Paper Company keeps him on the payroll.

✳ The dastardly **Gravy Jones** is one of the city's most notorious Baddies, and travels around in the Gravy Boat, a 26-ton road tanker full of piping-hot gravy. He can also shoot boiling-hot gravy from his hands, and briefly turn his own blood to gravy to enter one of his famous Rages. Several of the city's major gravy brands are rumoured to have approached him with lucrative contracts, but it seems his heart belongs to Crime.

Staying Safe

On the one hand, you can't ignore the fact that Eroica is constantly being terrorised by Baddies. On the other hand – if we're honest – it's pretty easy to stay safe from them. Nine times out of ten they'll be focused on robbing a bank or raiding a storage depot, with minimum civilian injury. The problem comes from the subsequent fights with Heroes – once a proper ruckus starts up, it tends to ricochet around the city like a ball bearing in a washing machine, levelling buildings as it goes.[1] And while I'd love to assure you that you're guaranteed

---

1 There's a reason construction companies make such a fortune here.

rescue by a noble Hero should debris tumble your way, you're better off stacking your odds by standing near an advertising billboard if trouble kicks off. Companies will tolerate a certain amount of human collateral damage, but they won't stand for their branding being damaged.

As a general reassurance, it's worth noting that, even for baseline humans, *it's incredibly hard to die here.* For some unfathomable reason, falls that would end a person elsewhere just leave light bruises here, and blows to the head that should cave in skulls simply *clonk* people into a gentle sleep. Minor injuries[1] can be forgotten about in a matter of hours, and barely any injury is fatal. It's got to the point where the Heroes find it hard to take funerals seriously anymore. Four times out of five, the departed Hero returns somehow.

 ## Eating and Drinking

✳ If you're into enormous portions then one of Eroica's **Hero Buffets** is the place for you. At these cavernous dinner barns, food is cooked in industrial quantities and carried out by the bucketload to be guzzled by ravenous Heroes on breaks between missions.

✳ Alternatively, if you can scare up the right underworld contacts and fancy roughing it, you might be able to join one of the **street cookouts** regularly thrown by Baddies, where an entire neighbourhood will be treated to the spoils of a dastardly raid. I wouldn't lower myself to this sort of thing, but Eliza went and said she quite enjoyed it.[2]

---

1 Which in Eroica can mean anything up to and including high-calibre bullet wounds.

2 *I did – until some psychotic Adonis in tinned-soup livery descended on rocket boots and opened up with a flamethrower. As he bathed the alley in flames, he muttered some grim one-liner about standing the heat and getting out of the kitchen, but everyone was too busy screaming and fleeing to listen. – ES*

✳ If you're really flush, treat yourself – and perhaps a date – to a five-star meal at **Excelsior**, the rotating restaurant atop the Grundlinger Typewriters tower. It's where Eroica's CEOs go to toast their daily successes, and rarely a dinner service goes by without an attempt by a Baddie to storm the restaurant from the outside,

— TESTIMONIALS —

As a little girl, I always dreamed of being saved from a fire by a Superhero, but I didn't see it panning out this way. I mean, she looked the part – she was gorgeous, with red vinyl wings and the logo of Mad Charlie's Furniture Warehouse curled around her thighs. But as she carried me away from the blaze, she kept whispering to me about the great prices on offer at Mad Charlie's, and it got really off-putting. Even as she set me down on the street she was trying to get me to sign up for a loyalty card, and I just wanted to get away.

— *Adele Spunt, 42, Cook*

Interesting, but not advisable as a family destination. The kids loved it when we saw our first Hero, flying alongside the monorail from the spaceport and waving at us, but it got awkward when he started mouthing the name of a fast-food chain and miming eating a burger. Big disappointment on the second day – when we saw the Ram Raider try to rob a bullion van we thought we were in for a real spectacle, but the pursuing Heroes just gave up as soon as they were outside their sponsor's territory, and she got away with the gold. The food's pap too, and the prices are sky high, so don't expect many great meals out.

— *Eugene Gruftoe, 28, Librarian*

and their subsequent foiling by one of the Grundlinger Seven. It only adds to the fun: after all, nothing quite sets off a romantic meal like two titanic figures battering the paste out of each other in the sky beside your table. It's like meat fireworks.

Fashion

While you risk getting sued for a life-ruining sum if you have the audacity to dress as an existing Hero (and bearing in mind costume redesigns, there are patents filed on thousands of outfits), the general Heroic aesthetic has permeated everyday fashion on Eroica to the extent that even the most buttoned-down professional will incorporate a cape or a pair of tall boots into their outfit. Try accenting a casual ensemble with a pair of light pauldrons to make it Heroic, or accessorise your evening attire with a gem-studded headpiece and a set of mighty gauntlets. At the end of the day, you have to find the look that's right for you. There are clearly no IP restrictions on dressing as a Baddie,[1] but if you do so, prepare to accept that you've invited a maelstrom of comical yet painful mistaken-identity situations into your life.

Entertainment

Entertainment is a tricky subject in Eroica, as it's hard for much to surpass the everyday life of the city in terms of thrills. Nearly every athletic pursuit conceivable has been rendered meaningless by the participation of Heroes, and sports *without* Heroes just seem boring here. Television is big, however, and still a recent enough innovation that people are amazed by it. Weekly high-budget documentaries about the recent activity of the Heroes command a huge audience who follow the

---

1 Indeed, many Baddies make their costumes as easily copiable as possible, and it's not unusual to find whole gangs of youths on poorer blocks wearing the mask of their favoured Baddie. Classified by the city as terrorist 'antiheroes', but calling themselves Henchfolk (or so Eliza tells me), these deluded kids will carry out astonishingly bold infrastructure raids in the name of their idols.

regular spectacles[1] with the conviction of soap-opera addicts. Recently, advances in special effects have allowed for more fantastical programming, set in worlds where nobody has any powers at all. Called 'normoes' by their fans, these short dramas are seen as horror stories about what would happen to society if nobody was better than anyone else.

---

1 'Marvels', they call them.

CHAPTER THREE
Spume

1. WELCOME TO SPUME

No destination has distilled the essence of high adventure quite like the nautical fantasy realm of Spume. With salt spray misting your face as you lean from the bowsprit of a galleon in full sail, it's impossible not to feel a freedom as unconstrained as the endless waves. And indeed, there's everything to play for here – just so long as you respect the Pirate's Code.

? Why Spume?

Sooner or later in any jaunt through the Worlds, you'll hit water. And once you hit water, there's every chance you'll hit Spume. Because if you set sail from *anywhere* with the right sense of perfectly measured recklessness, these horizons will suck you in. Drive a boat like you've stolen it – or better yet, steal a boat – and you'll end up here.[1] Nobody is sure why 'theft, but wet' is even a genre, let alone one so primal as to occupy this central space among the Worlds. Nevertheless, it is what it is, and Spume embodies it with breathtaking purity. An expanse of tropical archipelagos inhabited exclusively by Pirates, its deep, almost fastidious commitment to cliché has resulted in a destination that always hits the right notes.

It can take some getting used to. The contradiction between the recklessly egalitarian ideals of the buccaneering lifestyle and the Byzantine regulations of the Pirate's Code, which keep it viable, can be jarring at

---

1 Even if the 'theft' of a vessel is temporary and agreed with its owners in exchange for a reasonable donation, it works. I even heard of someone dodging the fare for a steamer on Chugholme and causing the whole shebang to end up on Spume because they felt too excited about getting away with it.

WHY MY HEART BELONGS TO SPUME
by Sid Tidy, ship's cook aboard the Gilded Gurnard

What convinced me to stay in Spume weren't the tropical weather, nor the gold: no, me hearty, it were the people. In me old job as a recruitment consultant, I were surrounded by complete bastards pretending to be reasonable people. Now, I be part of a crew o' reasonable people who spend all day pretending to be complete bastards. Sure, 'tis not the easiest life, but every day brings surprises, and the shore leave be *off the chain*. Last week I went ashore for a few cold ones with the hearties, and ended up stealing a cannon off the Navy. Proper mental, we be. Mad lads. One word o' warning, though: if ye come here, accept that ye may never go back. I still technically be on a stag weekend that started six years ago. I were going to go home, but Cap'n Beefshanks here needed a new cook, and I thought, *Why not?* Not sure what happened to the rest o' the lads, now I comes to think of it. Mike be definitely a skeleton – he loves it – and I think Colin be a Captain now? That's the thing about Spume – so long as ye be a good Pirate, ye can be anything here. So what are ye waiting for? Come aboard, shipmate!

first.[1] But stick with it long enough to learn the rules and you'll discover a way of life that – within a number of sensible parameters at least – has no limits.

Spume offers a wealth of simple pleasures, from sea views and accordion-heavy portside ambience to endless supplies of rum and seafood.

---

1 I should know. On my first visit I assumed an 'anything goes' mentality, and immediately shot a man in the leg for garnishing my drink incorrectly at Hardtack Mulligan's Bar & Grill. Over the following month in a rat-clogged brig, while Eliza explained my misunderstanding to the Council of Free Captains (CFC), I learned otherwise. I have to say, they were terribly reasonable about the whole thing in the end, freeing me in exchange for agreeing to . . . certain terms.

MAP'S EDGE

MAP'S EDGE

Yonder

BIG WINDY

The Stormwracks

The Yohos

DOLDRUM

Remittance
Island

MAP'S EDGE

MAP'S EDGE

And for those wanting to delve deeper into weirdness, it delivers in big, Pirate-sized spadefuls. There are sunken wrecks crusted with corals, city-sized leviathans, and skeletons you can have dinner with, if you can bear their company.[1] So, whether you fancy a laid-back cruise through turquoise shallows, hunting treasure on specks of paradise, or braving storms and black powder on a sloop full of deceptively sane madmen, there's a Pirate's life out there waiting for you.

 ## 'Can't Miss' Experiences

1 Battle a Kraken

We all remember that moment of childhood disappointment when we realised the sea monsters drawn on old maps were just tall stories. Prepare to leave all that disappointment behind in Spume! The monsters here are *real*. The Seven Seas teem with leviathans, of which the famous Kraken are the undisputed showstoppers. A lengthy dispute over marine stewardship policy between Skeleton Pirates and normal Pirates has made Kraken hunting more of a hot-button topic in recent years,[2] but there's still no shortage of 'squidbuster' fleets heading out from the major ports, and they're always looking for fresh deckhands.

2 Fight in a boarding action

We've all had the daydream: swinging from a rope with a flintlock in your hand and a cutlass between your teeth, hollering the naughtiest words you know as you prepare to cause havoc on the enemy's deck. On the seas of Spume, this isn't a daydream: it's a fairly ordinary start to the week. Ship-to-ship combat is almost oppressively frequent along the major trade routes, and is still a thrill to behold, even with the strict conduct for nautical confrontations set out by the Pirate's Code.[3]

---

1 They're really boring.

2 They had to politicise it, didn't they?

3 Controversially, some captains are now only allowing their crews to use foam cutlasses when there are tourists aboard, with rumours that this will soon be mandated by the Council of Free Captains. Critics are calling this a classic case of Pirate's Code Gone Mad, but I for one can see the sense in it.

3 Find buried treasure

Until recently, searching for treasure among Spume's island chains was a fruitless business, as all the good stuff had been dug up. Thanks to canny amendments to the Pirate's Code by Captain Bartholomew Threelegs, however, the booty game is back in business. Each year, Captains are mandated to bury between 12 and 40 per cent of their loot and then leave a map in a bizarre place for their rivals to find.[1] If you're in search of treasure, why not try organising a tour with one of the following many certified Guide Captains listed in the Port Remittance visitor directory?

4 Go out on the lash

Spume's land-to-sea ratio means the average Pirate lives at sea for nine tenths of the year – and living on a boat can be as claustrophobic as it is stressful. As such, when a ship stops in port and the crew get a chance to stretch their peg legs, things get *hectic*. The world's astonishing variety of rums – from molasses-heavy headache juice to ice-clear spirits fit for royalty – are consumed by the gallon, and the accordions ring out in cacophonic chorus. A night of shore leave on Spume is either impossible to forget or impossible to remember – but never anything in between.

 ## Region by Region

Just 4 per cent of Spume's surface is dry land, spread across the ocean like raisins scattered by a miserly baker. Between these specks of sand and rainforest is water – hundreds of millions of square miles of it – divided up into the Seven Seas.[2]

1 The Yohos

This idyllic archipelago, with its white-sand beaches untroubled by hurricanes or raids, is where Pirates go to relax, retire and raise families. The Pirate's

---

1 Best one I saw was by Captain Liz Blacktooth, who tattooed the map to her loot on the arse of her long-term rival's pet ape. They had the map right under their noses for years, but never saw it until the ape got the shits and they had to shave its rear end, revealing a dotted line and an 'x' marking the spot.

2 Eagle-eyed travellers will note that there are, in fact, only five seas. But this is just not polite to point out to the Pirates, who are adamant about there being seven.

Code forbids all but the most lighthearted violence here, and limits cursing to mild blasphemy, plus meaningless exclamations like 'Son of a Dutchman!' and 'Hornswoggle me Nutmegs!'. There's still some rough and tumble – the kids have to learn their trade somehow – but all in all, it's a cheerful place, suitable for travellers who like their rum watered down to child strength,[1] and who prefer to remember holidays with fridge magnets rather than scar tissue.

2 Doldrum

In a realm where sail power is universal, Doldrum – that great patch of breezeless ocean at the centre of the map – is a place considered universally worthless. It sits there like a big patch of sick nobody wants to clear up, caked over with grumous scum and dotted with the bleached, creaking hulks of becalmed ships. Nevertheless, from the albatrosses who circle above to the slimy things that gather below the water to breed, it's a top-tier destination for nature fans.[2]

3 The Stormwracks

In contrast to the Yohos, the Stormwracks are Spume on Hard Mode. These islands jut from the sea like rotten teeth, swathed in thorny jungle and brooding beneath the smoke of countless volcanoes. Their shores are encrusted with ramshackle port towns, where Captains take their crews to carouse, gamble and fight in the brief gaps between roaming the seas. While the Pirate's Code still applies here, it's definitely an adventure destination, where daylight robbery is considered a mandatory pursuit, and one grog too many can mean waking up naked, under indentured servitude to a glowering brute.[3]

---

1 Don't underestimate these Spume kids, though — the little bastards can put it away. I got in a drinking contest with a nine-year-old and the little git utterly bladdered me.

2 I must admit, I hadn't heard much about Doldrum until someone told me all about it on my way to a wedding — I have to say he was an odd bloke, but he really sold it well.

3 Not in the good way, either. It may sound like the stuff of cheap romance novels, but more often than not it involves a vast amount of deck maintenance and very little in the way of teaching twinkly-eyed ruffians the ways of love.

TALKING LIKE A PIRATE

Pirates make talking the salt-stained patter of the high seas look easy, but remember they've had a lifetime of practice. It's harder than it looks.[1] For newcomers, it's best to start with the odd contemplative 'arr' if you really must get involved, before throwing in the odd 'jimlad' or 'matey'. Intermediate learners may choose to start completely mangling all use of the verb 'to be', while experts can begin throwing whole phrases into conversation, such as these classics selected from the *Landlubber's Lexicon*, a free pamphlet issued to tourists by the Council of Free Captains:

SPLICE YON GURNARDS, ME JIMMY-LIVER FOR
I'LL GLUP A SACK O' NECKBLIGHT AVAST YE!

Do you want to go for a drink?

BY YONDER WOUNDS O' NEPTUNE, I'LL BE
GUTSLIT AFORE I BLITHER YE TO OLD HEMPEN
JACK!

You can trust me.

SALT-TACK BILLY-CLOTHS AND CLEAVE ME
GRUNIONS, FOR TO SEE WILY JOHN TAR ON THE
SEA-DAD'S WATCH!

**Even the CFC don't know what the fuck
this means.**

---

1 Case in point – 'shiver me timbers!' can be either an exclamation of mild surprise or a demand for vigorous manual stimulation, depending on the company you're keeping.

4 Yonder

The Sea of Yonder, and the windswept islands scattered across it, are the domain of the Skeleton Pirates:[1] walking, talking cadavers who have very literal trouble holding their drink. Thanks to their indifference to oxygen, the Boneys[2] live as much beneath the waves as on them, and conduct breathtaking aquatic tours from their capital in the drowned city of Thalassinor. Just don't be fooled by their bony grins: your average Skeleton Pirate is obsessively political, extremely sincere and about as gifted with humour as they are with skincare techniques.[3]

5 Map's Edge

The colossal viridian expanse of Map's Edge dwarfs the other seas, encircling them like the fist of an angry blue giant. But despite its immensity, it's astonishing to note that this sea contains almost nothing. No islands more interesting than little hillocks of sand and gull shit, and certainly no settlements. Apart from the odd lost Captain, nobody spends any time in Map's Edge, and so it's barely worth mentioning.[4]

SPUME

---

1 Of course, under the terms of the Code, nowhere on Spume is technically anyone's domain, but you get the picture.

2 Eliza says I can't use that word, as it is apparently disrespectful. I don't care: it's what everyone else calls them, so I say it's authentic.

3 I guess you could say they aren't very . . . humerus.

4 So – you know I mentioned the CFC freeing me after the incident at Mulligan's? Their clemency was on the condition that I give them full approval over the copy in this guidebook, so I had to be careful about what I included. However, these footnotes went in after they made their edits, so let me say this clearly: Map's Edge isn't empty. Not by a long chalk. If you listen to enough rum-chat among the old salts of the Stormwrack taverns, you'll hear the same: there's danger out there. Real danger. The kind that comes at the tip of a rusty machete, and which laughs with rotten-toothed malice at the Pirate's Code. I've seen it, and I'll never forget it.

2. UNDERSTANDING SPUME

A Brief History

The true history of Spume is hard to piece together, since it's not written down: paper and parchment are hard to come by in this watery place, and what little exists is usually reserved for making treasure maps. As such, the Pirates recount their history entirely through sea shanties, in which the details are almost entirely drowned out by repetitive refrains about heaving ho and lifting jugs of grog. After listening to thousands of hours of this nonsense, earthly historians have collected this sequence of best guesses as to the eras of Spume's past.

1 The Prepiratical Era

Spume is occupied by a thriving maritime empire, which grows rich through harvesting Kraken on an industrial scale. But the strain of maintaining order over many distant islands takes its toll: sailors turn rogue, congregating in hidden ports and plundering trade at their leisure. These are the first Pirates, and before long they begin to outnumber the empire's navies.

2 The Curse

Ruined cities – perhaps relics of a drowned civilisation – are discovered on the seafloor, and a vast quantity of gold is found within. It turns out to be . . . haunted.[1, 2] Those who take it are stricken by an awful curse: they become animated skeletons, immortal and unable to satiate their hunger or thirst. The social disruption caused by the sudden influx of miserable skeletons is the last straw for the empire: mass

---

1   *Floyd, what does this mean? It sounds an awful lot like bullshit to cover up something dreadful. – ES*

2   Look, there's something about 'Riddles from the Silver-antlered Ones' in the songs, but I think it's just the writers being silly. What's so hard to accept about haunted gold, Eliza?

SPUME

76

mutinies spread, all government collapses, and soon only Pirates – and Skeleton Pirates – remain.

3 The Golden Age of Piracy

For generations true anarchy reigns, as Pirates rob other Pirates in a global feeding frenzy. It's so action-packed, nobody bothers to write anything down at all.

4 The Silver Age of Piracy

The Golden Age proves not to be sustainable. With piracy so lucrative, fewer and fewer people bother to engage in building ships, refining gunpowder or farming food. Scurvy becomes a crippling pandemic, and timber becomes almost as valuable as gold itself.

5 The Bronze Age of Piracy

After a drawn-out nadir of economic auto-cannibalism, civilisation on Spume flatlines. Ships become vanishingly rare – most pirates sail on sprawling rafts constructed from detritus, and fight with spears and clubs rather than cannons and flintlocks. Starvation and disease are rife, and some crews become entirely feral, drifting the seas like swarms of flotsam-borne rats.

PARANTHROPUS PEIRATES

Back in the Prepiratical Era, Pirates were declared *hostes humani generis* – 'enemies of all humanity' – by the empire they preyed upon. The Pirates thought this was quite cool, however, and adopted the descriptor themselves. But what sense did it make in the Golden Age of Piracy, when human civilisation had been entirely replaced by Pirates? To the Pirates, it was simple: if they had been declared 'enemies' of humanity before, then surely they had become non-human by definition. And with humanity now functionally extinct (since everyone had become a Pirate), buccaneering anthropologist Professarr Andronicus Skinner named Pirates a new species – *Paranthropus Peirates* – in a taxonomic ruling that no biologist has yet dared to challenge.

6 The Council of Free Captains

Realising that life on Spume is on the edge of a precipice, the last reasonable mariners form the Council of Free Captains (CFC) and declare a ceasefire across the Seven Seas. They hold a summit with the Captains of the Skeleton Pirates, who have become fierce isolationists, and agree a set of ground rules for the conduct of piracy: the Pirate's Code. Under the Code, crews must split their time between thievery and the meaningful creation of resources, and observe strict guidelines as to which circumstances are suitable for behaving with lawless abandon.

> *Oooooh, I'll tell ye the tale of the birth o' the Code*
> *Heave to, my boys, heave to!*
> *The good word that governs the barnacle road*
> *Drink up, my boys, drink up!*
> *'Twas old Captain Dolan who first wrote it up*
> *Ohhhhh, raise the capstan!*
> *Told us how much to brew, and how much to sup*
> *Ohhhhh, weigh anchor!*

— True History of the Pirate's Code,
lines 1–8 out of 534,120

Spume today

After a marathon recovery, Spume is currently in what the CFC calls the Platinum Age of Piracy: the delicate sustainability policy enshrined in the Code has been honoured, and while resource scarcity is still a concern, the increasingly efficient and responsible nature of Kraken-hunting and the development of an undersea salvage industry by the Skeleton Pirates are making life more comfortable all the time. Now, with the advent of tourism, fresh gold – always the most treasured resource in a world of Pirates – is finally entering the economy. And while there was an initial period of awkwardness while the CFC figured out the rules for robbing

DAYLIGHT ROBBERY?

Building a utopia from the gristle-strewn mayhem of a society founded entirely on violent crime is no mean feat, but the Pirate's Code proves it can be done. Just don't make the mistake of thinking the crime has *stopped* – it's just been rationalised. So while you'll definitely be robbed during your time on Spume, you can avoid a lot of pain by knowing how it works:

✳ Always carry two coin bags – one obvious and ostentatious, containing exactly 17 per cent of your monthly salary, and one auxiliary, containing the rest of your cash, as well as Exemption Form 23-Arrrr, available from the CFC. Pirates will take care to only rob the former.

✳ When travelling on certain ships or staying in certain ports in the Stormwracks, more senior Pirates *may* rob from your auxiliary coin bag, citing Counter-exemption 499. If this occurs, don't panic – just submit a reimbursement claim to the Department of Buccaneering on Remittance Island, using Form 213-B. You should receive at least 80 per cent of what was robbed within twenty-eight days.

visitors, these have now been formalised and are no longer the cause of any diplomatic crises. With the Seven Seas returning a greater bounty every year, and the trustworthy, hooked hand of the CFC at society's moral tiller, now is the perfect time to visit Spume.[1]

---

1 This line was, admittedly, inserted into my copy by the CFC, but I really didn't like that prison, so I let it stand. Needs must when the devil drives and all, eh?

Climate and Terrain

If you've been paying attention so far, you'll probably have got the picture: there's a lot of sea on Spume. In fact, there's not much else.[1] As for climate, Spume is especially maddening: the bright white sun moves in different directions on different days, and there are no less than six possible equators, each of which migrates over time. The good news is that, because you're technically never more than 23 degrees north or south of an equator, you're always in the tropics. On the other hand, it makes the weather *insane*. Only the most scholarly Pirates even pretend to comprehend Spumish meteorology, and climatic maps tend to look as if a child has been given a bag of military-grade crank and told to

YE OLDE FORESTRY COMMISSION

You wouldn't think there'd be much need for forestry management in Spume, but you'd be wrong. Mangrove swamps spread for miles around many of the larger islands, while lush rainforest tends to spring up on any flat ground past the tideline, and sheer demand for shipbuilding timber means it all has to be carefully stewarded. Still, the real work of the CFC's Forestry Commission is out at sea: a whole fleet of ships patrols Spume's smallest islands, trimming back all foliage until only a single, iconic palm tree remains. It's this attention to detail that makes Spume as magical as it is.

---

1   I mean, it's all basically the same, isn't it? Just a load of wet water. Eliza insisted I do a section on climate and terrain anyway, but I don't think it's necessary. It's a bloody Pirate world – if you're reading this in the hope that I'll suddenly reveal a massive desert, you'll be sorely disappointed. Of course, I say that, but according to the primer Eliza gave me, there is in fact such a thing as a marine desert. I reckon that's bollocks – if there are no cactuses it can't be a desert, end of story.

draw a ball of string. As a tourist, however, all you need to know is which areas tend to be calm and which are stormy – let the Pirates figure out the rest.

Wildlife

The odds are, if you can imagine a ridiculous form of marine life, it probably exists on Spume. The Pirate biologist Tobias H. Beastcounter once tried to compile a full bestiary, but died at the age of ninety-three having got halfway through the section on crabs. These volumes alone took up half the hold of his ship. So, rather than attempt to summarise Spume's frankly bewildering biodiversity, it's best to focus on some of the more charismatic, dangerous or culturally important species.

✳ The **Palmback** (*Hyperchelonus Peudinsularis*) is a turtle-like colossus, measuring two miles or more fully grown, which spends most of its time basking at the surface. They are infamous for looking and behaving exactly like islands – until they submerge. As a result, Palmbacks are one great reason not to go island-hopping without an experienced guide.

✳ **Sea Serpents** (*Anguis Megamaritimus*) are aquatic snakes, and are common as muck on Spume, with the smaller species commonly spitted and grilled as street food.[1] The larger kinds, however, can grow to phenomenal sizes, and can crack the keel of any boat that runs into them in full sail. They're not dangerous to humans, although it can be faintly stomach-churning watching one swallow a whale whole.

✳ With more than ten-thousand kinds of **Shark** (*Elasmobranchii Orders*), Spume is a paradise for fans of the bitey lads. From the almost cuddly, faintly pathetic **Custard Sharks** (*Selachimorphis*

---

1 I have fond memories of the first time I tried what the Pirates refer to as 'the saveloys o' the sea' – if you can get past the fact that you've got to prise the fangs off first, they're great eating.

Tragicus) of Doldrum, to the sixty-foot **Greater Whites** (*Carcharodon Gigalodon*) that ply the deep channels south of the Stormwracks, there truly is a shark for every occasion. What's more, they are adored: many Captains will encourage them to follow their ships at sea, becoming familiar to the point that they'll take meat from the sharp end of a hooked hand.[1]

✳ Without a doubt, the most emblematic denizen of the depths is the **Kraken** (*Pseudarchiteuthis Imperator*). Much has been written about these vast creatures, but it all boils down to the fact that they are really, really big squid.[2] That's impressive enough on its own, but even more remarkable is their sheer economic utility: the internal structure of a kraken is maintained by bone-like structures with a composition almost identical to wood, while their excrement contains a petrochemical blend indistinguishable from tar. Their mouthparts produce a fibre that can be spun into sturdy rope, while glands in their gut produce all the necessary ingredients for gunpowder. All in all, they contain everything you need to build a Pirate ship, and they taste great too – which is why so many Pirates ply their trade hunting them.[3]

 # People

Pirates

Paranthropus Peirates culture is incredibly cosmopolitan: it favours no ethnicity, gender or sexual preference, and encompasses a huge range of religious beliefs. This egalitarian approach to identity makes it all the more bizarre that

---

1 Admittedly, this practice is also the reason why many pirates have hooks for hands in the first place.

2 According to the primer Eliza has forced me to read, they are in fact 'Pseudo-architeuthimorphic parazooids presenting features common to both Bryozoans and Siphonophores, but with astonishing emergent complexity'. However, since I have no idea what the hell that means, let's just agree on squid.

3 Hilariously, the same primer reckons the Kraken aren't natural at all. It says 'if you were going to engineer an organism in a hurry to facilitate the survival of civilisation after a catastrophic rise in sea level, you could do little better than the Kraken'. Come on, seriously? This is meant to be a textbook, not science fiction.

PETA

Perhaps the biggest source of acrimony between Pirates and their undead cousins surrounds the issue of Kraken. While the Pirates argue that hunting the beasts forms a vital part of both their economy and their culture, the Skeletons are insistent that the only time a Kraken should be fought is when a belligerent specimen (usually a large female in breeding condition) attacks a ship – and even then, many Boney[1] captains will refuse. To this end, they have formed an organisation known as PETA – Pirates for the Ethical Treatment of Architeuthimorphs[2] – which lobbies for stricter harvesting laws and pickets hunts with swarms of small boats.

1 *Please stop. – ES*
2 Slogan: 'Release the Krakens!'

it's mandatory for everyone to at least attempt an utterly ludicrous accent. But that's the secret to Spumish personal freedom: you can be anyone you like – so long as you're a Pirate first and foremost.

Skeleton Pirates

The Skeleton Pirates (technically *Paranthropus Peirates Skeletos*) are a strange bunch. The CFC certainly consider them fellow Pirates, since they pursue an existence based on ritualised maritime theft. Nevertheless, the longevity and melancholy inflicted on them by the Curse has made them rather more . . . pious. The political schism between Skeletal and Non-Skeletal Pirates is rooted in fundamental disagreements over the ontological complexities of Piracy, which have long become far too nuanced and labyrinthine for outsiders to follow. In short, the Boneys[1] feel the CFC has lost sight of the values of sustainability on which it was founded.[2] Rather than

1 *FLOYD. – ES*
2 It's fair enough, I suppose, since they'll be roaming the Seven Seas for centuries to come.

squander limited timber reserves by building new ships, for example, they tend to salvage old ones – or create serviceable vessels from the carcasses of sea monsters that have died of natural causes.[1] For the most part, the Skeletons prosecute their moral conflict through activism, stunts and passive-aggressive pranks. Frequently, Pirates will come across bogus treasure maps left by the Skeletons, which will lead them halfway across the sea only to find a chest containing a snarky political slogan signed with the Skeleton symbol.[2]

The humans

There are absolutely, definitely, 100 per cent *no* humans on Spume. Everyone is a Pirate. To reiterate: there are no humans at all, and it's certainly not worth going looking for them.[3]

---

1 Be wary when booking tours aboard such craft, as Skeleton Pirates have no sense of smell.

2 A boneless face over two crossed, floppy arms. It's understood that this was a sort of 'see how you like it' move, in response to the Pirates' refusal to give up the skull and crossbones as their own symbol. And believe me, you've not seen rage till you've seen a woman who's braved a ten-thousand mile quest only to find a scrap of parchment reading 'it turneth out ye real treasure was ye friends ye mayde along the way'.

3 The official position of the CFC is that there is no organised non-Pirate culture in the whole world. But then, that's exactly the impression they would want to give to prospective tourists, isn't it? And while I'm not going to flat out say there are hundreds of thousands of hostile humans living in the expanse of Map's Edge (which is not nearly so empty as the CFC insists), I'm trusting you, dear reader, to put two and two together here.

3. PLANNING YOUR TRIP

When to Visit

It would be pointless to offer advice on when to visit Spume based on the weather. You basically need a PhD to comprehend the forecast for a given region, so it's best just to stick a pin in the calendar and hope. Regardless, there are several annual and regular events that it's advisable to time a visit around.

The CFC AGM

On the last day of the Pirate year, every member of the Council of Free Captains sails to the vast compass that protrudes from the sea at the spot known as Allpoints[1] in order to discuss the future direction of piratical society. The actual council meetings, conducted on the upper surface of the compass, are interminably dull, but the jamboree the crews throw to keep themselves occupied while the Captains do their business is *fantastic*. Barges selling deep-fried seafood ply their trade between the ships, while travelling entertainers move from deck to deck by zipline.

Talk Even More Like a Pirate Day

Held each day at the start of whatever feels like it might be autumn, this maddening festival sees every Pirate on Spume dial their linguistic bullshit up to eleven and talk complete bollocks for twenty-four hours. It's great fun to experience – just don't try to accomplish any meaningful transactions on the day in question, or you'll be hopelessly bamboozled.

---

1 Oh, did you think that was just a nice little flourish by a cartographer? No, it's a massive stone compass sticking out of the sea, and nobody has any idea who put it there.

The Looting of the Governor's Mansion

While Pirates are fundamentally opposed to any kind of central government, they realised long ago that life would get dull without a formal nation state to oppose. Enter the Governor, a hapless Pirate chosen by lottery each year, who must live in an enormous, treasure-stuffed mansion in the Yohos protected by a wholly inadequate 'Navy'.[1] After a brief off-season, during which the Governor is mandated to hold several society balls, the mansion is declared fair game, and the looting – which is open to all, including tourists – begins.

The Pirates progressed from jostling the Governor to what I would definitely classify as 'rough shoving', and soon had him hoisted above their heads. I was – of course – just trying to work out whether it would be code-appropriate to rush in to the rescue, when I realised the Governor was laughing.

'Thank fuck for that, lads,' he gasped as he tore off his epaulettes and cravat. 'This is some other sod's job now. Now, who looted the good rubies?'

A rotund Pirate near the back of the crowd raised her hand (which was a corkscrew), and a cheer went up.

'Ha, Winehand Sally,' said the now ex-Governor, 'I should have known. Well, you can put that thing to use tonight, as the bloody drinks are on you.' The Pirates cheered again and stampeded off into the tropical night, leaving the mansion abandoned to the breeze once more. For now, at least, all government on the planet had technically been eradicated.

— FROM THE TRAVEL JOURNAL OF FLOYD WATT

---

1 As Captain Olivia Ravenswain argued in her famous address to the CFC when the tradition of the Governor was initiated: 'If the Navy did not exist, it would be necessary to invent it.'

Getting Around

Spoiler alert: it's boats.

Eating and Drinking

If you're fussy about eating seafood, this really isn't the World for you. While it's just about possible to get by on land-based foodstuffs here, you'll get bored of tropical fruit pretty quickly, and for many Pirates a vegetarian meal just means 'a few less sardines than usual'. One plant-based substance that *is* virtually universal[1] is rum, acting not just as a drink but as a marinade, a condiment and – for many – a hobby.

SPUME'S
BEST BARS and RESTAURANTS

Mad Tamzin's Hell for Fish: *Rickety shed in the Stormwracks, where creatures you've never heard of are dunked in rum by a woman with hands like bin lids, then hurled alive onto white-hot coals for your delectation.*

Steel Neil's Meal of Eels: *Hardcore establishment run by Neil himself, who now has so many metal body parts he can barely operate a stove, but who will still sell you a wheelbarrow of live eels for a doubloon.*

Vegetables, I Suppose: *Half-hearted 'vegetarian' restaurant, where meals are sourced by desperate cooks scavenging from a patch of rainforest out the back of the kitchen. On days when their luck is poor, be prepared for the head chef to try to persuade you that an octopus counts as a fruit.*

---

1 Other than the dreaded 'Sea Weed', that is.

Since Spume's natural reserves of gold ran out long ago (and much of it turned out to be haunted), tourists now represent the only fresh influx of gold into the economy – meaning that as a visitor you will *definitely* be robbed. It's worth noting that any currency is good here,[1] so long as it contains at least 25 per cent gold. Once a coin enters Spume, it's counted as a doubloon – and that's that. As a result, you can find coins from hundreds of cultures on Spume, from Hierarchian Leaderbucks to Bison Groats and Chugholme Shillings. Depending on where you've come from and where you're headed afterwards, you can make a small fortune using Spume's weird economy to game the exchange rate between worlds.

THE BITTEN COINS

The CFC has taken some fascinating measures to stimulate the economy of Spume during chronic gold shortages, but surely the most eccentric is the tradition of the Bitten Coin. Under this scheme, gold increases with the number of consecutive Captains who have owned it, as it means it has been stolen more often. Captains traditionally test the quality of coins by biting them, and since each Captain has a distinctive bite mark recorded at Remittance Island, the indentations on a piece of currency map out the chain of theft it has passed through, and therefore its value. Canny travellers can take advantage of this financial alchemy, if they can make sense of how it works.

OH, AND BY THE WAY: It's definitely a scam!

---

1 Just remember that you don't technically buy anything in Spume – you just pay to steal it. Property here really is theft.

DAILY SAMPLE COSTS

BUDGET: Less than 10 doubloons
Roustabout's quarters in the bilge of a sloop: **4 DB**
BBQ sea serpent and seaweed fritters: **2 DB**
Bottle of Jenny Blackblood's Killdevil Rum: **3 DB**
Ticket and bucket of rotten fruit for an anti-Navy political
    play: **1 DB**

MIDRANGE: 10–25 doubloons
Bosun's quarters on a mid-size carrack: **6 DB** (7 DB without rats)
Fresh pineapple and turtle-meat kebab: **3 DB**
Bottle of Old Bart's Foul Tymes Rum: **5 DB**
Kraken-spotting daytrip from Thalassinor: **4 DB**

TOP END: More than 25 doubloons
Captain's suite on a luxury galleon: **15 DB** (including hat rental)
Flame-grilled Kraken steak and actual vegetables: **12 DB**
Bottle of Gilded Fran's Angel Juice Rum: **19 DB**
Permit to shoot a man in the arm for no reason: **42 DB**

Don't Forget to Pack . . .

Vitamin C tablets
Scurvy is a worldwide pandemic on Spume due to the chronic shortage of fruit and vegetables, and is a major concern if you're planning on staying for more than a couple of weeks.

Nautical supplies
While gold is a must-have for travelling on Spume, remember that common shipboard materials are worth almost as much in a pinch. Metals in particular are extremely hard to come by, so a bag of nails will make you plenty of friends.

Crackers for parrots
It's a rare Pirate ship that doesn't possess at least one parrot, and they *always* want crackers. They also want pieces of eight, but it's a fool's errand to give a bird money.

DRESS TO TRANSGRESS – SPUME FASHION

To be a Pirate, you need to look the part. Spume has an astonishingly deep unisex fashion culture where anything goes, and while you've got no hope of keeping up with seasonal trends, the buccaneering wardrobe leans on a number of perennial staples:

* A cool shirt: Extravagant lace cuffs are de rigueur for Captains, while stripy tops of various kinds are the standard for crews.

* Headgear: While you can get by with a salt-stained rag knotted behind the skull, some of the hats constructed for more senior Captains can outvalue the ships of their lesser competitors, and can require two shipmates just to hold aloft.

* Beards: Common status symbols, with colour and style denoting social status. False beards can be acquired at exclusive boutique hirsuteries by those declining to grow their own.

* Peg legs, hooks and prosthetics: Even the lowliest roustabouts will wear a false eyepatch for special occasions, while committed fashionistas will undergo elective surgery to allow for more outlandish body-part replacements – exotic fixtures such as egg-whisk hands and telescopic shins can be seen at the trendier bars in the Stormwracks.[1]

* Pets: Primates and parrots are the most common, although statement pieces including land crabs, bats, ravens and pangolins are seen from time to time. Pets are considered best kept on shoulders, so Pirates will often sport massive single epaulettes incorporating perches, feeders and even small hutches.

---

1 Generally speaking, the more senior and experienced a Pirate, the more prosthetics they will have. There is usually a practical limit to levels of replacement, but Pirates still sing the legend of Captain Jurgen Bunchfist, who supposedly went 'full sawdust', only being declared dead a week after his shipmates realised they had replaced his last original body part with a block of wood.

Cutlass holder

If you're going to truly get into the Pirate spirit, you'll need a cutlass. And if you're going to climb ladders and swing on ropes with one, the traditional place to hold it is in your teeth. So invest in a leather mouthguard. The Pirates may make it look easy, but be advised: hospitals on Spume are essentially pubs with slightly more blood, so you don't want to end up in one with a cut-up mouth.

Proper documents

Technically, any human on Spume is designated *hostes pirati generis*, and is thus eligible for execution on sight – so you'll want to make sure you pre-print a certificate proving that you are a Pirate, in order to ward off any overzealous buccaneers.

Manners and Etiquette

Let Pirates take the lead in confrontations

The Pirate's Code is unfathomably complex, and takes a long career on deck to fully understand. While it can be easy to get carried away during a grog marathon and decide it's the perfect time to threaten a man with a cutlass, you will almost certainly cause grievous offence if your etiquette is anything short of perfect. When in doubt, wait for a Pirate to threaten you, and then escalate according to their lead.

— TESTIMONIALS —

We had a great holiday in Spume, until it came to checking out of our accommodation. As I handed back the keys, the hotel's Captain called me a good-for-nothing piss weasel, and my wife Sandra got quite upset. She aimed a flintlock at him, and he got extremely offended, grabbing his copy of the Pirate's Code and pointing angrily at a paragraph of really small text. Even the cabin boy on duty told us we should be ashamed of ourselves, and we left under a bit of a cloud.

— *Kenneth Sausage, 42, Bin Engineer*

Leave only footsteps, take only memories (and treasure, where permitted)

When island-hopping, especially with Skeleton Pirates, be careful to pay proper respect to the environment. Don't litter, don't snaffle souvenirs without asking, and certainly don't start campfires unless instructed to do so. These fellows take resource conservation very seriously, and will be quick to reprimand you if you help yourself to anything except looted gold.

Don't shoot albatrosses

As an extension of the above, *please, for the love of all that's good, do not take potshots at albatrosses*. For reasons unknown to science, the death of one of these extra-large birds can kill all wind in a fifty-mile radius, potentially adding days to the length of a voyage.

Forget the 'w' word

People make many assumptions about Pirate culture when travelling to Spume, and, to be fair, many of them prove to be completely accurate. Nevertheless, one of the more poisonous misapprehensions is the idea that women (or people of any other gender) occupy anything short of an equal role to men in Pirate society. Call a Captain of any kind a wench, and you're liable to be hauled under a boat on a rope. Not that big a boat, perhaps, but it's still not a risk to take unless you properly love barnacle abrasions.

4. SUGGESTED ITINERARIES

📋 1. TREASURED ISLANDS: (2 WEEKS)

From the Yohos to the Stormwracks

This tour eases visitors into the Pirate life, taking them from the balmy and non-threatening Yohos, through ever-increasing levels of maritime mischief, to the Stormwracks themselves.

DAYS 1–2

Starting off in the merry fishing village of Avafite, spend a couple of days orienting yourself before heading off to sea. If you're into daytime drinking, the local Scoundrel's Academy runs great activities for the kids to enjoy while you get trolleyed.[1] Before you leave, make sure to catch an evening meal at a tavern holding a scheduled 'brawl' – areas for fighting are clearly marked with red paint, so you don't have to endure a sweating gunner's mate crashing through your dessert if you don't fancy it.

DAYS 3–6

Once you've got your sea legs ready, book passage on a pleasure sloop heading to the Stormwracks (the *Wobbly Dogfish* and the *Maiden's Belch* are tidy, well-run ships), and learn some colourful shanties from the crew. There are plenty of great day excursions to be had at the ports along the way: we recommend Madame Flannigan's Parrot Farm & Used Ape Sanctuary. Less recommended is the pungent immensity of the Hedstrom & Sons fish tinnery, while at the very bottom of your sightseeing list should be the wheezing racket of Port St Boafus' sixty-strong accordion orchestra.

---

1 Be aware that your children will learn skills such as 'punching' and 'threats' on such outings, however.

BEST BARS IN KEELHAULYER

As in most port towns, Keelhaulyer's taverns hang clear, Code-mandated flags above their doors stipulating the level of general mayhem accepted within. This helps tourists avoid unnecessary violence, while allowing the authentic 'all you can beat' experience for true thrill-seekers.

Rancid Bob's Appalling Teahouse (White Flag – fisticuffs prohibited)
Pleasant establishment, if a little rough around the edges. What makes it appalling are the teas, which are brewed from mushrooms collected at random by Bob himself. They can do anything from putting you into a two-day coma to making you see the face of the devil in your own shoes.

The Broken Arms (Yellow Flag – mild peril)
Classic Stormwrack tavern – superb for old salts telling blood-chilling tales of mutiny on barren seas, and a decent selection of ales on tap to boot. Can get a bit Beast Mode after midnight, but the locals know better than to do anything more than shake a fist at tourists. The upstairs is a tattoo parlour run by a Skeleton, whose cursed designs will growl threats at you for years to come.

Ironshin Nancy's Haus of Fights (Red Flag – heavy fighting)
Where Pirates go to settle old scores, in brawls presided over by the metal-legged proprietress herself. Famous for its boast of 'a ten-minute fight every five minutes', it's rarely a quiet night at Nancy's, and you're likely as not to leave through a window, smeared in someone else's blood.

The Carnival of Fists (Black Flag – enter at own risk)
This isn't even really a tavern. It's just a windowless barn floored with gravel, where gigantic people go to hammer seven shades of shit out of each other. It's not even apparent whether they serve drinks. It doesn't matter. Only violence lives here.

DAYS 7–9

After crossing into the Stormwracks, you'll spend a couple of days in the lawless port of Keelhaulyer,[1] where the roughest, toughest Pirates gather to swap tall stories over pints of methanol-heavy spirits. Staying at one of the town's spit-and-sawdust boarding houses (Bad Molly's or the Two Eyepatches are good options), you'll have a few days to soak up the town's madhouse atmosphere and rambunctious nightlife.[2] If you want a breather amidst the excess, be sure to take a walk to nearby Confidence Cove, where Pirates suffering from low self-esteem go to encourage each other in massive group therapy sessions.

DAYS 10–13

When you can resist the call of the waves no longer, sign on with one of the crews headed out of port[3] and experience the brand-new madness of living in a leaky wooden coffin packed with hard-drinking people who roar all day. Ships sail all over Spume from Keelhaulyer, but a natural destination is the storm-tossed region known as the Bundlemarr Heptagon, just a week's sail west. Making it through the Heptagon is hair-raising to say the least – but there's simply nothing like hauling rope in the driving rain, singing a song about lost love and public executions, as leviathans breach to starboard by the light of St Elmo's Fire.

1 Of course, everywhere on Spume is technically lawless, but it's mandatory under the Code to refer to all Stormwrack ports as 'lawless' in order to preserve their rough mystique.

2 A discreet note: despite the 'rum, sodomy and the lash' line that gets thrown around about life in the Stormwracks, it's worth pointing out that only the rum is compulsory, and even then alcohol-free options are available. If the other two do happen to be your thing, you should know that Keelhaulyer has a well-regulated, heavily unionised sex industry, which its participants take great pride in. Rest assured, there are plenty of opportunities to get Jolly – and ethically – Rogered in these parts.

3 Please, please remember to make sure you sign up under a temporary contract.

'It's coming right for us,' I hissed in panic, as the beast surged towards our carrack under a moving hill of water.

'Fear ye not,' intoned Captain Rattleribs, raising a bony hand for calm. ''Tis just her way. She be happy to clap eyes on us, that be all.'

Even when the first of the Kraken's house-width tentacles lummoxed onto the deck, the Skeleton stayed calm, sauntering over and patting the leathery purple flesh as if it were an old, beloved hound.

'Arr, me fine old lass,' he said affectionately, as the beast's great eyeless beak-mount loomed up beside our deck, 'I've missed ye!'

For a moment, I thought he had genuinely tamed the thing. But then it let out a scream like a train full of old modems crashing into a pig farm, and tore away the mainmast with a flick of a tentacle.

'I think you should probably get the cannons out,' I warned, as I felt the blood drain from my face with fear.

'No, no,' said the Captain wistfully, as the monster began smashing the deck into splinters around him. ''Tis just her watery way, is all.'

Nodding sagely as if I understood (reader, I did not), I ran for the lifeboats, just as a second Kraken emerged from the sea on the other side of the deck. Casting off from the rapidly disintegrating carrack, I swore I heard Rattleribs booming with joyful laughter.

I next saw the Captain that night, as I was about to light a fire made from the bleached timbers of the lifeboat. My leaky boat had only made it a few miles, and I'd been forced to maroon myself on what was clearly a one-man island.

Even so, here was Rattleribs, wading out of the sea with crabs scuttling from his ribcage, and his usual enamel rictus somehow looking like a dopey smile. He was in such a good mood, he didn't even lecture me on my use of the island's sole palm tree *to provide kindling. I was confused to say the least, but offered him a spot by the fire nonetheless.*

'It were a male,' he said at last, after we had sat in awkward silence for some time.

'Hm?' I replied, concentrating on trying to grill a limpet.

'Ye second Kraken,' Rattleribs explained. 'It were a young fella, come to meet his fair maiden o'er the banquet o' me ship.'

'But they sunk it, Captain.'

'Aye, that's as maybe. But after all these years, I finally got the chance to watch 'em court. He had a hectocotylus like Neptune's trident, so he did. 'Twas the most beautiful thing I ever did see.'

Then it dawned on me. I didn't remember much from the zoological primer Eliza gave me, but I knew that 'hectocotylus' was the fancy word for octopus dick.[1]

'Captain,' I said gravely. 'They fucked your ship to bits.'

'Aye,' he beamed, 'and I could expire happy with the knowin' of it, if only 'twere possible for me to die.'

Once again, I nodded as if I understood, and carried on grilling the limpet. The Skeleton Pirates are a strange lot.

— **FROM THE TRAVEL JOURNAL OF FLOYD WATT**

---

1 Some anatomical diagrams can't be unseen.

DAY 14

If you make it through the Heptagon without being dashed to driftwood, your Captain may take you north to Big Windy himself: the colossal, unexplained weather system that looks exactly like a human face, and which constantly huffs out hurricane-force winds like an incredibly angry football manager made of clouds. And if you're not ready to go home after all that? Well, who knows – perhaps you've got what it takes to be a Pirate after all.

2. THAR SHE BLOWS! (10 DAYS)

Skeleton-guided Kraken Hunt in Yonder

Since they don't need to breathe, the Skeleton Pirates are as happy below the waves as above, and make perfect guides for those who want to see the best of Spume's wildlife.

DAY 1

After arriving in Yonder at sunset, spend the evening taking in the tranquil emptiness of island life. Poke a crab, shout at a monkey. You know, island stuff. While you're at it, get pumped up to kill a Kraken, because you *know* that's what you're going to do before this holiday is over.

DAY 2

After a dawn pickup via a quaint wooden submersible, descend to Thalassinor, the sunken city of the Skeleton Pirates. Thalassinor's ancient, drowned skyscrapers stand in a sunlit wonderland of coral, with every surface that isn't regularly cleaned sprouting a colourful profusion of marine life. This includes the Skeletons themselves, and many residents consider it a fashion statement to be as festooned as possible in barnacles, sponges, tubeworms and Sea Weed. There are many pressurised, air-filled spaces in the old buildings, where you can enjoy relaxing chamber music played by a skeletal quartet on eerie bone instruments, while looking out at the city's vibrant coral gardens. It will all be very peaceful, but don't worry – *that big squid's still gonna die.*

DAY 3

If you've managed to pay the CFC a 'licence fee' to turn a blind eye towards the use of modern SCUBA gear,[1] or if you're willing to resort to the rather drastic option of taking Cursed Gold and becoming a Skeleton yourself, you can leave your quarters and take a walking tour of

---

1 Piratical dive technology is not recommended, being essentially a wooden barrel on the end of an air hose.

the reefs with a Skeleton guide. Out in the blue, you can marvel at the shoals of brightly coloured fish, and feel slightly baffled at the sight of enormous, corroded statues of people who seem to have antlers. Just don't touch any gold you find scattered by the feet of these statues or you *will* become a Skeleton for ever. After an evening of crushingly dull mandatory lectures from the Skeletons, on topics ranging from responsible tourism to the philosophical inadequacies of regular Pirates,[1] you'll be able to catch some sleep before rising at dawn to board your tour vessel – a traditional Skeleton Pirate ship made from the ribcage of a leviathan. That's right – you're going Kraken hunting.

DAYS 4–7

The ship will make sail for the Doldrum on a three-day voyage. While aboard, those with a taste for the spooky may choose to drink tea infused with traces of Cursed Gold. While the quantity involved won't be enough to turn you fully skeletal, it will make your bones shine through your skin under moonlight and give you a host of melancholy thoughts about the sea. Whether you've gone full Boney or not, once you reach the edge of the Doldrum you'll have the chance to walk out on the surface of the Glop itself, where you can encounter its many mucous-heavy denizens under the watchful eye of a Skeleton naturalist. By now, you'll probably be making polite yet regular enquiries to your hosts about when the squid-busting will start.

DAYS 8–10

When you've had enough of watching miserable creatures haul themselves across a yawning expanse of slime, it's time to board the ship again and set sail for a three day Kraken-hunting expedition, at their breeding grounds in the Pontoppidan Deeps. It's at this point that you'll read the small print on the itinerary and be crushed with disappointment that you're hunting the Kraken to watch them, rather than fill them with harpoons. Even so, be *certain* to know where the lifeboats are.

---

1 Mostly the latter.

CHAPTER FOUR
Chugholme

WELCOME TO CHUGHOLME

Or, alas, not. Poor Chugholme. Until recently this was – for me, at least – one of the undisputed jewels of all the Worlds. It was a thoroughly civilised place, where one could enjoy the finer things in life – gilded with the trappings of fantasy, no less – without being troubled by baser concerns. Now, however, Chugholme has rather gone to the dogs. It's been under a no-go advisory by the authorities for months now, and Eliza has insisted on abandoning the double-length chapter I had initially penned for it. Nevertheless, I refuse to let its passing go unremarked, so I'll use the thousand words Eliza has accorded me 'if I really feel I must' to celebrate what it once was.[1]

Chugholme: An[2,3] Eulogy by Floyd Watt

Chugholme, the great capital of the Pretanian Empire, sat proudly at the heart of its domain, importing luxuries, treasures and coal from every corner of the world, and exporting good manners in return.

Around it sprawled the bucolic delights of Chalmondesleydale[4] – a comfortable county with no dirty coal mines, which managed to maintain the vibrant social claustrophobia of a well-to-do rural community while still covering hundreds of square miles. In Pretania, social standing was everything, and the manors of Chalmondesleydale were where

---

1 *You've already rinsed 120 of them, mind. And on what I have to say is the most atrociously pompous paragraph I've yet to see you produce. Well done, I guess? – ES*

2 Sorry, Eliza – is it 'a eulogy' or 'an eulogy'?

3 *Figure it out yourself. I'm not going to edit a word of this chapter. I'm just going to bin it on press day, so write what you like. – ES*

4 Pronounced 'Chalmondesleydale'.

the most eligible of the eligible went to court, scheme and dance their silk socks off. There were balls every night: wild galaxies of lace and candlelight that attracted swarms of brooding bachelors like moths – for it was always debut season in Chalmondesleydale.

City Living

And then, when you became jaded with even the wonders of the countryside, you could travel into the city – with its steam-cranes, its steam-mills, its steam-groceries and steam-newsagents – to experience truly imperial splendour. As your train pulled in to one of Chugholme's four-hundred railway terminals, you'd see crowds of the young tearaways who called themselves 'Steampunks' on the station concourse,[1] guffawing and competing to see who could affix most cogs to a hat.

FULL STEAM AHEAD!

Perched at the giddy pinnacle of industrialisation, Pretania was an empire powered by coal – and by steam. Even though more advanced technology had long been in reach, Empress Pretania,[1] in all her wisdom, always understood that an aesthetic is an aesthetic, and so passed ordinances that severely restricted electric technology. As early as the fifth year of her reign, electricity was only being used for spectacular crackling orbs in the laboratories of eccentric scientists, and to power the Mk IV 'Bulldog' electro-truncheons employed by Pretanian police forces in the imperial colonies.

1 I met her once, by the way.

1 They were mostly boarding-school kids enjoying a break from their studies.

Once in the heart of the city, one was at leisure – providing one had a little cash to flash. There were few things more genteel than sipping fresh tea from fine porcelain in the saloon bar of the Botherstone Club while watching zeppelins unload at the steam-warehouses across the river. Yes, it was a little silly that most of the clientele wore goggles at all times for no discernible reason – and I really did never get the business with the platform boots – but it didn't do too much to detract from the atmosphere of refinement. The banter, needless to say, was tremendous.

The aforementioned zeppelins weren't on one-way routes, either. For a reasonable sum of Pretanian guineas, you could book passage to anywhere in the colonies, and enjoy the capital's suite of luxuries in a more tropical climate.

All Good Things . . .

Of course, that was where the trouble started. A few years back, you started hearing about trouble overseas: rabble of one kind or another, using cannibalised engine parts to make armies of crude steam-mechs.[1] There was simply no *elegance* to what they were doing, but it was effective: places started dropping off the map, and it happened more and more often.

Then, suddenly, the trouble wasn't overseas any more. Out of nowhere, a militia called had occupied half of Chalmondesleydale, and there were columns of smoke-puffing assault vehicles advancing on Chugholme itself. Pretania had seen off invasions of tentacled aliens in five-legged walkers before now, but this was a different story. Battalions of commoners – largely conscripts from the northern mining towns – were sent out to repel the transgressors, but most simply dropped their weapons and turned coat. The city fell within days.

---

1 Their gripe was something about independence, or the means of production – I can't remember, to be honest.

Chugholme Today

I know trouble when I smell it, so I was out of there pronto.[1] The last I heard before I bugged out, the Imperial Palace had fallen into enemy hands, and its giant golden lion statues were in the process of being dismantled. After that, I heard plenty more – but all from excitable adventure tourists who had found a way past the entry blockade, and who told too many tall tales to be believable. Reports of invading steam-brigands from all corners of the empire seemed conceivable, but the yarn I heard about a volunteer brigade of *Orcs*, of all things, seemed ludicrous.

Who knows who is in charge of Chugholme now, but it seems tourists are emphatically not welcome there. Not to worry, though – I'm sure it's only a matter of time before business as usual is resumed, and you can see for yourself what a spiffing place it is.

---

1 Although I was devastated to forfeit my reserved table at the Botherstone.

CHAPTER FIVE

SPACE

*(**S**ector of **P**seudofictional
Astro-**C**ultural **E**nvironments)*

1. WELCOME TO SPACE

Considering it's mostly made out of nothing, there's a mind-bursting wealth of sights to see in SPACE. From the many strange worlds in its depths to the wonders of the twinkling void itself, the sky isn't even close to the limit when you holiday here. Big enough to hold a lifetime of surprises, but not so massive that it's scary, SPACE is a destination you'll never get tired of.

? Why SPACE?

If you've got the sort of wanderlust no forest or ocean can satiate, you need to get your arse to SPACE – the Sector of Pseudofictional Astro-Cultural Environments. And if you're put off by the long acronym (I know they can be intellectually intimidating), fear not: the good news is that unlike *real* space, SPACE couldn't be easier to understand.

While most of the Worlds are restricted to single planetary surfaces, with space travel either technologically infeasible or just not worth bothering with, this destination is dramatically larger, containing a plethora of stars and planets, and loads of interplanetary societies.

NATURE ABHORS A VACUUM

In grudging recognition of the astrophysicists, I'll say this: the 'vacuum' that fills SPACE is pretty odd stuff. It's only moderately freezing, it soaks up stellar radiation, and in some places you can just about breathe it. It even carries sound, so you can hear the ace engine noises that all the SPACEships make.

Astrophysicists grumble about 'everything being way too close together', and the region being 'not *proper* space', but as far as I'm concerned they're just missing the point.[1] SPACE is just as packed with magic as any of the other Worlds – it just so happens that the magic here involves spaceships. Or rather, SPACEships.

Thanks to SPACE's strangely forgiving nature, the technological barriers to entry for starfaring are surprisingly low. As a result, dozens of cultures have reached beyond their planets of origin to trade, explore, bicker and battle in this strangely crowded abyss. Travelling among

WHY SPACE IS THE PLACE FOR ME

By Sam Turbo, Ensign on the independent trading vessel Rowdy Ronald

I always dreamed of being an astronaut as a kid, but it turned out that not only did you basically have to be a living god to do it (I couldn't be bothered with that), but space was also a complete nightmare full of freezing emptiness that would murder you at the first opportunity. So I became a recruitment consultant instead. When I came to SPACE, however – on an adventure holiday with my estranged father – I realised that my dreams *were* possible after all. You see, this place isn't that scary: the distances aren't mind-shatteringly vast, the aliens are basically just people with strange faces, and the holographic, monster-based board games are really cool. Hell, in my early years on the *Ronald* I even accidentally forgot to put my helmet on before opening the outer door of the airlock (lol), and ended up floating in the big empty! It was a bit dicey, but the crew got me back in again soon enough using the SPACE Rope, and we all had a good laugh about it. Everything's a good laugh out here – I think I've found my orbit.

---

1 They may think they're clever, but really – when it comes down to it, what are astrophysicists but overqualified geographers?

PULP
NEBULA

'THE GALAXY'

H
VA

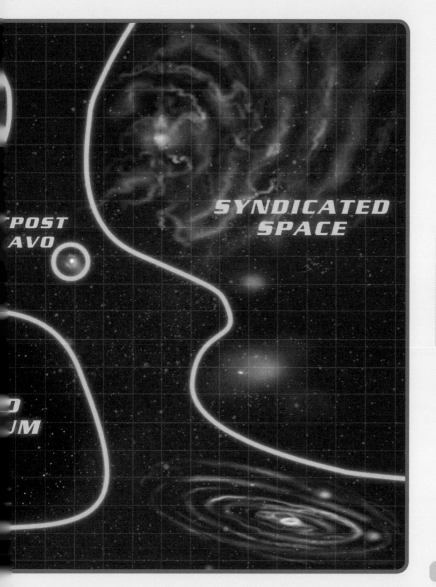

POST
AVO

SYNDICATED
SPACE

JM

them means meeting humans – and strangely familiar aliens – from bizarre civilisations, and living constantly on the edge of information and sensory overload. It's a place where technology is sufficiently advanced as to be indistinguishable from magic, and where even on a slow day you can achieve five impossible things before breakfast. So get yourself a SPACEsuit and travel, with the stars your destination.

 ## 'Can't Miss' Experiences

1 Take a giant leap for mankind

Although pretty much every world in SPACE has been discovered by *someone*, only a tiny fraction of the asteroids, moons, comets, planets and unexplained artefacts within its limits have been officially surveyed by *us*. Which means they're up for grabs, right? And with durable plastic flags available from plenty of gift shops for a modest sum, it's never been easier to claim a distant body of rock as property of the Earth.[1]

2 Outwit an alien

Although the sentient aliens of SPACE are basically just humans with minor anatomical differences and/or a different skin colour, they are at least interesting in that each of their cultures is defined by one or maybe two overwhelming character traits, and none of them are as cunning and plucky as humans.[2] Starfarers familiar with these wily beings – such as the celebrated Captains of Syndicated SPACE – know the ins and outs of alien psychology like clockwork, and regularly engage in duels of wit and intrigue with these creatures while negotiating trade and diplomacy out in the black. Get chummy enough with one of the Captains while on board ship with them, and who knows – they might even give you a turn on their giant communications telly!

---

1 *Floyd, isn't this both a) alarmingly colonial, and also b) entirely against the ground rules we agreed for your travels? Those flags are meant for sports games, not fucking conquest. And don't you dare tell me it 'doesn't count because they're only plastic'. – ES*

2 *Wow. There's just so much to unpack in that last statement. It's a work of art. I don't know where to start, so I reckon I'll just let you continue. – ES*

3 See things other people would never believe

The many star systems encompassed by SPACE include just about every gorgeous conjunction of stellar bodies[1] imaginable, and with everything so close together, there's virtually nowhere you can stand (or float) and not be blasted to mental smithereens by the view. Planetary night skies swarm with nebulae, shooting stars and strange moons, while days can boast between one and nine suns in a range of spectacular colours, depending on what's nearby. It's all extremely pretty.

'And why should we cede mineral rights to the Go'ka Cloud to you fod-zeh humans?' growled the Olang elder on the big screen, the orange flanges of his nose wrinkling in exasperation. Sitting in the bridge's command chair, Captain Aquitaine steepled her fingers and breathed deeply, tension radiating from her as she pondered her answer.

'Excuse me,' I murmured, sidling over to the big chair despite First Officer Murray's look of annoyance (the big galoot had been trying to keep me away all afternoon, saying I was 'too drunk' to be on the bridge), 'but I've done this before. I reckon I can sort it out.' The Captain shot me a look of assent, and before Murray could block me, I took the microphone and looked up at the Olang on the screen.

'Because, you orange git,' I said, gnashing the words with relish, 'Captain Aquitaine has three stealthed attack craft just astern of your vessel. What do you think of that, eh?'

The situation was solved. Captain Aquitaine put her palm to her face in relief, and the Olang offered her the tight-lipped expression and raised eyebrow which I'm fairly sure is a gesture of submission in their culture. I don't know why I ever gave up this diplomacy lark, I'm amazing at it.

— FROM THE TRAVEL JOURNAL OF FLOYD WATT

SPACE

---

1 *Yuck. I don't ever want to hear that sequence of words from you ever again. – ES*

4 Investigate a mysterious distress signal

Despite the relative safety of travel among the stars, there's still no accounting for accidents, stupidity and hubris: switch on even so basic a device as a radio in open sky and you'll receive hundreds of pings from crash sites, derelicts, imperilled colonies and mysterious ancient artefacts. Pretty much any of these can make for a fantastic day out, although admittedly sometimes that will involve an ambush from SPACE Pirates or an encounter with a nest of writhing Xenads.[1]

Region by Region

The star systems of SPACE hold far too many planets, moons and structures to detail individually. Even the interstellar empires are too numerous to outline here, with more than thirty civilisations having ten or more systems to their name. Nevertheless, there are some broad regions worth identifying to the prospective astronaut.

1 Outpost Bravo

Our main access point to SPACE is via the gargantuan, leaky station at its centre, known as Outpost Bravo, which has become a hub for travel throughout the entire region. Bravo is the home and workplace of the hapless Space Men[2] (*see People, below*), but given its location, it's also a popular neutral ground for trade and negotiation, and virtually every species and government in SPACE has an expat community here. The Space Men are a bit stressed out by all this happening on their turf while they're trying to do their Missions[3], but they stay sane so long as the civilian population keeps mostly to its assigned districts.

---

1 Neither things are as bad as they sound. The SPACE Pirates are largely recent immigrants from Spume and are thus way too polite to be much genuine trouble, while the Xenads haven't been *proven* to lay their eggs in anyone's mouth.
2 *I really can't cope with the capital letters every time I read this, so this is henceforth the style when referring to them and them alone. - ES*
3 Who can fathom the Missions of the Space Men?

2 The Pulp Nebula

Not far from Outpost Bravo sprawls a huge, pink-tinged nebula – one of the regions where SPACE's ultra-thin atmosphere gathers into a pocket of breathable air – with a dozen or so moons concealed in its depths, all orbiting the enormous gas giant Grum. This Pulp Nebula (so-called for its resemblance to a giant, burst-open fruit) is home to an astonishing ecosystem, where thick, warm air has allowed life to flourish in the expanse between worlds. Asteroids on which drifting seeds have taken root have become floating, forested mountains, while gigantic Astrocetaceans and jungled-over derelicts drift together through flamingo-coloured skies. It's a wild place, and the moons within it are hotbeds of savage adventure populated by Barbarians, Lizardmen and more.

3 Syndicated SPACE

Almost half of SPACE is looked after by the Syndicate, a conglomeration of human and alien states with a vast shared fleet of starships that's either an armada of science ships or a navy, depending on who you talk to. Certainly, the Syndicate is a peaceful society – but largely because they outlawed war a while back and threatened to annihilate anyone who so much as thought about starting a beef within their sprawling territory. It seems fair to

I put one leg up on the boulder and sighed, gazing wistfully at the immensity of the twin suns as they sank towards the hazy desert horizon. All was silent, except for the faint susurration of dust devils out on the plain. Soon, the smallest of the two stars would vanish completely. I coughed meaningfully and shot a quick glance over my shoulder. Grudgingly extinguishing her cigarette, the hired musician picked up her French horn and began to play the sad music I had requested, but the moment wasn't quite what it could have been.

— FROM THE TRAVEL JOURNAL OF FLOYD WATT

me. Each Syndicate ship is run by an incredibly charismatic human Captain,[1] with a diverse senior management team under them, as well as a few-dozen randos with handguns.[2] Their missions, despite being much-celebrated as voyages of exploration, rarely seem to discover anything new. Indeed, 90 per cent of mission time tends to be spent having weirdly episodic encounters with well-known alien species, or solving outbreaks of bickering among the crew.

4 Hard Vacuum

This harsh, sparsely inhabited region of SPACE is home to the only people Earth astrophysicists respect. Universally human, the societies of Hard Vacuum refuse to use commonplace technologies such as teleportation and faster-than-light travel, since they insist they *just aren't possible*. These people even get irritated with the forgiving nature of the SPACE around them, and have embarked on massive engineering projects to make it colder and emptier, and to make planets in their territory more barren[3]. Still, even though their lives are lonely, dry, grim and difficult, the Hard Vacuumers take a great deal of pride in being more 'legitimate' than the colourful patchwork of cultures elsewhere in SPACE, whom they dismiss as mere fantasists.

5 The Galaxy

Although it's not technically a galaxy at all, this clump of 284 star systems is the biggest single-civilisation grouping in SPACE, and so I suppose we have to respect what its inhabitants – the ever-brash Stellar Warriors – call it.[4] Comprising weirdly uniform planets, each with a single terrain type, the Galaxy is ruled over by a startlingly incompetent, vindictive dictatorship, forever snatching defeat from the jaws of victory against a small band of armed insurrectionists. For their own part, these insurrectionists could have dismantled the monstrous

---

1   My favourite is Captain Karl Bludgeon, by a mile.

2   But the guns can be put on a setting that just makes people sleepy, so it's not a military force, OK?

3   It's called "terrorforming".

4   As far as I can tell, the designation is largely about bragging rights. This way, people can boast about being the best pilot in the Galaxy, or making the finest soup in the Galaxy – or whatever – and it's harder for people to disagree.

superstate decades ago, but they can't stop scrapping among themselves over the issue of whether 'girls are allowed to fight'. Honestly, the whole situation's maddening (and that's not even getting into the Sword Monks or their completely mental religion).

Despite the Syndicate's repeated demands to stop fighting, the Warriors don't know any other life – and besides, as they've said many times, the Syndicate is more than welcome to come and stop them if they reckon they're hard enough.[1]

---

1 'Who would win out of the Syndicate and the Galaxy' is always a cracking debate. And for the record, if all the best Syndicate Captains teamed up, they could totally defeat the whole Galaxy in an afternoon. It's just beneath the Syndicate, is all. They're classier than that.

2. UNDERSTANDING SPACE

 A Brief History

Oh right, this'll be easy, then. Just summarise the entire history of a few-thousand planets in a few-hundred words, shall I?[1] OK, fine. But I'm only going to give you the beginning, then skip to the end: the sagas that make up much of SPACE's history are so long and complex they can only be told via the interminable means of opera, and we've certainly not got time for that.

Nobody is quite sure when humans first began to cruise the void, but every culture in SPACE – aliens included – remembers the Space Men being there already when they reached the stars. The Space Men, however, claim to have no idea where they came from, or – if they're really honest – what they're doing. Ask them directly and they'll just start babbling on about the Mission while getting increasingly anxious.[2] There are rumours, however, that SPACE was inhabited long before even the Space Men. The Captains of Syndicated Space regularly encounter artefacts and derelicts belonging to a people called the Forebears, who apparently lived *ages* ago – but beyond that, almost nothing is known about them.

Floyd's Note
For ages, when people told me about the Forebears, I thought they were talking about Four Bears, and I got incredibly confused – sounded like the shittest creation myth ever. So, to be perfectly clear, there are no bears involved in the history of SPACE (apart from the Multibears of Ursinos VI, that is, but there were way more than four of them).

---

1 *Floyd, you have to at least try. – ES*

2 They're really not OK, the poor bastards.

SPACE Today

SPACE has had its ups and downs, but especially since the Syndicate banned all war outside the Galaxy, it has been a fairly tranquil place. Indeed, other than the Blundakh plague on Pletphah VII, the unexplained horror nimbus around Star Omega Six, and the other few minor, episodic crises one expects to crop up from day to day, there's never been a better time to visit. Or to claim planets in Earth's name![1,2]

Climate and Terrain

Except for the region of Hard Vacuum, whose fastidiously bleak inhabitants have gone out of their way to make their local environment as true to its name as possible, SPACE is not a true void at all. As such, it has weather like any other atmosphere, but considerably weirder, from the devastating firestorms of solar flares to the astonishingly pleasant phenomenon known as astro-snow. The planets and moons, of course, each have their own climates and landscapes, although they tend to fall into several common categories:

✳ **Earthlike** planets look uncannily like humanity's real-world home, only with randomised coastlines and maybe some different bugs. Perfect if you want to pack light.

✳ **'Palette swap'** worlds are often alien home worlds and, reflecting the nature of their inhabitants, tend to look like earthlike planets, but with different coloured foliage, water and sky.

✳ **Poly-Badlands** planets, often encountered by away teams

---

1 About that: if you run into any disgruntled diplomats on Outpost Bravo grumbling conspiratorially about a supposed 'land grab' by me on Earth's behalf, just ignore them. They don't know what they're talking about. And Eliza (since I know you're reading this), don't pay any heed to talk of me bribing Syndicate Captains to look the other way on all the flag-planting. Aliens talk a lot of shit, you know?

2 *Hmm. Right. – ES*

from Syndicate ships, resemble lifeless deserts, full of strange rock formations. The terrain is not made from rock, however, but from a strange, naturally-occurring form of expanded polystyrene, which tends to wobble alarmingly when a Captain is slammed against one while being strangled by a rubbery-skinned alien.

✳ **Single-biome** planets, common in the Galaxy region, are entirely covered in one extremely unimaginative terrain type, such as swamp, snow or lava. Sometimes they are also palette-swapped, but don't be fooled.

Wildlife

One might expect SPACE to be packed with incomprehensible wild beasts. But, just as is the case with its technologically advanced aliens, most of its fauna is startlingly comprehensible, being just a couple of anatomical degrees removed from familiar animal life. Nonetheless, there are some interesting specimens out there:

THE VAST AND THE CURIOUS

Spend enough time in a nebula and you'll almost certainly encounter the marvellous Astrocetaceans, more commonly known as SPACE Whales. While nothing like whales biologically (they appear more like gigantic, gas-filled worms), these filter-feeding drifters are well named, thanks to their enormous size, mournful foghorn cries and inquisitive, intelligent nature. While they are content to feed on astroplankton, however, their sheer scale means they will often swallow up anything not capable of getting out of the way fast enough – such as Space Man rocketships that have suffered equipment failures. It's not uncommon to look through the translucent hide of an Astrocetacean and find a colony of glum, bearded Space Men dejectedly banging on the walls of the body cavity in the hope you'll let them out.

✳ The bizarre **Astrofish** (*Piscis Stellaris*) appear remarkably similar to terrestrial fish, swimming through the void in the thicker nebulae and congregating in shoals millions strong. When they exhaust the food in one gas patch, they'll build up speed and leap into the void, where they'll freeze solid and drift until they hit another patch of air. Consequently, they're a dreaded navigational hazard, and any SPACE Captain lives in terror of a fish strike, when thousands of frozen Astrofish will start punching through their vessel's hull without warning.

✳ The creatures known as **Xenads** (*Pseudoscolopendra Badejo*), resembling giant centipedes, are thought to have been engineered by the Forebears either as a bioweapon or a truly horrendous prank. With their reputed habit of laying eggs in the mouths of unfortunate travellers, they tend to be exterminated as soon as a colony is discovered. And hey, even if they don't lay eggs in mouths, they're still pretty horrible, so it's no tragedy.[1]

✳ The **Multibears** (*Ursa Plethora*) of Ursinos VI nearly threatened to end all life in SPACE. Seemingly innocuous, almost rather cute orange bears, they had the unfortunate habit of duplicating at terrifying speed whenever someone looked at them, and soon multiplied to fill nine entire star systems. Amazingly, it turned out that in this one case in the entire history of apocalyptic catastrophes, the solution to the problem really was to ignore it until it went away.[2]

✳ **Beings of Pure Energy** (*Energia Etcetera*) are repulsively common in SPACE, and come in many varieties, differentiated largely by the colour of the whirly balls of lightning they're made up of. Everyone

---

1 *Has anyone tried talking to them? I don't want to point out the obvious, but they look exactly like the Scolopendrakin on Mittelvelde, who were also exterminated on sight as vile monsters, until they turned out to be thoroughly decent people (and they definitely don't lay eggs in anyone's mouths, for the record). – ES*

2 Even so, to this day it's illegal to turn a telescope towards any of the systems once blighted by the Multibears, just in case they're still there.

gets really excited when they come across their first BPE, until they realise it's essentially just vermin that looks like a shit special effect, and which is determined to dive into their personal electronics and fuck them up beyond repair.

People

Once again, while there's no hope of introducing the vast range of SPACE's cultures within the confines of this guide, there are certain groups you're almost certain to come across.

The Space Men

The Space Men are a culture of intense, square-jawed, *utterly identical* human men.[1] It's believed they're all descended from a single ace pilot, although wherever he came from has either vanished or is yet to be discovered. Either way, he was stranded on a tiny asteroid, and injected himself with an untested serum which turned him into a self-replicating organism. His millions of weird identical sons used floating debris to turn that asteroid into the city-sized structure known today as Outpost Bravo, and the rest is history. Although physically strong and mathematically gifted, the Space Men are weirdly helpless, endlessly getting into dire predicaments that they don't quite have the wits to fix. They're also extremely anxious about fulfilling the original Space Man's Mission,[2] although none of them have much of an idea what it was, beyond vague exploration. Professionals to the last, they wear their SPACEsuits at all times, talk using radio slang even in face-to-face conversation, and huff down cigarettes non-stop. Although they're neither SPACE's most accomplished inhabitants nor its most popular, they happened to

---

1   They reproduce by budding, just like yeast. It's extremely odd. The newly budded Space Men aren't even babies, just sort of . . . crunched-up, muscly little men born with the minds of their progenitors, who slowly expand over the course of a few weeks. They're prolific budders too, so it's lucky they've such a titanic mortality rate, or they would overcome the whole sector.

2   The Space Men are very anxious about *everything*, given the sheer amount of amphetamine rations they feel compelled to chew their way through.

end up building their base in the centre, so now they're lumbered with running this neutral ground for everyone else.

Robots

The Space Men are assisted in their work by a species of self-aware yet astonishingly primitive robots. These automatons – self-assembling copies of the original Space Man's mechanical companion – despise the Space Men, and the Space Men harbour a thunderous (and wholly reasonable) collective paranoia over the intentions and integrity of the robots. While grim tradition dictates that every Spaceman works with a lifelong robot partner, these partnerships are almost always dynamos of mutual loathing. Because of this, the two communities stay well away from each other outside of formal Mission time, with the robots of Outpost Bravo living in a greasy, sparking warren of tunnels, as far from the Space Men as possible.

SPACE Pirates

Once upon a time, armed seizure of cargo by rogue crews was a major hazard to those travelling in SPACE. But with the abolition of armed conflict across most of the sector at the behest of the Syndicate, most privateers headed to the rowdier environs of the Galaxy for richer pickings. This left something of a vacuum, into which stepped several retired Captains from Spume.[1] They brought with them their philosophy and methodology of piracy, and while it took them a while to master the art of sailing the nearly void, they've become rather successful. When a SPACE Pirate vessel threatens a boarding

---

1 I have no idea how they got from Spume to SPACE, of course. Certainly, the suggestion that I accepted bribes from Spume to allow certain individuals to relocate is simply bunkum, and fodder for the credulous mind. .

SHADOWS IN THE VOID

Despite the enlightened technological nature of its inhabitants, SPACE is a place that lends itself well to ghost stories. All over the sector, you'll occasionally hear tales of ships half-glimpsed: phantom vessels cloaked behind shimmering force fields, which project fleeting images and thoughts into the minds of the crews who encounter them before vanishing without a trace. Some say these ships are an alien species yet to be formally encountered, while others argue they are the Forebears themselves, still around after all these years, silently observing their domain. Either way, they're really creepy.

action, most Captains would rather instantly capitulate and pay for them to go away than endure the time-consuming, theatrical nonsense of Spume-style buccaneering.

Aliens

There are around seventy known species of sentient alien, with virtually all of them conforming to a fairly standard humanoid configuration:

✳ The sweating, gargle-voiced **Hunglrrrrgh** (aka the dogmen)[1]

are an honourable people beloved to the Stellar Warriors; their thick coat of reeking fur seems to give them the impression that it's fine to walk around completely starkers. I suppose it would be fine if the fur at least covered their big grim balls.[2]

✳ The deathly dull **Hephaestans**, who co-govern the Syndicate with humans,[3] literally just look like people with a bit of make-up and weird hair. I'm told they've got slightly odd necks, but I'm not really seeing it.

---

1 *It's literally only you who calls them that. – ES*
2 *They're not balls, you fool! They're external kidneys! – ES*
3 Ugh, seriously, they're astonishingly boring. All they talk about is maths.

PEW! PEW! WHOOSH! PEW!

Part of the joy of the Stellar Warriors' obstinately martial culture is their utter refusal to abandon weapons and tactics that make next to no sense in a high-tech SPACE combat environment. Their greatest heroes, the Sword Monks, insist on fighting with the blades that give them their name, while the outcomes of even the largest fleet engagements, between dozens of mile-long vessels, will always be decided by the actions of squadrons of tiny fighter craft. Everyone wonders why the Warriors maintain this archaic, inefficient means of fighting, until they take a ride in the passenger seat of an Insurrectionist C-7Z and realise it's the most thrilling thing a person can experience with their trousers on.

✳ The **Olang** are the orange-skinned, bat-nosed chief rivals of the Syndicate – a crafty bunch who constantly manage to work around the peacekeeping efforts of their adversaries and cause mischief.[1]

✳ The **Unk** are a warrior race[2] of tusked, grey-skinned bruisers who used to be the Syndicate's main antagonists, forever causing trouble, until war was banned. Now they are under the protection of their former enemies, and have honest jobs as security staff on many Syndicate vessels.[3]

---

1 Their bloody lawyers are always pulling contracts out of their arses 'proving' the Olang have rights to various SPACE-bound resources, but the canny Syndicate Captains always see through their nonsense.

2 *Important: do they call themselves a 'warrior race', Floyd? Because if not, that is really not an OK term to use. – ES*

3 *Oh shit. It's only just hit me. They're . . . they're Orcs, aren't they? This is Mittelvelde all over again. – ES*

3. PLANNING YOUR TRIP

 When to Visit

Given the sheer number of different calendars in play across all of SPACE, there's no one time it's best to visit, although there are some local cultural landmarks you simply have to see if you can:

Punch Moon Destruction

It's hard to grasp exactly what the Dictatorship that runs the Galaxy actually stands for, but one thing it *loves* is building nonsensical superweapons. And the insurrectionists love blowing them up just as much. To ensure cultural continuity, therefore, every five years the Dictatorship begins constructing the Punch Moon, an artificial planetoid armed with a giant extendable boxing glove, with which it threatens to knock a civilian planet's lights out. The insurrectionists will typically spend most of the half-decade construction period arguing about whether ladies should be seen flying fighter crafts, and then scramble at the last minute to exploit the Punch Moon's traditional glaring weakness. The Moon's detonation is an unrivalled fireworks display,[1] and the celebration afterwards lasts for as long as it takes an insurrectionist leader to insist that only men should do the flying next time.

Hephaestan Shag Week

Every twelve years, the frighteningly boring Hephaestans undergo a hormonal transformation that means they spend a week desperate to either fight or bang everything around them. In fairness, they're perfectly respectful of others' consent, but it's still extremely irritating when you're trying to enjoy a nice evening at an Olangian seafood buffet, only to find a half-dozen pinch-faced logicians running a train on the salad bar.[2]

---

1 Sadly, falling debris usually exterminates all life on the planet the Moon was constructed around, but that's not something to worry about during the shindig.

2 I mean, who fucks a salad?

DON'T MISS: *AESCHYLUS ONE*

If you fancy an extremely strange cruise with elements of a giant murder-mystery party, I recommend a trip on the *Aeschylus One*, a battleship turned refugee vessel from a planet whose human occupants were overthrown by androids who looked exactly like people. The ship now wanders round SPACE in a slow circle, with everyone aboard constantly trying to work out which of their peers is secretly a robot. Of course, the tragedy is that the *Aeschylus'* organic crew all died of anxiety decades ago: everyone who remains is a robot, pretending to be a human, who's paranoid that *everyone else* is a robot.[1]

---

1 When dining with these people, it's incredibly funny to say 'bleep bloop' in the middle of sentences, and then swear blind that you didn't say anything when questioned. Really messes with their heads.

 ## Getting Around

Getting to even the furthest reaches of SPACE is a trivial business, with trade routes connecting Outpost Bravo to almost every conceivable destination. From the enormous gleaming vessels of the Syndicate, which stop regularly at Outpost Bravo for trade and resupply, to the million-plus ramshackle private vessels known to the station's docks, you'll have no trouble finding a conveyance option to match your budget. Just bear in mind that if you want to go somewhere really dicey, or you've got sod all in the way of dosh, you're going to end up on one of the cantankerous, leaky red rocketships of the Space Men, at which point you're playing Russian roulette with your life.

Eating and Drinking

The restaurants of SPACE between them boast a veritable galaxy of Michelin stars (or at least their cosmic equivalents), meaning a smorgasbord of opportunities for the budding gastronaut. And while shipboard fare can be a little ... algal, especially among more austere cultures, you'll find you're never more than a few light minutes[1] from a slap-up feed.

SPACE'S
BEST BARS and RESTAURANTS

The Ves Banyopp Taverna – *Once renowned as the ultimate hangout for the rowdiest lowlifes in the Galaxy, this legendary dive is now somewhat cleaned up for the tourist crowd, with memorabilia all over the walls and a bar crowded with preening wannabes. You can still get threatened by a geezer with an anus for a face while ordering if you feel you really need to, but it'll cost you a pretty penny these days.*

Finale – *Tacky but moderately amusing chain restaurant claiming to be at the end of time, where you can watch the universe 'explode' (actually a clever sound and light show) as you eat. Don't be fooled into paying through the nose for the meat that supposedly 'implores you to eat it' – it's actually just a waiter under the table, doing a silly voice.*

Hroopenblups – *An extravagant alien-friendly cocktail bar in Syndicated SPACE, run by a lady with three nostrils and an otherwise ordinary face. Great spot to drink glowing neon-coloured mixed drinks while checking out the extravagant fashions on display, or watching Syndicate Science Dreadnoughts launching from the nearby drydock.*

The Grand Concourse – *Public space on Outpost Bravo, where alien residents hawk their home cuisine. Some foods are genuinely weird*

---

1 *Floyd, you do realise one light minute is eleven-million miles, right? – ES*

– you simply must try the inevitable bowl full of live, glowing tentacles when it's offered – but many are as disappointingly familiar as the aliens themselves, for example the classic 'apple with antennae instead of a stalk.'

Recreation Chamber Thirteen – *Austere watering hole where the crew of Outpost Bravo go to drink. At all times of day, you'll find this cramped, windowless hole rammed with rows of Space Men, cheek to jowl but not talking; just pounding back artificial ethanol and sweating. Just about the only concession to fun is the fact that the music – atonal, psychedelic drone rock – is turned up so high that the patrons can't hear each other howl to themselves in existential despair.*

☀ Floyd's Tip

Space Man cuisine isn't really much to write home about, having been designed entirely for efficient sustenance over pleasure. The Space Men will take fresh food then grimly hoy it into the hoppers of a giant machine that grinds, blasts, boils, pulps, leaches and presses it, before spitting out a row of tiny pellets. Despite seeming to absolutely shatter the law of conservation of energy, it seems a Space Man can obtain an entire day's nutrition from just three of these pellets – an orange one, a green one and the unspeakable 'dinner wafer'.[1] The Space Man regimen can be interesting to try once,[2] but that's generally where the fun should end.

Currency

With only a few minor exceptions, all planets in SPACE accept the universal currency known as Starbucks, which take the form of small golden rectangles. These are minted and regulated by the Egh – an alien

---

1 It's just more amphetamines.
2 Especially if you like the idea of being able to see the accusing, spectral forms of long-dead Space Men in your peripheral vision.

species whose defining characteristic is that they are obsessed with money – and come in denominations starting at 14.99 million. Regrettably, you see, the Syndicate's recent initiative to expand their fleet of Science Dreadnoughts[1] tenfold has necessitated the printing of quite a bit of new money, and inflation has become a bit of an issue.

DAILY SAMPLE COSTS

BUDGET: Less than 10 billion Starbucks
Zero-G bunk in the crew section of Outpost Bravo (smoker's berth): **5bn SB**
One day's Space Man Misery Rations: **1.5bn SB**
Ten minutes in the Outpost Bravo Imagination Hole: **2bn SB**
One day's flight aboard a Space Man rocketship: **7bn SB**

MIDRANGE: Between 10–50 billion Starbucks
Homestay with a family of Jalllooare Sandranchers: **42bn SB**
Tall glass of premium green SPACEmilk: **14bn SB**
Rental of a co-pilot seat in an insurrectionist fighter craft: **31bn SB**
Passage aboard a supposedly crap freighter that ends up outflying military vessels: **36bn SB**

TOP END: More than 50 billion Starbucks
Officer's quarters on a Syndicate Science Dreadnought: **112bn SB**
Exquisite seafood from a planet with loads of consonants in its name: **56bn SB**
Ticket to a Syndicate Captains' gala dinner (includes tickets to an Unk Fight): **173bn SB**
Single Teleportation: **60bn SB** (also technically costs your life as you are broken into your component atoms and then 'printed' elsewhere, but . . . y'know. Don't think about it too hard)

---

1 *Is that really what they're calling their battleships? I thought the Bison King lacked subtlety, Floyd, but the Syndicate really take the cake. – ES*

DRESS TO FLOURESCE: SPACE FASHION

When choosing your outfit for day-to-day life among the stars, it's better to fall on the side of the outré – among aliens in particular, there's a running joke over which species can wear the most ludicrous costumes and still be taken seriously by humans. Inevitably, this long-running competition has accidentally spawned some genuine fashion miracles, and so alien communities on human stations and vessels tend to be something of a haute couture extravaganza. Here's how to copy their look:

* In general, silver fabrics are always a good choice, while sequins, headdresses and extravagantly weird make-up are all highly recommended.

* Diaphanous fabrics are almost always a good shout, but shiny plastics can be a hit if you've got the confidence to pull them off.

* Glowsticks. Everywhere you can stick them.

* If you're not dressing to impress, there are practical considerations. Cold is often an issue, especially on poorly insulated Space Man vessels, so a good knitted jumper is advisable at the very least.

* Magnetic boots are also a good call, as, while artificial gravity is de rigueur in most off-planet situations, you don't want to be left drifting like a poached egg if you find yourself on a ship without it.

IN SPACE, *EVERYONE* CAN HEAR YOU SCREAM

If you're spending time in the districts where the Space Men sleep, be prepared to endure the constant sound of worried barks and shouts – these poor sods are tormented by nightmares and fitful sleep, and the walls of their bunkhouses are paper-thin. There's a reason why the cheapest accommodation in the station can be found here.

 ## Don't Forget to Pack . . .

Translatron
These superb gizmos, sold at kiosks run by Egh entrepreneurs on Outpost Bravo, allow the wearer to understand any language spoken in SPACE.[1]

Towel
One of the SPACE's local guidebooks claims towels are completely essential packing for any visitor to the region, but I don't really get the hype. I mean, they're all right after a shower, or for wiping up sick after you've quacked a gutful in zero-G, but that's about it.

A beach ball
On a SPACEship in distress, with just seconds to go until the hull breaches? 'There's no need to panic', as they say! Just inflate this bad boy and keep it with you. Then, even if you do get blasted into the void, you'll have a good few huffs of air to last until someone can throw you a SPACE Rope and haul you to safety.

Phillips-head screwdriver
Funny story, actually: I was on a Space Man rocketship headed to Syndicated SPACE when I spilled coffee on the controls and they

---

1 *Floyd, it's a complete grift, mate! They're just lumps of plastic! And, like, have you never stopped to realise that everyone, in every World, speaks English anyway? I mean, that struck me immediately, but you do you. – ES*

jammed up completely.[1] The bloody vessel started plunging towards the heart of the nearest star, and I must admit I got fairly worried. But then, would you believe it, this fellow just showed up out of *nowhere*, wearing a ridiculous bow tie and a flappy coat, and waved a screwdriver at the dashboard. Fixed it instantly, then vanished again. No idea who the hell he was or what he did,[2] but I've carried a screwdriver with me ever since.

 ## Manners and Etiquette

Say how impressive everything is

Especially among the Space Men, it's worth downplaying how familiar you are with advanced technology, if only out of politeness. You see, the sheer *quaintness* of their technology will astound and delight you: it's all shiny chrome and chunky, colourful buttons, along with green-screen computers, glowing orbs and cream plastic panelling. It might seem pathetic and obsolete, but the Space Men are very proud of their machinery and will be very upset if you laugh at it.

Shit in secret

For an unknown reason, Syndicate crewmembers have a mortal terror of being seen going to the loo. For this reason, the toilets on their ships are all hidden, ingeniously disguised as laboratories or store cupboards. This can be maddening at first, but it lends a weird speakeasy mystique to the business of taking a dump, and can be great fun when you get used to it.

---

1 Well, actually, it was wine. But still – those Space Men and their shoddy kit!

2 I suspect he was a Wizard.

4. SUGGESTED ITINERARIES

📋 1. A TASTE OF SPACE: (6 DAYS[1])
At Home with the Space Men

This budget holiday will give you a sample of all SPACE has to offer in the jankily cosmopolitan environs of Outpost Bravo.

DAY 1

After navigating the bustling crowds of the station's arrival hall, the rest of the day is set aside for acclimatisation to the cosmic lifestyle. Despite being largely a utilitarian structure, with many areas cold, grubby and lit by dim CRT monitors, you'll find the Outpost also has some outstanding beauty spots, if you know where to look. Spend the afternoon in the docking complex watching sleek, finned rocketships cruising to and fro, or watching nebulae swirl through the misty glass ceiling of a relaxation dome, before hitting one of the entertainment districts for an exotic evening meal.

DAY 2

It's time to get used to the stale scent of astronaut sweat and cigarette smoke, as you head to the warren-like expanse of the crew quarters to experience the spartan life of the Space Men. These neurotic hunks spend most of their time working at primitive computer terminals, furthering their inscrutable 'Missions', and to be fair, their time off isn't much more fun either, being spent either frantically working out, dozing fitfully in rows of grimy sleeping bags or smashing back machinery-flavoured spirits in the Recreation Chambers. It's probably more rewarding to watch than to join in.

1   SPACE weeks are six days long.

AN ANNOTATED GUIDE TO OUTPOST BRAVO

❶ Diameter of the station ....1 mile

❶ Population of Outpost Bravo: 635,000

Split of population:

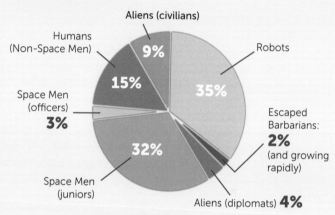

❶ Most powerful processor speed on the Outpost .... 18 MB

❶ Average cigarettes smoked per day, per Space Man 28

❶ Average daily menu for a Space Man... Green pellet, orange pellet, "dinner wafer" (drugs)

❶ Alien species represented ....Loads

As the station lights dim for the night cycle, why not take a trip to the Imagination Hole, where 'advanced' hologram projectors can recreate scenes straight out of your head. The Space Men have mostly stopped using the Hole out of fear, since it keeps showing them images of their dead ancestors pointing fingers in condemnation, but these visions rarely occur to tourists, so you'll probably be all right. Alternatively, enjoy live music featuring a disproportionate number of theremins, participate in some furtive Megagambling activities, or head to the Fight Dome, where you can watch twitching, sweat-drenched Space Men have fist fights with aliens to the accompaniment of a live orchestra playing discordant battle music.

DAY 3

Spending too much time with the Space Men can be overbearingly stressful, so head to the station's outer ring, where the civilian population lives. Studding the circumference of the ring are the botany domes, where trees, crops and lush tropical foliage are grown beneath the stars, which are fantastic spots for a picnic – so long as you can handle the Barbarians (see below). If that's not your cup of astro-tea, take in the hubbub of the Grand Concourse, where dozens of alien vendors have made an insane three-dimensional maze of stalls. The low gravity settings mean you can swim between them like an astrofish with an appetite for tourist tat – but don't get your trajectory wrong, as some of the food sellers are frankly reckless about signposting fire hazards.[1]

DAY 4

If you're after a unique experience, you might want to visit the labyrinthine robot habitation district[2] known as Bleeptown, in the levels of the station surrounding its engine core.[3] Expecting artificial intelligences with almost godlike intellectual capabilities, visitors often find these bulky mechanical citizens quite endearing, with their rasping voices,

---

1 *You could also argue that some visitors are frankly reckless about getting lunchtime-pissed and then passing out in zero-G, before drifting slowly through the flames of a barbecue and catching alight. – ES*

2 *Some might say 'ghetto' – ES*

3 The reason this area has been left to the robots is that it's saturated in radiation from the engine's amateurish shielding, so either find lead-based fashion choices or bring plenty of anti-rads.

SAFETY FIRST

By our standards at least, Outpost Bravo is an absolute death trap, with unshielded reactors, wonky airlocks and alarming structural weaknesses all over the place There are quite a lot of dangerous alien life forms stowed away in the recesses of the station too, either brought back as spores from away Missions or escaped from labs, so be sure to stick to well-lit areas when traversing the station. Most notably, some of the botany domes have been infested by Barbarians from the nearby moon of Grondorra, who insist on constantly pillaging crops, while there's a cabal of vampires living in one of the engine rooms, feeding casually off the Space Man engineers. Nobody's quite sure where *they* came from, but they're bad news.

spinning head-mounted radar dishes and propensity for reading out long strings of numbers. Whatever you do, though, don't patronise the robots – they seem *this close* to starting a violent uprising against the Space Men, and the last thing the situation needs is a well-intentioned tourist sticking their oar in.[1] If robots aren't your thing, you can always head to one of the station's alien quarters to enjoy a 'psychic' experience with an Olang mystic.[2]

DAY 5

It's worth taking a trip deep inside the station to view Outpost Alpha, the tiny asteroid where the original Space Man was stranded, and which has been kept intact at the heart of Bravo as a sort of memorial. There's a

---

1 *Floyd, in what world does ordering a robot to breakdance for your amusement not count as 'sticking one's oar in'? – ES*

2 Your mileage may vary: I paid through the nose for a man with a wrinkly ear to give me a 'vision of the future', and all I saw was some lady with antlers beckoning me through a load of fog. Nice try, mate, but I could do that myself with dry ice and a couple of tree branches. He wasn't fooling me for a moment.

— TESTIMONIALS —

Outpost Bravo? Outpost their fucking bedtime, more like. I don't know who sent these clowns to SPACE, but they're made of the Wrong Stuff, and it'd be an act of mercy to take them back at this point. I wanted to take my grandson for an exciting retro sci-fi break, but I didn't count on the kind of exciting that involves superheated steam and engines shaking themselves apart. These jokers want to spend less time being complete lunatics and more time fixing their bloody station. Nice views, though – I'll give them that.

— Roger Loaves, 72, Engineer

Did anyone else find Outpost Bravo incredibly creepy, or was it just me? Seriously – that Outpost Alpha exhibition was properly sketchy about what happened in the early days, after that bloke got stranded on the asteroid. Was he really the sole survivor? What did he eat for all that time alone? And what's the deal with all the ghosts? Don't tell me it's just the Space Men who see them – they're everywhere in the deeper parts of the station.

— Kelly Pigeon, 34, Artist

My husband and I had a fantastic homestay with Gluthoor, a Klambian empath who runs a little boutique just off quadrant three of the hab-ring. They've knocked down a lot of the Space Men's bulkheads to make a bit of room there, and it's becoming quite a pleasant little district, with a park, a theatre and some decent shopping. We were lucky enough to be there when the station was passing a school of Astrocetaceans, and one came right past the window of our apartment. Unforgettable.

— Maureen Bouffant, 43, Marketing Director

neat recreation of the Space Man's original rocketship, and a little exhibition about the settlement's early days, as well as the Space Man's SOS transponder, still broadcasting after all this time, with no reply from home.[1] Another must-visit location is the Bridge: a pod full of wheezing machinery and bleeping computer terminals that serves as the nerve centre of the whole Outpost. Here, dozens of Space Men rush around the haggard, chair-bound figure of the Captain, trying their best to do duties they barely understand. If you're lucky enough to be there for a Red Alert, you may even get to experience 'the shudders': the entire structure is built on a bed of hydraulic springs, so it can jerk around with sparks flying out of every console during a crisis.

DAY 6

On your last day, it's time to experience the void itself, as you rent a relatively safe SPACEsuit and head outside for a two-hour SPACEwalk. Most visitors opt to spend their walk staring at the stars in quiet contemplation while praying that the pump on the other end of the air hose doesn't break down. However, if you're more of an adventurous type, you can make a good few Starbucks by heading out with a rake and doing your best to dislodge some of the metal-eating starnacles that infest the station's hull.

 ## 2. THE PENULTIMATE FRONTIER: (2 SPACE WEEKS)

Trekking with the Syndicate

It's all very well mucking around on Outpost Bravo, but if you want to see SPACE in style there's simply no other way to do it than with one of the Syndicate's legendary Captains.

---

1 Privately, many suspect there's a good reason that Mission Control has never phoned back. After all, we only think the Space Man was his civilisation's greatest pilot because that's what his identical descendants tell us. Honestly, if he was much like the bunch of dolts who currently run Outpost Bravo, I can imagine why his people wanted shot of him.

DAY 1

After arrival at Outpost Bravo, hang out at the docking complex until you spot a crew of extremely professional-looking SPACEfarers in svelte jumpsuits, with colours corresponding to their jobs. This is the crew of Captain Tess Aquitaine, and they'll be your hosts for the next few days. They'll probably be negotiating a legal dispute with some sort of alien, but when they're done, introduce yourself and board their majestic Science Dreadnought, the *SSD Intrepide*.

DAYS 2–5

Once aboard, you'll spend a couple of days being wowed by the *Intrepide*'s swanky interior, jazz-infused lounges and erotic hologram entertainment. Unfortunately, you won't see much action. Although Eliza rates Aquitaine,[1] I think she's dull as dust, as she solves every crisis she encounters with talking, and emotions other than rage. Still, this trip guarantees at least one CSS (Challenging SPACE Situation), chosen from the following list:

✳ Intervention in a civil war between two species of alien who share a planet but have different-coloured noses; they must learn to get along despite their differences.

✳ Capture of an away team by a giant blue octahedron; the shape only lets them escape once they discover the true meaning of compassion.

✳ Visit to the sad planet Lachrimosa, where the ship's clown on the *Intrepide*, Blumboid, helps the gloomy Lachrimosans rediscover their sense of fun in time to avert the self-destruction of their world.

✳ Resolution of an interminable squabble between the bridge crew over who left the SPACEmilk out of the fridge.

1 *I said she's better than Bludgeon. That's not hard. – ES*

☀️ Floyd's Tip

Feel free to sleep through your assigned CSS: you won't miss much. Pretty much all of the action on Aquitaine's missions could just as easily take place in a supermarket as on a SPACEship, and you'll be lucky even to see the lasers fire once. Even then it will be to do something soft like set off fireworks.

DAY 6

Captain Aquitaine will drop you off at Klapdran's, a dilapidated SPACE pub (or SPACE bar - ha!) in the outskirts of Chiasmus Quadrant,[1] where you'll meet up with your second Captain (and by far my favourite) – the legendary Karl Bludgeon. When you meet Karl, he'll almost certainly be having some gigabeers with the boys from the bridge and wearing some kind of badass jacket over his regulation tunic. Grab him a drink and wait for the inevitable fistfight with one of the pub's rowdier alien groups to kick off. Karl will win.

DAYS 7–11

After boarding Karl's ship (also confusingly called the *Intrepide*), you'll meet its crew of handsome roustabouts, and join them for an altogether more boisterous tour of the stars. While Karl is bound to respect the ban on war enshrined in Syndicate law, he's subject to a special exemption allowing him to have fist fights whenever he likes, so the CSS options on his part of the trip are considerably more exciting than Aquitaine's:

✴ A trip to Blethrigar, homeworld of the Ranidans, where Karl will wander around aimlessly with a ripped shirt until one of the world's rubbery inhabitants (who despise nudity) tries to lamp him. Then he has a fist fight and goes home.

---

1 It's not as dilapidated as some of the rougher bars in the Galaxy, but it's nasty enough.

SPACE

✳ Crisis in which Karl's Hephaestan first mate Hrup falls into the clutches of Hephaestan Shag Fever and won't stop fucking a wardrobe. Karl tells him to cut it the hell out, but Hrup doesn't listen, so they have a fist fight.

✳ Journey to a planet of purple-skinned aliens where women are treated as property. Karl fist fights its emperor in order to win the right to make out with as many consenting aliens as he likes. Nobody is freed, however.

✳ Encounter with a cloaked Olang warship threatening the *Intrepide*, until Karl dons his Nuclear Knuckledusters, leaves the airlock while holding his breath and has a fist fight with it.

DAY 12

After a brief detour that hardly bears mentioning,[1] the *Intrepide* will take you back to Outpost Bravo, from where you can return home, inspired by Bludgeon's heroic services to the Syndicate.

 ## 3. CONTRASTING SPACES: (5 OR 192 DAYS)

Hard Vacuum and the Galaxy

This itinerary might seem grim at the start, but the long haul is worth it, if only to appreciate the knockabout fun afterwards as you join the most enjoyable civil war in the Worlds.

DAY 1

Meet with the crew of Sisyphus VII, a joyless border outpost at the edge

---

1 *I beg to fucking differ, Floyd. I saw the cargo manifest, and I know full well Bludgeon sold five platoons of Unk 'security officers' to the Stellar Warriors and pocketed the cash himself. He's a hair's breadth from being a goddamned slave trader, yet you still love him because he's got a cool jacket and a winning smile. Don't give me that bullshit about it being his 'evil universe counterpart' either – he trots that out every time he commits an atrocity, and you believe it. – ES*

of Hard Vacuum, as it prepares the cargo ship *Boulder 3* for yet another gruelling journey to Sisyphus VIII, the next station along the chain. The hard-faced, malnourished astronauts will give you interminable briefings about how dangerous SPACE is, but don't listen to a word of it – no matter how much they want SPACE to be difficult and scary, it's all just wishful thinking. Just give them a knowing smirk and move into your berth on the *Boulder 3*.

DAYS 2–189

While the journey to Sisyphus VIII could be achieved in minutes with even a low-end faster-than-light drive, the Hard Vacuumers insist on doing everything at sub-light speeds. This means you're in for twenty-seven incredibly cramped, depressing weeks on a 'real' SPACE mission, cooped up with a load of humourless bores. You're not even allowed to open a window to let the breeze in. You will come to be able to tell each crew member by the smell of their farts, and you will grow to hate them all.

DAY 3 (OR DAY 190, IF YOU'RE HARDCORE)

Luckily, when you can't handle any more, and you feel The Madness might be closing in, you can bail out at any moment. I lasted until the second day of the voyage – but who knows, you might stick it out for longer!

Either way, when you're ready, punch the pre-agreed code into your SPACEphone and a battered freighter will show up in a blaze of light, having crossed the light years from its home port in a matter of moments. This will absolutely *enrage* the Hard Vacuumers, and they'll bang on the windows of the *Boulder* to complain that FTL travel isn't possible. After that, they'll get *even angrier* when they realise the freighter's pilot can hear them banging, and is laughing with derision. Take your leave of them, making sure to get your own back for the farts by leaving the door open on the way out.[1]

Once aboard your new ride, you'll meet its pilot – the dashing rogue

---

1 They will be apoplectic that they aren't asphyxiating.

IN-FLIGHT ENTERTAINMENT

While onboard, make sure to kick back and take advantage of the onboard creature comforts. You can play a sci-fi version of Connect 4, where the counters are little holographic monsters, or chat with what's-his-name the Sword Monk about his bonkers religion. He might even cajole you into firing a handgun in the close confines of the guest lounge while wearing a blindfold, claiming it's a mystical experience. Alternatively, switch on the megately and watch a SPACE Opera beamed directly from the Galactic Capital – I recommend *The Saga of Nasty Daddy*, a three-part epic following the life of the naughty boy who grew up to be the armoured colossus at the right hand of the Galactic Dictator himself.

Jimmo Smirk – and his nine-foot-tall dogman friend, Gnnnnnnnngh. The pair are smugglers, flying right under the noses of the Dictatorship with a hold full of contraband, and they live aboard the ship with a Sword Monk whose name I can't remember since he waved his hand in front of my face once too often.

DAY 4

On day five, Jimmo, Gnnnnnnnnngh and Thingy will take you to the Ves Banyopp Taverna, on the planet of Thrasheroo, for a big night out. Things will get hairy and limbs will be severed – the Sword Monk can't hold his bloody drink *at all* – but by the end of the night you'll all have declared each other best mates, and someone will have ended up nearly copping off with a relative. When Jimmo realises he's way too pissed to fly his ship back to orbit, you'll all climb inside a dead animal to stay warm for the night, and wake up feeling like death.

Honestly, Ves Banyopp was too much for me, and I had to head home at this point. I think I was meant to be going to some kind of swamp to learn sword fighting from a muppet, but I really couldn't handle it on that level of hangover.

CHAPTER SIX
Grondorra!

WELCOME TO GRONDORRA!

Wind-blasted plains, steaming jungles, peril and pleasure and awe: all await you on Grondorra! Here is a grandeur too brutal to be tamed, and where there is no beaten track – save that which you beat for yourself with the flat of a sword. It's not an easy destination, but it never fails to reward the mighty.

? Why Grondorra!?[1]

If destinations were meals, then perhaps Mittelvelde would be a hearty stew and Spume a rich bouillabaisse. Good, balanced dishes, nourishing the senses and the soul alike. Grondorra!, by contrast, would be a bucket of raw mince eaten with clenched fists at the heart of a thunderstorm. This primeval moon, at the heart of the Pulp Nebula, screams around the gas giant Grum in a cloud-scrapingly low orbit, packed with broadswords, magic, dinosaurs and (thanks to its situation within SPACE) ray guns and rocketships too. It's old school, to say the least. And yet it commands such primal romance, such jagged authenticity that even self-proclaimed sceptics will find themselves drawn to return again and again.[2]

Climate and Terrain

Grondorra is girdled by the Great Plain, a lunar sea of parched grass, fraying occasionally into skeleton-haunted desert or parting around

---

1   The exclamation mark is technically mandatory whenever discussing the place, but I find it ludicrous, and even Eliza agrees with me. I'm not going to bother using it anymore.

2   Honestly speaking, I was expecting to hate Grondorra, but I was very pleasantly surprised. It's an acquired taste, for sure, but I'm a fan. With this world, for once, what you see is what you get. Frankly, I needed that.

volcanic jungles. The Plain is pocked with the remnants of a thousand civilisations – some mere ruins, others still clinging to the stagnating decadence of former glory. But between them is only emptiness . . . and Barbarians.[1] Grondorra crashes regularly through Grum's debris rings like a roustabout being hurled through a plate-glass window, plunging ordinary days into orbital bombardments of rock and ice. Volcanoes vent the moon's guts as they compress under gravitic stress, while Moonquakes are near-constant, from minor trembles to city-swallowing cataclysms.[2] Still, there's a fun side to it all: Grondorra's tiny size gives it extremely low gravity, meaning even complete duffers can run marathons with ease here. Even better, the planetary radiation that gives such 'dramatic'[3] sun tans also paints breathtaking aurorae across the night sky, allowing for some 'oohs' and 'aahs' to go with all the 'AAAARRGHs' on your holiday.

 # History

Grondorra's history is a nightmare to unpick, as its thin soils conceal an ocean of ruin: the bones of once-mighty civilisations lying atop one another in a planetary mass grave. There are even gods down there – or at least monsters horrible enough to mistake for them.[4] Answering the question of who was here first, however, is akin to trying to work out who started a drunken argument. However, several discoveries of ancient rock paintings suggest that before everything got complicated, the first Barbarians shared the world with the Deer Folk, a people they represented as deer-headed humans with slit-pupilled eyes.[5]

GRONDORRA

---

1 We'll get to them.

2 Of course, this doesn't necessarily mean the cities stop . . . citying, but it does often involve the residents rapidly evolving into shrieking troglodytes.

3 *Cancerous.* – ES

4 Spend five minutes among the Barbarians and you'll hear about bloody Gak, the ant-faced god. Apparently, he lives in a deep hole, and they despise him.

5 This is odd, to say the least, because the only deer-headed humanoids on Grondorra these days are the atrocious Stagmen, created by a depressed Sorcerer who wanted something to loathe other than himself. He did a good job with these braying, punch-drunk cretins.

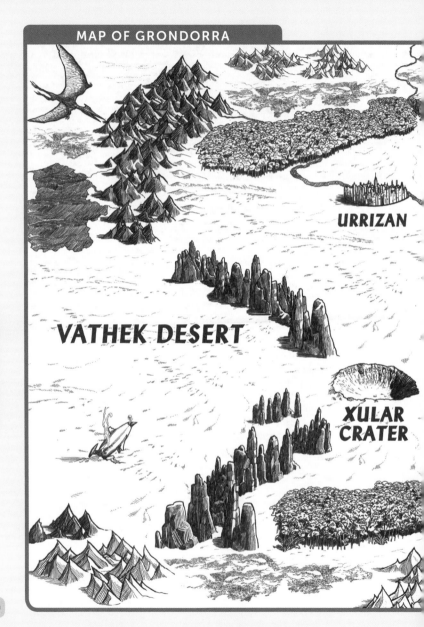

MAP OF GRONDORRA

URRIZAN

VATHEK DESERT

XULAR
CRATER

Mt. GRUM

RESEARCH STATION ZETA

Only one culture has remained a constant through all of Grondorra's wild history: the iconic Barbarians, as raw and ruthless as the moon itself. They are . . . big. Thanks to the low gravity, the Barbarians grow large enough to consider seven feet dumpy, and are stacked with rippling pecs, thighs like overfed pythons and abdominal muscles like a child's drawing of a window. They are extremely erotic, if you're into that sort of thing.

But despite their sheer physical presence, these Nietzschean beefcakes believe the mind is the greatest muscle of them all.[1] Indeed, the Barbarians spend much of their time deliberating over the question of what is 'good in life' – usually by oiling up, swaggering into cities and taking whatever they want. It's a strange means of contemplation, but it never leaves them short of an answer. They are hedonists, unconcerned with anything except the pursuit of experience and its seizure through individual prowess.[2]

DON'T FORGET TO PACK: OIL

Even if you're not a particularly beefy sort, you'll draw a lot of funny looks in Barbarian company if you don't grease any exposed flesh until it glistens. This will confer the additional benefit of making you slip from the hands of any potential strangle-happy assailants.

---

1 One of the biggest heroes in Barbarian oral culture is Gukleth the Roaster, a woman paralysed from the neck down who demolished her foes not through hammering them flat with a hammer, but with devastating rhyming couplets.

2 They've got a crap sense of humour, mind. Don't fall for the old chestnut of 'the puzzle of steel', in which they'll set you a silly riddle about swords and then hit you really hard on the back of the head with a length of steel while you're confused.

PRAISE GRUM

Almost universally, the Barbarians worship the gas giant Grum, loving it just as much as they despise Gak, the ant-faced god. They understand Grum is just a ball of gas with no feelings or agency – but they love it anyway, because it's so big and impressive. When Barbarians find themselves looking down the barrel of old age, they may choose to muster their strength for a final feat. Taking advantage of the moon's low gravity, they will sprint right up one of Grondorra's tallest mountains, before taking a mighty leap from its miles-high peak. While nine out of ten warriors will simply soar away in a long parabola before becoming a smear of red somewhere in the desert, some are strong enough to achieve escape velocity, and will *literally jump into SPACE*. It's a hell of a way to go.

Occasionally, Barbarians will congregate in huge nomadic groups in order to storm larger settlements and socialise. During these swarming periods, Barbarians of all genders will mate enthusiastically, and when this results in pregnancy, newborns will be left gently in the wake of the horde's passing to be raised by wolves.[1] The hordes never last, however – the Barbarians know they are a sort of natural regulator to the development of civilisation,[2] and so always make sure to demolish their factions before long, in glorious infighting over loot.[3]

---

1 Fascinatingly, the syncretic evolution of dogs and humans has taken a wildly different path on Grondorra. The wolves here have remained wolves, and stay wild and hostile to adult humans. Nevertheless, they have learned that if they take in and nurture babies long enough for them to rejoin their fellow humans, they will be rewarded with meat.

2 Civilisation is like unprotected sex with strangers, the Barbarians say: it seems exciting enough in the heat of the moment, but it rarely ends well.

3 Spume could learn a thing or two from these folks.

Animalmen

Grondorra is famous for its proliferation of Animalmen – a species in which the heads and other components of animals are magically fused with extremely buff human bodies.[1] While some types of Animalmen don't do so well,[2] others (most notably the prolific Lizardmen) can be found in abundance. All the Animalmen love capturing people and are masters of stealth and ambush. Fear not, though: once captured, it's remarkably easy to astound them into thinking you're a magician, which usually allows for a prompt escape.

Space Men

Grondorra has its *own* moon,[3] the grey, barren ball of rock known as Clax. It's home to a miserable colony of Space Men from Outpost Bravo, determined to survey the savage moon as part of their inscrutable Mission. You'd think their technology would give them a considerable advantage on this primitive world, but any head start is mitigated entirely by their dismal luck and frequent blunders. Their faulty rocketships are constantly crashing, leading to the Space Men getting captured by Animalmen, or ending up bare-chested and fighting off swarms of eels or other vicious creatures. The Space Men pity the Barbarians for their savagery and simplicity, while the Barbarians piss themselves laughing at the fastidious, fragile masculinity of the Space Men and their complete refusal to admit they're struggling.

---

1 Usually this is as straightforward as animal head/human body, but there are exceptions: the unpleasant Toadman is simply a large toad with human feet, while the Badgerman resembles a human with the weird, beanlike nose of the well-known woodland creature.

2 The tragic Anteaterman must spend all day huffing termites through his stupid little pipe of a face in order to avoid dying of starvation, while the Slothman's brain is completely unable to cope with the speed at which his human limbs move, and spends most of his time staring sadly into the middle distance as his body thrashes and flails.

3 A moon-moon, to be precise.

PULP FRICTION:
ANIMALMAN IDENTITY POLITICS

Whenever discussing Grondorra's smorgasbord of Animalman species, the question of whether it's right to call them 'men' comes up. The answer, as I discovered in the battle arena of the Crayfishmen, is complex.[1] While I thought I was being open-minded in calling them Crayfish*people*, in recognition of the range of genitals the flimsiness of their loincloths did little to conceal, the snippies insisted on my calling them men.[2] Oh, and go easy on animal jokes. It's all too easy to let loose what you think are a series of real thigh-slappers after a jar or two of the local rotgut. But before you ask an Anteaterman 'why the long face?' or jokily refuse to play cards with a Cheetahman, think long and hard about whether you are the first person to do so.[3]

---

1 *Well, it's not really, is it Floyd? It would have been really fucking simple if you'd actually listened to the briefing, and I wouldn't have had to beg them to let you free. – ES*

2 *One: 'snippies' is really not OK – we've been through this. Two: you're the one who's confused, mate. By and large, all Animalmen identify as male regardless of anatomy, so they're men. That's it. I don't care how progressive you think you're being - it's their decision. I wouldn't mind, but they told you this again and again, Floyd. – ES*

3 *Well, that explains why you were so anxious to know whether cheetah bites were infectious that one time, doesn't it? – ES*

The Urrizanians

At any given time on Grondorra, you'll find a couple of ancient civilisations in a state of advanced senescence, staggering through civilisational twilight in a forlorn wait for the Barbarians to put them out of their misery. For tourists, the dying civilisation *du jour* is the city state of Urrizan. This crumbling metropolis, groaning under the work of a million sculptors, was once populous and powerful – but glory is long behind it. The city is choked with bureaucracy and tradition to a point where you don't so much immerse yourself in culture as slowly suffocate in it, and its citizens are stuck in a rut of joyless decadence, consumed with the observance of a million clapped-out rituals. These rituals involve an amount of human sacrifice that would be horrifying if it wasn't for the sheer incompetence of the priestly caste.[1] Urrizan's altars are heaped with virgins just one minor intervention away from salvation, and infiltrating the city to free them has become a beloved pastime for young Barbarians and tourists alike.

Sorcerers

In the depths of Grondorra's Vathek Desert, the notorious Sorcerers build their towers. Genius magicians who've wandered away from ancient empires after discovering immortality, these undying tinkers love the peace and quiet of the desert, as well as the access to *loads of skeletons*.[2] Whether they're content to ponder the mastery of the dead or they branch out to try their hand at making legions of Animalmen or other weird monsters,[3] their lifestyle generally boils down to using their minions to acquire treasure, then having it all robbed by Barbarians.

---

1 Around 72 per cent of the population.

2 Rather predictably, the combination of amoral magic users working with no constraints and tombs full of mummified warriors has led to a serious problem with the Undead on Grondorra. It is a problem to which the solution, as usual, is Barbarians.

3 Please, for the love of God, stay clear of the citadel of Wrigglar the Worrying, in the western Vathek. She's spent the last thousand years trying to perfect 'a new kind of worm' (her words, not mine; looked like a normal worm to me), and will tell you about it at length if you so much as make eye contact with her.

Skeletons

It's hard to get taken seriously as a Sorcerer without at least a *small* cohort of Skeleton warriors. Still, they're a bit shit: Grondorran Skeletons are weirdly jerky, moving in fits and starts as if animated in stop-motion, and tend to be limited to following basic commands and rattling in a menacing fashion. Even so, there are rumours of stray Skeletons congregating in deep-desert ruins and developing impressive communal intelligence over centuries. It's hard to know the truth, however, as it's said that when the living intrude on their domain, they just slump into the dust and pretend to be archaeology.

 ## Wildlife

As a world celebrated for its primal character, Grondorra is chock-a-block with monsters of all descriptions[1] and is an unmissable destination for wildlife fanatics.[2]

✳ Grondorra's volcanic jungles are ruled over by the Dinosaurs, ignoble brutes as emblematic of Grondorra as the Barbarians themselves.[3] They're not like the dinosaurs of our own past, however. These lizards are terrible in every sense of the word: turd-drab, unreasoning hulks that live for nothing except ripping lumps out of each other in fetid swamps, and will go to outrageous lengths to snap a morsel of human meat between their house-sized jaws. None of

---

1 Eliza objects to me lumping all of Grondorra's fauna under the category of 'monsters', but I'm sorry – even the slugs here have jaws full of venomous, razor-sharp fangs. It's a monster world, and that's that.

2 Keen naturalists can read up on Grondorran wildlife in 'adventure textbooks' such as Fistfight Kalligan's Bestiary for Bastards and Ernst Blunch's Grondorra!: How I Fought Everything There.

3 Fascinatingly, the dinosaurs are not surviving relics of a bygone era, as was first presumed. Recent discoveries of advanced ruins in Xular now tell a far more interesting story, of a vanished society that just would not stop building hubristic dinosaur theme parks, despite their safety record. It seems at some point they went one theme park over the line, and while the dinosaurs survived, their creators did not.

them are nice: even the nominal herbivores won't think twice before dipping their heads from the treetops to guzzle a passing human.[1] Luckily, it's easy to keep a safe distance from these trudging, nut-brained dunces, since they move at the speed of local government and announce their presence with constant, needless roaring.[2]

✳ Travellers passing through the Badlands east of Urrizan are often advised to stick to established paths, lest they fall prey to **Medusae** (*Homo Craniophidia*): gaunt, cannibalistic humans with deep azure eyes and nests of writhing serpents rooted to their scalps. According to some textbook I got bored reading, the 'snakes' on their heads are in fact 'the motile fruiting bodies of a parasitic, cordycepomorphic

VICIOUS VEG

In focusing on Grondorra's lethal animal life, it can be easy to forget that even the plants will murder you if they get half a chance. From the Nazahak Horsetrap to Battle Kelp, Biff-wort and the notorious Shitkicker Lily, Grondorra's biomes are carpeted with aggressive flora. Even the desolate plains are not to be trodden lightly: too many travellers have strolled into seemingly harmless veldt only to hear a telltale thrashing and realise they are in a deep thicket of Grondorra's dreaded Punchgrass.

GRONDORRA

1 In fairness, they probably won't even think once, since they've got the neural architecture of a child's toy calculator.

2 The dinosaurs of Xular are so cosmically, elementally stupid that they can literally be baffled to death. I once saw a Lizardman confront a Megacarnossus with nothing more than his own scaly hands; as the rot-reeking abyss of the beast's mouth descended from the clouds, he simply clicked his fingers to focus the monster's attention, and performed the classic illusion where it looks like someone has pulled off their own thumb. The dinosaur stopped in its tracks and made a noise like a seal being hit in the gut with an iron girder. Its grape-sized eyes rolled up in their sockets, and it keeled over stone dead, blood trickling from its ear-holes. It had died of confusion.

mycelial mass' – whatever that means[1] – and feed off the brain tissue of their still-living hosts as they wander aimlessly through the labyrinth of rock. Definitely worth avoiding.

 ## Eating and Drinking

It's probably not a surprise to hear that Grondorran cuisine is . . . fairly meaty. Even within the jungles, only a handful of plants aren't lethally poisonous, and the plains offer only a few desultory herbs and wild onions. As such, vegan travellers are essentially out of luck. Even *drinks* here tend to be a fairly fleshy affair: Grondorra's most popular soft drink is a brew called Greh-ve,[2] while most alcoholic drinks are made from either fermented beast-milk or some kind of blood.[3]

GRONDORRA'S BEST BARS and RESTAURANTS

The Sword & Sorcery – *Outside of getting rat-arsed in tents, there isn't much of a bar culture on Grondorra. Still, a few years back, an offworld entrepreneur tried to start a town-sized megapub called the Sword & Sorcery, sticking it right in the middle of the Great Plain in the hope of drawing passing Barbarian traffic. Unfortunately, it has been so successful it tends to be burned to the ground on a weekly basis.*

The Gilded Urn – *Preposterously high-end fine-dining establishment in Urrizan. During the rare moments when the city isn't in the grip of dysfunctional famine, this restaurant serves overpoweringly floral wines and impossibly labour-intensive delicacies such as hummingbird tongues and candied ape's breath.*

---

1 *Waggly, mind-controlling mushrooms, Floyd. – ES*

2 By amazing coincidence, this translates exactly to 'gravy', because that's what the drink is.

3 If you're wondering: 1) yes, mammalian Animalmen produce milk, 2) yes, I've tried it, and 3) no, I don't want to talk about it.

COMMUNAL EATING, BARBARIAN STYLE

When you enter a Barbarian feasting tent, you'll usually be greeted with a cheery *Garunka-gak!* (death to the ant-faced god!) from the patrons. It's best to respond rapidly with *Ganosh-grum!* (praise to Grum!), or you may be taken for an Antman in disguise and eviscerated on the spot.

To get a seat, you must wrestle one of the incumbent diners to the ground. Obviously, you should seek to persecute any other tourists present, but since the Barbarians respect courage almost as much as prowess, some good sports will feign injury in order to give you a 'surprise' victory, should you challenge them.[1]

The feast will usually start with a round of raucous toasts, plus maybe a fight and quick song about Grum. After that, the meal itself comprises three dishes: *Rastacah-runn* ('red vegetables') – the meat of a herbivore, such as a horse or a dire antelope, which counts as a vegetable to the Barbarian palate.

Lidhmugh ('fightmeat') – the centrepiece course, which must be an animal capable of killing an adult Barbarian.

Yolledd ('sweetness') – foods violently stolen from other people, garnished with looted jewels and precious metals. These foods are almost always meats, rather than desserts as you might expect; the sweetness comes from the satisfaction of taking them.[2]

---

1 Others will respond to a challenge by battering a spoon into your heart with the heel of their hand, however, so there's an element of luck involved.

2 Interestingly, the Barbarian word for 'theft' – Yuth – is the same word used for 'harvest'.

Lug-glug-lugl[1] – *Although the Lizardmen are largely insectivorous, you'll be astonished by what these scaly culinary geniuses can do with the contents of a shaken bush. At this rustic establishment in the deep jungle, you can enjoy candied tarantulas, stir-fried weevil grubs and antcake, all while enjoying the sight of captured Space Men duking it out with swarms of small but angry creatures in the Combat Holes.*

Getting Around

Clearly, given the technological state of Grondorra,[2] not to mention its general aesthetic, muscle power is the only way to get around. The low gravity favours travelling on foot, but if you're planning on doing any looting, it's worth springing for a pack beast. Fast travel necessitates booking transit aboard a Space Man rocketship, however, which will seem terribly exciting until you're crashed in a swamp, choking on chemical smoke and desperately trying to thin a swarm of scorpions with a faulty ray gun.

Currency

Among the Barbarians, gold and valuables are hoarded only as markers of status, and the idea of using money as a token for the exchange for goods or services is laughable. As such, the only way to acquire anything is to take it by force or be given it as a gift,[3] and so what you can get largely depends on how massive and charismatic you are.

---

1 Pronounced like a cartoon character chugging a bottle of oil.

2 After all, the wheel was only invented recently – and it's a single giant stone wheel, used by the Barbarian king Qelzadd to crush prisoners of war.

3 Think about this for more than a few minutes and the sheer amount of cognitive dissonance involved will start to fold your brain over on itself like grim meat origami. Several economists have travelled to Grondorra to try to comprehend the Barbarian financial mindset: without exception, all have either been slaughtered or gone completely mad and become warriors.

STATUS	ACCOMMODATION	
You are physically fragile and entirely unlikeable	Sleeping in the dust at the edge of a nomad's encampment	
You are modestly strong, with a winning smile	A night in a medium yurt, on a stack of used wolf pelts	
You are a granite-jawed titan; people weep to behold you	A night beneath a tent of golden silk, fanned by a legion of adoring eunuchs	

Suggested Outings

The botched sacrifice

Join up with a group of young Barbarians, infiltrate Urrizan's Holy Quarter as dusk falls, and don priestly robes to attend the weekly sacrifice at the Temple of Krung the Foul. Wait for the very last moment, as the knife hovers above the victim's chest,[1] then toss a banana skin beneath the executor's feet and dive to the rescue. The virgin will be secured with manacles of such poor quality that they pop apart in your hands, and the temple guards will literally fall over each other in their scramble to catch you. After that, it's simply a case of escaping the city via a thrilling raft ride through an underground river and a bit of catacomb-blundering before you emerge into the Eastern Badlands. You're likely to face moderate quantities of Skeletons, but a good spray of Lazenby's

---

1 As you wait for said moment, you might as well enjoy the sheer ineptitude of the rest of the ceremony, which is easily mistakable for pantomime.

FOOD & DRINK	ENTERTAINMENT	SOCIAL PRIVILEGES
A quick slurp from a Wirrux's udder	Watching a fight from the back of a crowd	Capture, followed by ten years chained to a millwheel
Several mouthfuls of raw goat meat	Hire of a rusty sword and shield for a raid on a Sorcerer's tower	The right to punch a camel square in the jaw
A diamond-encrusted bucket of dinosaur nuggets	Travel on a palanquin, borne on the shoulders of forty less-fortunate tourists	A crown, entitling you to seize your destiny by toppling an ancient civilisation

Skeleton Repellant will see them off.[1]

Lasers and lizards

Stay with the Space Men at Research Station Zeta, their sweaty outpost deep in the Fireheart Jungle. Zeta has poor air con and is plagued by tropical diseases and animal attacks – but you won't be there long. Simply imply that you've seen a strikingly beautiful woman wearing animal skins somewhere in the trees, and the Space Men will scramble to assemble a search party. As a matter of certainty, this search party *will* be captured by Lizardmen during a thrilling duel of spears and ray guns, after which you'll be carried to the scaly ones' picturesque treehouse capital. There, on realising you've fallen in with a bad crowd, your hosts will free you, letting you enjoy their exotic home in comfort and peace

1   The end of the trip rather depends on how well you get along with the would-be sacrificial victim. It's traditional for rescuers to fall in love with rescuees, but this is by no means compulsory – if there's just no chemistry, or either party isn't feeling it, things will likely end with an awkward peck on the cheek and a sheepish wave as you walk in opposite directions across the plains.

WASTES OF SPACE

There is one exception to Barbarian fiscal policy – when dealing with Space Men, the tribes have agreed on an extended practical joke. Stifling cruel laughs, the bemuscled berserkers swear blind that they use teeth as currency, pointing to the tusks and fangs they wear as jewellery to evidence the fact. Unfortunately, there are no animals on barren Clax, where the Space Men make their home, so if they want to 'buy' anything from the Barbarians, they are forced to use *their own teeth* to pay up. There are few sights sadder than that of a Space Man 'master trader' sighing miserably through increasingly empty gums while a smirking Barbarian asks him to up his offer on a sackful of meat.[1]

---

1   The poor Space Men. Although I pity them, I truly loathe them.

as the Space Men are carted off to the Combat Holes.

The Temple of Gak

For this trip, you'll travel with the warband of Brengann the Unstoppable, a relatively affable Barbarian lord. After a warm-up skirmish with a group of Lionmen, followed by a victory feast in which you'll be faced with the dark question of whether it's cannibalism to eat the meat of a Lionman,[1] it'll be time to embark on a gruelling, 200 mile yomp to the Great Temple of Gak, the ant-faced god. There, you'll fight your way through increasingly dingy sandstone chambers, against cultists who get more and more disconcertingly ant-like as you go. At the temple's heart you'll find, replete with blood and reclining on a giant pile of treasure, one of the avatars of Gak – a vast ant with human hands. When you see the avatar, don't think twice: just jam your sword into its neck and prise its head off in a fountain of gore. If you're quick enough to get there first, Brengann may allow you to keep it as a souvenir.

---

1   You know what they say: 'What happens on Grondorra, IS WEIGHED UP AT TIME'S BITTER END BY THE IRON HAND OF GRUM.'

— TESTIMONIALS —

I had a lovely week staying with a Sorcerer who'd converted the bottom of his tower into a B&B. It was a bit weird when I went to the kitchen for a glass of water at 3 a.m. and found him sewing a hyena's head onto a man's body, dripping glowing fluid onto the stitches. But everyone's got to have a hobby, you know?

— *Rex Blap, 42, Sales Consultant*

By Grum, it's hard to remember there was another life, once. I was weak then; a fool, in thrall to some manner of recruitment business. A few of 'the girls' decided to go on holiday to celebrate Siobhán's divorce; thought they'd go somewhere with lots of oil and muscles. Pah! They knew not the glory of Grondorra! And yes, muscles and oil are a large part of that glory, but there's so much more. Those so-called friends betrayed me: I ended up enslaved, chained to a millwheel for ten years, where I developed my astonishing physique. But it was not only my magnificent thighs that grew strong during that gruelling decade: so too did my mind. I learned the error of trusting in your friends — of trusting in anything except the steel in your own heart. Eventually, I grew strong enough to break free, using the millwheel itself to crush my captors, and now I wander the world, using this mighty disc of stone to secure everything I desire. Life on Grondorra is what I make of it, and so life is good! Now give me all of your possessions, or I will flatten your head with my millwheel.

— *Janet the Batterer,*
Headwoman of the Crimson Jackals

CHAPTER SEVEN

Mundania and Whimsicalia

The World of Wizardes

1. WELCOME TO MUNDANIA

Once upon a time, this was one of the most picturesque, charming – dare one even say 'twee'? – destinations among the Worlds: an ordinary place full of ordinary people, with a secret mirror-world of Wizardes. A fabulous tapestry, begging the curious to tug loose threads. Alas, that tapestry has . . . unravelled a bit. But the resulting mess offers a unique blend of grit and whimsy.

? Why Mundania?

Mundania's population has always been divided, thanks to its unique position as an entirely non-magical world laced with hidden regions where magic is emphatically real. The inhabitants of Whimsicalia, the magical world, are known as Wizardes,[1] and have always referred to their disenchanted counterparts as the Mundanes.

The real beauty of the situation was always that the Mundanes (with the exception of a regular trickle of gifted young people chosen to join the Wizardes) had no idea of the splendour existing right under their noses as they went about their drudgework, while the Wizardes could flit in and out of concealed Whimsicalia at will. To be their guest was like attending a speakeasy on a planetary scale: a drab exterior, revealing utter fabulosity to those with the password.

Alas, nothing lasts for ever. The awkwardness that transpired a few years ago was certainly unfortunate,[2,3] but few would disagree that it was bound to happen sooner or later. And besides, with the ceasefire having held for more than a year now, and most Mundanes returned to blissful

---

1 Not to be confused with the Wizards of Mittelvelde, who are a different kettle of fish entirely.

2 *Floyd, are you going to do the whole 'oblique hints in footnotes' thing all through the chapter, or just bloody admit what you did? – ES*

3 Yes, Eliza, I'm getting to it.

WHY MUNDANIA IS MAGIC TO ME

*By Jenny Moonwish, Demolitions Expert
for House Wurblyflop*

I always knew deep down that I was special, but I didn't realise just *how special*, until I got the letter. Looking back on it now, it seems unreal: I'd dropped out of college and was working at a recruitment consultancy, and one day this bat flies in and drops a scroll in my coffee. Says I've been summoned to a place called 'Greeblewhoz' (a magic school, apparently – how mad is that?) and that I'm to enrol as a matter of urgency. So I quit my job and head there, and I've not been there five minutes when this talking Skeleton gives me a scarf and tells me I'm in House Wurblyflop. I told the headmaster I thought I was a bit old to be starting school, but he said something about 'making up the numbers' and went back to frowning at his map. I've gotta say, my education was pretty brief – just a few weeks – and mostly focused on blowing stuff up. But it was blowing stuff up *with magic*! Floyd's told me to skip over what happened after basic training, and that's fine with me – our field trips were really scary. But things are looking up now; the trouble's over, and me and my surviving housemates are proper Wizardes! We get to hang out with all kinds of magical creatures and get all the bunglebean juice we want. It's a great painkiller. I know I can't ever return home, but the way I see it, my real family are all here in Whimsicalia, and *I'll kill for them again if I have to.*

ignorance of their situation, tourists are once again free to enjoy the best of both worlds.

I would be the last person to pretend this isn't a destination with some wounds,[1] and I must stress that sensitivity to the recent upset should be at the top of anyone's mind when touring Mundania. However, with the

---

1 *I should fucking hope not, Floyd. – ES*

right paperwork and a good instinct for avoiding trouble, visitors will find this a singularly enchanting place, where anyone – or at least those with the right powers – can do amazing things.

 ## 'Can't Miss' Experiences

1 Attend Wizarde school

The famed Greeblewhoz Academy has been training young Mundanes into magic users for centuries, and is a cornerstone of Wizarde culture – all the most famous Wizardes studied there, and nobody gets far in magical society without a 'Greebs' education. The institution isn't quite what it used to be – the recent unpleasantness rather curtailed its curriculum[1] and saw the fabled halls become a little more austere – but things are slowly getting back to normal, under the steady hand of Headmaster Candleflash. Tourists shouldn't miss the chance to be sorted into one of Greeblewhoz's ancient Houses by Mr Grinnywithers, the school's famous talking Skeleton.

2 Discover fantastic beasts and get trashed with them

While the Mundane world is covered in a dismal patchwork of commercial farms and suburban sprawl,[2] its magical pockets are full of deep, pristine forests and gleaming mountains, still thronging with the magical creatures that always lived there. What's more, many of these ancient species are highly intelligent, from hybrids such as Centaurs and Taszraks to Klatterlings, Bogberts and other strange peoples. All are long-term allies of the Wizardes, and – with the notable exception of the ancient Faeyrie, who have retreated into the deepest woods of late – they always tend to be up for a shindig.

3 Cast your first magic spell

Whimsicalia is absolutely dripping with magical energy, and tends to reveal at least a modicum of thaumaturgic capability in most

---

1 *By which Floyd means it became a training camp for child soldiers. – ES*
2 With the occasional patch of magically irradiated wasteland.

offworld visitors. Even better, the magic itself isn't that hard to use: under the watchful eyes of a Greeblewhoz tutor you can go from being a complete novice to levitating a small hound in a little under a week.[1] Of course, the magic won't stay with you when you go home – but isn't that as good an incentive as any to go back?

4 Play Grunche

Of all the games and sports that have evolved across the Worlds, perhaps none is more celebrated than Grunche. This joyfully anarchic pursuit requires a panoply of skills, as participants are levitated around the pitch in cauldrons by their teammates, barging into their opponents in an attempt to . . . well. OK. The rules take a good while to explain, but once you get the broad idea and realise that 90 per cent of play is irrelevant to who wins in the end, it's an utter hoot to spectate.

Region by Region

In this guide, we'll focus on the island of Albionus, the heart of Wizardely society. There are other countries, of course, but they seem mostly there to add flavour and frankly aren't as important.

1 Lundowne

Lundowne is the Mundane capital of Albionus, and – since the peace agreement outlawed unsanctioned portals – the only place tourists can travel between the Worlds, on the famous Dead Toad Road. It's also home to the official Wizarde ministry, the concealed Department of Magic, where simpering mages in brightly striped suits act as a figurehead government for Whimsicalia.[2]

2 Greeblewhoz Academy

Rebuilt and extended by countless generations of Wizardes, the once-humble castle of Greeblewhoz now sprawls over countless acres of pristine

---

1 I never got much further than making acorns smell a bit funny during my visit, but in fairness I had a very full schedule.

2 Still, whenever an eldritch detonation levels a street, they claim no knowledge of the perpetrators.

Greeblewhoz Academy

Bagfists House

CRICKLEDALE

Blacklox Prison

CHUMBLETON

MAGICAL LUNDOWNE

Dead Road

Pranslemead

Lundowne

highland in the far north of Albionus. That may seem a little big for a school that only takes in a few-hundred students a year,[1] but those students are very special people, and they deserve it. Besides, Greeblewhoz is more than just the Academy: it's the de facto capital of magical society.[2]

3 Chumbleton

Although it was razed to the ground during the war, the Wizardes made it a point of pride to rebuild the charming village of Chumbleton even more beautifully than before. On the edge of the Enchanted Forest, just a few miles from Greeblewhoz, its wonky, timber-framed cottages provide an ideal location for the Academy's elites to kick back with the rest of magical society.

4 The Enchanted Forest

Much of Whimsicalia is swathed in enchanted forest, but this stretch of primeval woodland is particularly . . . foresty,[3] and particularly enchanted. In its sun-stippled margins, one can enjoy lazy afternoons watching jewelled bees gather sparklepollen from the carpet of flowers, their low hum harmonising with the susurrations of the leaves. Just . . . stay in the margins. The heart of the forest remains the domain of the Faeyrie, and even Greeblewhoz headmasters are in the habit of asking permission before going too deep in.[4]

5 Crickledale

Crickledale, a county of chilly, rain-slick hillsides where the sky is enchanted into a permanent state of gloom, is the ancestral home of the Dark Wizardes. Here

---

1 The Mundanes were furious when they found out about it, given the underfunded, overcrowded nature of their state schools. I don't see the fuss, personally. Surely if they wanted it badly enough, they could have made giant castle schools for themselves?

2 Indeed, when Mundane intelligence agencies want to talk to real power, they forget the Department of Magic and head to Platform Zero at Empire Cross Station, where they await the arrival of the Greeblewhoz Express, a behemoth armoured locomotive bearing representatives of the Academy.

3 Note to self: come up with a better adjective before publication.

4 How do you know when you've gone too far into the woods? You'll know. Whether it's the sunlight giving way to a deep arboreal gloom, a gradual proliferation of cobwebs, or the sudden absence of birds and the emergence of more eerie calls, there's no way you'll miss your sign to turn back.

THE HOUSES OF GREEBLEWHOZ

BOLDERBIFF

Despite pages of rather unconvincing denial in the Academy's prospectus, this is where Mr Grinnywithers puts all the most heroic students. Bolderbiff members are brave, strong, handsome and charismatic, and tend to have brilliant self-esteem. They were natural choices as officers during the ~~recent bother~~ war.[1]
(*House Sigil: an owl with muscular arms instead of wings*)

JAGGLETON

Generally likeable but a bit awkward and far too smart to like yourself? You're a classic fit for Jaggleton. The house for high achievers and nerds, Jaggleton supplied many of the finest minds in Greeblewhoz's R&D dungeon, as well as many of the spies who worked behind Mundane lines during the . . . war.[2]
(*House Sigil: an octopus with horn-rim spectacles*)

SNYX

One look at the logo of House Snyx tells you all you need to know – this is the house for Cool Bad Guys. It's virtually impossible to be taken seriously in Dark Wizarde society without being a Snyx alumnus, and graduates favour an overabundance of capes and black leather in their aesthetic. During the war, Snyx trained assassins, saboteurs and commandos.
(*House Sigil: a spider smoking a cigarette*)

WURBLYFLOP

With a body of students outnumbering all the other houses put together, House Wurblyflop has always been a sort of catch-all bucket for students with reasonable magic potential but few other defining characteristics. During the war, Wurblyflop alumni were what an unkind commentator might call cannon fodder.
(*House Sigil: a slightly ill-looking hound*)

---

1 '*Recent bother*'??? Floyd, it was a WAR. And until you acknowledge that, I'm going to edit all the euphemisms out of your text, whether you like it or not. – ES

2 Fine – happy now, Eliza?

they gather, with their velvet capes and astonishing bone structure, to mutter about their own superiority to everyone else over meals of black wine.[1]

6 Blacklox Prison

Rising from the storm-lashed waters off the northern coast, Blacklox prison was built at the war's end by a combined force of Wizarde and Mundane engineers, and remains under shared control of both of Albionus' governments. War criminals from both sides are incarcerated here, but two in particular are especially notorious, kept in clammy cells far below sea level.

7 Drungsleydale Memorial Power Facility

The DMPF stands where the Mundane city of Drungsleydale used to, before a spell of terrifying magnitude turned it into a glass-floored crater. Now this defiant hulk of a structure provides electricity to most of northern Albionus, and forms the centre of an extensive research complex, kept under a veil of total secrecy by the Mundane government.

---

1 Dark Wizardes are not to be confused with vampyres, despite their similarly general moody sexiness.

2. UNDERSTANDING MUNDANIA

 ## A Brief History[1]

You know much of the history of Mundania already: a world divided, with the bulk of humanity toiling away in brutish ignorance of the realm of magical bliss lying just under their noses. Meanwhile, an elite slice of the species, chosen via genetic lottery, enjoyed access to this other reality, as custodians of its wondrous bounty. It was a totally fair situation and should have lasted for ever.

Deathwish and Miller

The situation couldn't last for ever. A sizeable faction of the Wizardes – the Dark ones – wanted to openly subjugate the Mundanes, while the 'Light' Wizardes simply wanted to manipulate them in secret and never share their stuff with them.[2] After simmering for centuries, this tension seemed certain to boil over when an ancient Crickledale aristocrat known as Baron Deathwish squared up to Beatrix Miller, a Greeblewhoz sixth former prophesied to be the champion of Light Wizardery. The seemingly inevitable conflict was averted, however.[3]

The paragraph Eliza has forced me to write[4]

All right, then. It wasn't so much that the Dark/Light conflict was averted as made irrelevant by a

---

1   *OK, Floyd, you've danced about long enough: out with it. – ES*

2   Interestingly, Dark Wizardes are far less hated in Mundane culture than their counterparts due to this very difference – there's a general sense that while they may want to keep their gleaming boots firmly on the neck of the Mundane world, at least they've always been honest about it. Plus, they're a bit sexier than normal Wizardes.

3   Nobody ever seems to give me credit for averting that conflict. If things hadn't played out the way they did, it would all have blown up and spilled into the Mundane world anyway – but everyone seems to have forgotten that now that I'm the scapegoat.

4   *Damn right. – ES*

much bigger crisis. Which was *a bit* to do with me. You see, around this time there was all sorts of rubbish in the press about my buying personal favours by selling guns to the Bison King on Mittelvelde. It was all a complete misunderstanding, but I was getting a lot of flak for the proxy oppression of Orcs and it was highly embarrassing. My solution was quite elegant: I made a public trip to Mittelvelde, found an underprivileged Orc that one of our freelancers had visited – Benedict, he was called – and offered him a scholarship, funded by my good self, at Greeblewhoz. I thought he'd love it, and the press would too.

It was all Benedict's fault

Unfortunately, Benedict *did not play ball*. He made it to his first formal dinner before stamping demonstratively on his Wizarde hat and storming out. I tried to follow him,[1] but he'd gone straight to Chumbleton and portalled to the Mundane city of Drungsleydale. There, he went to a pub, climbed up on a table and told the crowd that on a nearby industrial estate lay a gateway to a world where the solutions to all humanity's problems were being kept out of reach by a cabal of magicians. The crowd would have reacted in disbelief were they not being told this *by an Orc*. As it was, they went completely apeshit, formed a mob and rampaged through Benedict's portal to burn Chumbleton to the ground.

The War

As magical boltholes were discovered all over Albionus, mob incursions spread like wildfire. The Wizardes were quick to retaliate, enacting magical guerrilla violence across dozens of Mundane cities. The Wizardes were outnumbered, but their mastery of portal magic – and their willingness to fight with fanatic Greeblewhoz-trained teenagers – gave them the upper hand. After two years of vicious fighting, things came to a head when Beatrix Miller was captured, imprisoned at Mundane central command in Drungsleydale and scheduled for public execution. Then the unthinkable happened.

The Girl Who (Crucially) Did Not Die

At dawn, as the firing squad lined up, Baron Deathwish himself came screaming out

---

1 After staying for the cheese course, naturally.

of the sky in a flying cauldron, leading a squadron of elite Dark Wizards. Despite being Miller's sworn nemesis, the Baron found the prospect of the Mundanes winning the war unthinkable. He threw a magical shield around the girl Wizarde right as the first bullet struck her chest – earning her the moniker 'The Girl Who Did Not Die' – and had his minions form a protective circle around her as Mundane soldiers rushed in.

The Atrocity

Outnumbered and faced with the certainty of death or capture, the Baron suggested a monstrous gambit, and the pure-hearted Miller reacted with horror. She begged the Baron not to go through with his plan, but he did it anyway: siphoning the younger Wizarde's power and adding it to his own, the Baron unleashed a blast of energy that annihilated the city and its inhabitants. The exertion left both mages unconscious at the centre of the devastation, and when horrified Mundane reinforcements arrived, Miller and the Baron were captured.

Mundania Today

The Drungsleydale atrocity ended the war. The Mundanes couldn't stand more losses on that scale, and the Wizardes couldn't risk losing both their leaders, not to mention the hundreds of prisoners (wizoners?)[1] already incarcerated. A ceasefire agreement was signed, under the following stipulations:

　＊ Miller and Deathwish were to be locked away under the newly constructed Blacklox Prison.

　＊ All portals between Mundania and Whimsicalia enclaves were to be shut down, except sanctioned gateways in Lundowne, ending free movement between the magical and non-magical worlds.

1 *Floyd, this is not appropriate at all. – ES*

✳ 99.9 per cent of the Mundane population were to have their memories of the war, and of the existence of Whimsicalia, magically torn from their brains,[1] with only a thin sliver of government figures and military personnel permitted to remember on a need-to-know basis.

✳ Vague promises were made by the Wizardes about 'sharing some of their stuff'.

It's now been eighteen months since the ratification of the ceasefire, and peace has once more returned to Mundania. There are tensions, to be certain, and plenty of rumours of trouble to come, but while neither side has a strategic advantage over the other, the ceasefire endures.[2]

Climate and Terrain[3]

Albionus has a climate best described as underwhelming, and the landscape is mediocre at best, comprising spiderwebs of suburban sprawl and tracts of soggy farmland bracketed by carrier-bag-haunted motorways. Whimsicalia, however, is the country Albionus wishes it was, and which Mundane pensioners swear it used to resemble. Lush, dark forests blanket the land – broken here and there by pristine mountains – and cradle wide swathes of idyllic meadows. The weather is glorious in summer and dramatic in the colder months, with midwinter bringing a gorgeous spell of frosty stillness.[4]

---

1 This would come to be known as 'the Forgettening'.

2 There, happy now, Eliza? I'm sure that account of atrocities will do wonders for tourism, but at least you got the satisfaction of hanging me out to dry. Besides, I still maintain this wasn't my fault. I thought Benedict would love Mundania. How was I to know he'd take such a bizarre stance?

3 Feels a bit gauche to start talking about the weather after being forced to admit indirect culpability for the annihilation of a city, but there we are.

4 Crickledale is an obvious exception, being broodingly unpleasant year-round, but that's an aesthetic choice on behalf of its inhabitants.

Wildlife

As in Mittelvelde, dividing the fauna here between the categories of 'wildlife' and 'people' is difficult and controversial. It's generally safe to say that if an animal doesn't have a human vocabulary of more than a few-dozen words and isn't fond of complex tool use, it's probably not a person.[1] With that in mind, here are some of the fabulous creatures you can expect to encounter in the wilds of the magical world:

✳ While they are a little smaller and less overtly murderous than the beasts found in some more grandiose destinations, Whimsicalia's **Dragons** (*Draconis Fabulosa*) are undoubtedly the real deal, and can be found in a variety of environments depending on species.[2] Sadly, the population dwindled during the war, as scores of the things were unleashed over Mundane Albionus and got absolutely monstered by attack helicopters.

✳ The small, brightly coloured **Messenger Bats** (*Vespertilio Nuntius*) are the mainstay of the Wizarde postal system,[3] and a bat summons was traditionally the means by which prospective students were recruited from the Mundane world, thanks to their ability to flit at will between worlds (this also led to some fairly dark experimentation with miniature incendiary devices during the war).

✳ One of the few other animals able to travel between Mundania and Whimsicalia at its own discretion, the **Gomdrinn** (*Detritovora Mensa*) is a scavenging creature a little like an eight-foot-tall

---

1   Besides, miscategorising an owl with hands as an animal would be the least of my bloody reputational problems when it comes to Mundania, so I'm not too worried.

2   My least favourite is possibly the Gumsley Reeker, a large, flightless dragon that lives in marshland and absolutely honks of decaying vegetables, thanks to the rafts of detritus that tend to accumulate on its back while it marinates in stagnant pools.

3   Eel Mail, although efficient in a region with decent plumbing, never really caught on. Nobody likes an eel popping out of their loo with a scroll in its mouth, after all.

pangolin with butterfly wings, which can disguise itself as a coffee table if seen by a Mundane.

✳ At first glance, the **Grifter's Platypus** (*Ornithorhynchus Criminalis*) is not that different to its Mundane counterpart, save for its perpetually grubby-looking cream-coloured fur and the faint smirk on its duck-billed face. Where it really stands out, however, is in its capacity for theft – or 'clever buying', as keepers of the beasts affectionately call the habit. The Platypus will hoover up coins, gems and trinkets with merry abandon, storing them in a throat pouch with seemingly infinite capacity. Luckily, these pleasantly awful creatures saw only light duty during the war, just being released in Mundania to waddle round wealthy areas and cause mild economic disruption.

✳ Probably around half of Whimsicalia's magical wildlife is a **Chimera** of some kind – a mash-up of Mundane species, supposedly created by the Faeyrie at the beginning of the world. Sometimes the results are majestic: take the **Taszrak** (*Tigris Aegypius*), which is essentially a tiger with vulture wings and beak. Other chimera are more tragic. The **Jurgle** (*Hippopotamus Catastrophus*) – bless it – has the body of a hippo, but the head of a sparrow and the tail of a rat, while the abysmal **Gurbo** (*Beastus Shittus*) has a cheetah's face slapped haphazardly onto the back end of a turkey with tortoise legs. It's pathetic.

People

The Mundanes

The Mundane population of Mundania needs little introduction, since they are in essence much like you and me. Their culture is wholly pedestrian, bearing a remarkable resemblance to our own society, and stumbles along largely as it did before the war, thanks to the Forgettening.[1]

---

1 Admittedly, the Forgettening wasn't 100 per cent successful — even now, Mundanes have a baffling fear of wardrobes, as on a subconscious level they're always scared that their morning rummage for pants will instead reveal a teenage Wizarde with a knife between their teeth.

They have supermarkets and crap cars and a system of local government entirely preoccupied with disputes over bins. They have hopes and dreams and rich inner lives – but let's face it, you're not travelling to Mundania to watch a load of people sitting on sofas eating chips, are you?

Wizardes

Whether you love them or loathe them, the Wizardes are the stars of the show on Mundania. They are a civilisation that has grown up as a reflection of another, and which has always defined itself as something more carefree, more whimsical and more *fun* than the drudgery of its counterpart. Now, however, that whimsy has the air of a clown's tears. Watching the gnomish Professor Fleepdrop deliver a lesson on alchemy in his baggy mauve pantaloons, it's easy to be carried away by delight at the man's buffoonish energy as he capers with hands full of reagents. But then the smell drifting from a flask will remind him of the burns ward after the Battle of Whizzbang Lane, and his face will drop, haunted by the screams of the colleagues he left behind.

Magic-adjacent peoples

Although it can be easy to overlook them in favour of the tribulations of Mundania's human population, the purely magical inhabitants of this world are at least as numerous as their hominid counterparts (even taking the Mundane population into account), and were the original inhabitants of Whimsicalia.

✳ The Faeyrie: The original masters of magic and the oldest friends of the Wizardes, the Faeyrie are now very rarely seen outside of their deep forest glades. Although they are said to be astonishingly beautiful, few can tell the truth of the matter, since they wear heavy silk shrouds concealing their bodies. Only their strange antlers and silvery hands protrude from these garments, with long fingers constantly fiddling with cat's cradles of magical light.

✳ Bogberts: These wheezing, diminutive green creatures look like self-portraits drawn by very old men with even less artistic talent than self-esteem, and are nearly ubiquitous in Wizarde society. Indeed, as long as there have been Wizardes, there have been Bogberts waiting on them hand, fist and foot.

KNOW YOUR WIZARD(E)S

It's all too easy to presume that magic users are the same across all the Worlds – but don't be fooled! Here's a handy guide to telling apart Wizards from Mittelvelde and Wizardes from Whimsicalia.

	Mittelvelde	Whimsicalia
Pronunciation	*Wizz-'rds.*	*Wih-zaahds.*
Hats	Conical, floppy, battered.	Sometimes fezzes, sometimes floppy velvet ones, sometimes trilbys with feathers.
Aesthetic	Posthuman vagrant.	Extreme, eccentric wealth, portrayed entirely through charity-shop purchases.
Tools of the trade	Gnarled staffs, filthy clay pipes.	Ornate wands, pocket-sized magical familiars.

✳ Klatterlings: Similar to Bogberts, but redder and fightier, and they live in holes.

✳ Centaurs: If the Centaurs had not remained neutral in the war, it might have gone very differently indeed. Horses with the top halves of extremely muscular humans in place of their necks,[1] they are preposterously strong, fiercely loyal and stuck in a state of constant low-level fury due to the unfortunate biomechanics of their digestive systems.

---

1 In most cases, at least. One in a hundred centaurs is born with the front half of a horse on a pair of human legs, and while centaur culture considers the arrival of such a creature to be a blessing upon a family, befitting months of lavish gifts, one suspects this tradition has evolved more as a coping mechanism than an actual reflection of good fortune.

3. PLANNING YOUR TRIP

When to visit

Most Mundane festivals are drab, patriotic affairs designed to drum up threadbare merriment in a population beaten down by post-war austerity. But for the people of Whimsicalia, every day is magical: since the Wizarde calendar is scheduled along vaguely pagan lines, there's almost always an excuse for a lavish party due to the position of the moon or the stars or whatever. Even so, there's one party whose pleasures simply can't be overegged.

The Grunche World Cup
Every four years at Whooshbury Stadium, teams and fans gather from all over the world (dressed in wildly camp magical exaggerations of national dress, naturally) to really Grunche it up. There are fireworks in the sky and on the pitch, as romance and rivalry flares between one-dimensional teenage sport gods. Non-magical tourists are permitted to attend, but given the prevalence of jolly terrace chants about killing all Mundanes, it's worth having a thick skin.

Getting Around

Travel links around Albionus for Mundanes comprise predictably sensible modes of transport – cars, trains and the like. Getting about in Whimsicalia, by contrast, gets far more exotic. Since the dawn of magic, Wizardes have been finding ways to accomplish dull tasks with zero effort, and transport is no exception. Portals can be opened from place to place (within magical enclaves) for a reasonable sum, while more

THE RULES OF GRUNCHE

✳ Each team has nine players – three Drangles, two Snicklers, two Billybiffs, a Tanglebob and a Bamboozler – seated in enchanted flying cauldrons.

✳ In play are an assortment of balls, hoops and skittles too numerous to list, as well as a crate of flying, downy-feathered frogs called Flitcroaks. Some of the balls appear to be sentient. Sometimes there's a flying hammer that swears at people before cracking them across the temples. But sometimes there isn't. Either way, fear of the Winged Hammer appears to be a major element of the game.

✳ As far as can be discerned, most of the game's scoring system is concerned with the Drangles manoeuvring the various implements of play into crucial areas, or through the assortment of hoops and brackets affixed to the stadium walls. The Drangles tend to accumulate between fifty and a hundred points per match this way.

✳ Opposing them in these endeavours are the opposing team's Billybiffs (armed with fist-sized wooden lumps on the end of ropes) and the Tanglebob (who has a net and a crossbow).

✳ While all this is happening, the two pairs of Snicklers compete to capture as many Flitcroaks as they can, with each one being worth a trillion points.

✳ It's not certain what the Bamboozler's job actually is, but it seems to involve drugs. It doesn't really matter since, like every other player besides the Snicklers, they are just part of an elaborate sideshow that takes place as four people frantically search for frogs.

hearty travellers might try renting flying cauldrons[1] or more esoteric enchanted vessels such as bathtubs and refuse skips. Oh, and don't ask if you can ride a Centaur, as they will make *such a fuss*.[2]

Floyd's Tip

If you want to travel by portal without paying the fees, there are ways – but they come with risks. Not *all* of the secret portals used by guerrilla fighters were closed up after the war, and many connection points remain hidden in plain sight. Seriously intrepid travellers may choose to use them, but must remember that many are set with gruesome magical traps that can swap your hands and your feet, turn your blood to porridge, or make a live squid materialise in your trachea.[3]

Eating and Drinking

Mundania is developing a decent fine-dining culture now rationing is coming to an end, but it will never hold a candle to the epicurean delights of Whimsicalia. Thanks to the dizzying range of ingredients native to magical Albionus, the limitless culinary techniques presented by the use of magic and the sheer flamboyant inventiveness of the Wizardes, Whimsicalia's food is some of the finest in all the Worlds.[4] Mundania also boasts a sumptuous range of drinking

---

1 Do be aware that they take some practice, though. They tip bloody easily, you see, and that's no laughing matter when you're rocketing over a jagged mountain at half the speed of sound.

2 *Floyd, I thought this argument was over. It's not about whether it's anatomically possible – it's about whether it's OK to command a stranger to give you a piggyback. And it's not OK to do that. – Eliza Salt.*

3 It's a terrible way to go.

4 Indeed, the fact that Wizardes could use magic to cheerfully ignore such concerns as intensive agriculture, distribution logistics and even the laws of thermodynamics in their food economy was one of the main instigating factors in the war. When your civilisation is only ever three meals away from anarchy, it's irksome to find your neighbours have been conjuring pastries from thin air for hundreds of years, I suppose.

options, from Salamander Shandy and blue Mungleberry Wine to Brattleperk's Singing Ale[1] and the narcotic known as Bafflejuice. Wizarde-brewed alcohol seems to offer all the benefits of regular booze with none of the downsides. There are no hangovers, boorish behaviour or slow descent into an endless nightmare of terrible decisions and poor health. As such, it's extremely popular with children as well as adults.

WHIMSICALIA'S BEST BARS and RESTAURANTS

The Talking Hat at Chumbleton: *This famed Wizarde inn and gastropub favours dishes made with faintly spooky ingredients. Pumpkins and toadstools are perennial favourites, while tourists with an open mind will be delighted by its 'swamp wings' – toad legs, fried and served with hot sauce that makes your nose glow like a pink LED.*

The Flattened Toadstool: *At Chumbleton's edges, there are seedier establishments – at the Toadstool, rebellious Greeblewhoz truants share cheap bunglebean juice just tables away from the Bogberts who toil happily to serve them at the Academy, and it's rowdy without being threatening. More dimly lit establishments play host to gatherings where tourists are not welcome, however, while Centaurs and other forest creatures loiter with tins of cheap greaselager on street corners on the outskirts of town. Don't go there.*

Mama Owlbrows' Teahouse: *Charming cottage teahouse and youth hostel just inside the Enchanted Forest, where enterprising*

---

1 It sings raucous songs about getting drunk (in the most direct sense of the verb) in an increasingly small and ecstatic voice as you drain the mug. Quite disturbing, actually. Is it alive? Can it think? What if it doesn't want to be consumed, but feels compelled to sing anyway? As is so often the case in Whimsicalia, it's best to adopt my motto: 'Don't think about any of it too hard.'

witch[1] Jay Owlbrows serves tea and cakes to talking animals and happily welcomes guests to their table. Of course, the cottage also has a backroom where larger, more ferocious talking animals – like Klatterlings and Skullbears – arrive quietly and depart with bundles of long, carefully wrapped hardware, but it's best not to pay attention to that.

Currency

Mundane currency is bog standard – little embossed brass coins and plastic sheets with unsmiling politicians printed on them. Once in Whimsicalia, you'll be looking to swap your money for Faeyrie groats, forged by Klatterling smiths from exotic gold alloys. Coin denominations are tricky: the system was complicated even before the war, but when the Mundane government tried to press the Wizardes to adopt the metric system as part of the ceasefire agreement, they doubled down on their currency's complexity out of spite.

WHAT'S IN A GROAT?

* ✳ 43 grabblers make a gilly-farthing
* ✳ Three-and-a-half gilly-farthings make a large-farthing
* ✳ 17 large-farthings make a short-farthing
* ✳ 4 short-farthings make a whammo
* ✳ 7/12 of a whammo is a groat

---

1 It's worth understanding that 'witch' is not a gendered or ethically loaded term in Mundania – it's more of a lifestyle descriptor, applied to people living one step removed from formal Wizarde culture who spend a lot of time boiling plants in tumbledown shacks.

DAILY SAMPLE COSTS

BUDGET: Less than 1wh,3g,1(s)f,6(l)f,2(g)f,21g per day
Attic bunk in a witch's cottage – **???**[1]
Cauldron-taxi from Greeblewhoz to Chumbleton – **???**
Jumbo bag of Mr Nincomplod's Fabulous Fizzy Bee
    Arses – **???**
Hour of levitation tuition – **???**

MIDRANGE: Between 1wh,3g,1(s)f,6(l)f,2(g)f,21g and 4wh,2g,2(s)f,12(l)f,1(g)f,14g per day
Dungeon-level suite at Greeblewhoz – **???**
Wizarde's fee for a 200 mile portal jump – **???**
Nine-course meal in a magical inn – **???**
Ticket to see the Pranslemead Grozzlers play Grunche – **???**

TOP END: More than 4wh,2g,2(s)f,12(l)f,1(g)f,14g per day
Penthouse at the Smoking Spider country club in Crickledale
    – **???**
Overnight berth on the Greeblewhoz Express – **???**
Endless food and enchanted cutlery – **???**
Full magic tuition at Greeblewhoz (comes with scarf) – **???**

Don't Forget to Pack . . .

Family heirlooms

There's no getting around the fact that at some point – especially if you dress as well as me – you're going to end up fifteen minutes into a conversation with a Wizarde who has mistaken you for another Wizarde. If you want to avoid the awkwardness of explaining that you're a non-magic user, it's worth having a small family heirloom on hand which you can pretend has a magical backstory going back generations.

---

1 Eliza, I'm sorry, but I really can't work out the maths for this bit. Can you get someone to do it, please?

DON'T MISS: GREEBLEWHOZ MIDWINTER BANQUET

While most of Greeblewhoz's nightly feasts are off-limits to visitors due to the fact that they can get . . . quite political, the famous Midwinter Banquet is open to tourists. Running dusk till dawn on the longest night of the year, this utter gut-buster has been known to defeat the appetites of visiting giants and is the pinnacle of Wizardely hospitality. Here's a sample menu from last year:

6 p.m.
An intimidating number of hors d'oeuvres: Bogbert fancies, vol-au-vents from a never-emptying tray, enchanted salmon, 'imp bollocks'[1]

7 p.m.
Pre-dinner desserts: warlock creme, gremlinflower sorbet, wibblyplip pudding, sausage & mash panna cotta, the custard hose

7.45 p.m.
Opening speech by Headmaster Candleflash

8.15 p.m.
The pumpkin course: pumpkin soup, pastries, bread, sweets, stew and fritters

9 p.m.
The weird pies course: glitter gravy, roast beast, steak and Brattleperk's, frog larynx, pumpkin

10.30 p.m.
Opening speech by Headmaster Candleflash will probably end

---

1   pickled walnuts.

11 p.m.
The magic meat course: steamed giant spider legs, greased gryphon eggs, dryad salad, ghost venison

11.15 p.m.
First-term performance reviews for all students, and presentation of this year's potential Chosen Ones, as well as house prizes

11.59 p.m.
Minute's silence for the fallen

Midnight
Space reserved for dramatic reveal of Dark Wizarde masquerading as teacher

1.30 a.m.
Comedy roast of Dark Wizarde[1]

2 a.m.
Starters begin anew: salamander caviar, flying chicken wings, Professor McBungus's Tap-dancing Fungus, jungle soup

2.30 a.m.
Traditional midwinter roc roast with all the trimmings

3 a.m.
Final course of cheese and fruit

4 a.m.
An entire bucket of sausages is slapped in front of each guest

5.30 a.m.
Guests retire, Bogberts begin clearing up the worst of the sick

---

1 Once upon a time, this sort of revelation would tip proceedings into chaos, but with the Light vs Dark tensions a thing of the past, it's all just a good laugh these days.

Indigestion remedies for horses

Despite the limitless healthcare resources offered by the magical arts, Wizardes only really know how to ease digestive complaints in the human part of a Centaur. If you want to make some very firm friends among the half-equine community, stock up on horse drugs. Recreational ones, too.

A knife forged from a horseshoe

Apart from the whole affair with the lingering aftermath of a global conflict, Mundania is a relatively safe place to visit. Even so, you wouldn't want to visit a planet swarming with guerrilla-trained magical creatures and *not* take a cold iron blade, would you?

Manners and Etiquette

Mundanes didn't forget everything

While the Forgettening may have erased Mundanes' specific memories of the war, it did nothing to lift the profound trauma dealt to their subconscious minds. As such, exclamations like 'Hey presto!' and 'Alakazam!' will not only alarm people, but may prompt a PTSD response, while describing an idea as a 'wizarde wheeze' will get you punched in the face in broad daylight.[1]

Don't try to free the Bogberts

Dressed in rags and stooped from constant labour, the Bogberts horrify many travellers, and I've lost track of the number of times well-meaning backpackers have tried to start slave revolts on their behalf. It never works, however. The Bogberts were enchanted with a spell so that they simply *need* to toil on others' behalf, and are in fact happiest in Crickledale, where the Dark Wizardes make no pretence of offering them civility or decent living conditions.[2]

---

1 The infamous 'wizarde wheeze' was a cloud of poisonous gas released in East Lundowne, which turned all its victims into huge, dying rats.

2 It's almost like some kind of BDSM thing, to be frank. I watched a Bogbert get chastised by its master for failing to clean his riding boots correctly, and as it scurried to fetch the punishment stick, I was certain I saw it rubbing its moist green hands in glee.

Don't make Deathwish/ Miller jokes

Wizardes love to make jokes drawing on the former enmity between supporters of the Girl Who Did Not Die and the acolytes of Baron Deathwish. This once-deadly feud lost its meaning during the war against the Mundanes, and even became a source of jovial competitiveness. Indeed, it all seems a big laugh until you, a tourist, decide to chip in. Then, no matter how good your punchline, the room will fall silent and you'll find ranks of scar-riven faces staring at you with eyes that have watched comrades burn alive. You wouldn't know: you weren't there.

4. SUGGESTED ITINERARIES

 ## 1. BEST OF BOTH WORLDS: (6 DAYS)

Lundowne to Pranslemead

If you've got limited time but want to see the full contrast of Mundania's dual worlds, this tour is for you, showing kids and adults alike there's still plenty of fun and wonder to be had.

DAY 1

After arrival in Lundowne, check into the Queen's Arse, a midrange hotel with poky rooms smelling faintly of cigarette smoke. Dinner is a heaving plate of grey curry with overboiled rice, after which you will collapse into a heavy sleep.

DAY 2

After a dismal fried breakfast, stop by the Department of Magic to admire its whimsical, multicoloured facade. The Forgettening altered the Mundanes' brains to make them unable to fully perceive it, so you'll be free

---

WHY WON'T MY MINIBAR OPEN?

Those in the Mundane government spared the Forgettening are constantly paranoid about the possibility of Wizarde terrorism, and have passed regulations to ensure that cupboards, chimneys and other spaces commonly used as portals by Wizardes remain boobytrapped and bound by chains. So if your fridge won't open, it's for your own safety.

DTR

For centuries before the secret, magical 'Platform Zero' was built at Empire Cross Station, the cobbled medieval alleyway known as Dead Toad Road was the main permanent portal between Mundane Lundowne and its Wizarde quarter. Accessed through two pub back rooms – one at the Mundania end and one at the Whimsicalia end – it was a place where Wizardes went to shop and dally in the atmosphere of the city, and where many of Lundowne's magically gifted youngsters would get their first taste of the astonishing world awaiting them. Now, however, Dead Toad Road has a markedly different atmosphere. The pubs have been built up into a pair of heavily fortified, opposing checkpoints, and the alley's shops now ply their trade under the watchful eyes of armed guards, temporarily freed from the Forgettening in order to keep the peace. For tourists, travelling legally from one world to the other means traversing the checkpoints at DTR.

to chortle at their baffled, uneasy expressions while you take plenty of snaps. When you're done, head to what used to be the Ape and Statue pub at the head of Dead Toad Road to begin your transfer to Whimsicalia.

You'll need to have plenty of documents with you, which you should arrange via your travel agent at least a month prior to departure. If everything checks out, the customs process – including security interviews, random searches and intimidation by dogs – can be over in as little as an hour. It will take a while for the customs Warlocks at the former Broom & Bogbert to process your entry application, so take your time to enjoy some shopping for magical goodies.[1] Once entry is granted, head to your lodgings – a spare room in the mansion of a quirky magical academic, complete with a talking suit of armour and some kind of lovable ghost.

---

1 Since DTR is no man's land, the shops are completely tax-exempt, so despite the gorgeous black-beam facades on the buildings and the candlelit rooms full of leather-bound tomes, the area has taken on the strange atmosphere of a duty-free lounge.

DAY 3

Today is all about shopping and as much sightseeing as you can fit in. Lundowne's Wizarde quarter is fairly pokey, but there's still more than you can see in a day: the bunworks on Spunsugar Street, the trinket market in Abnorm Alley, and the statue of Miller and Deathwish in Cracklebrak Plaza are all must-visits, though. When dusk falls, you'll travel out to the suburbs to have dinner with the Bozzlebees, a family of ordinary Wizardes. They're a large and light-heartedly rambunctious clan, so expect plenty of tomfoolery and levitating cutlery during the meal – just don't crush the mood by remarking on any of the empty chairs and untouched meals.

DAY 4

After a long lie in on day four, your hosts will conjure a one-use portal to Chumbleton, where you'll check in to one of the guestrooms at the Talking Hat. Take the afternoon to explore the town and its environs – but do hire a local guide.[1]

In the evening you'll board a chartered flying bathtub, headed to the Bolderbiff Trust Magical Nature Reservation in Albionus' northern highlands. At the reservation you'll be hosted by the titanic gamekeeper Bagfists, who looks after the park from a dilapidated cottage that he shares with his Nine Tame Alligators.[2] He'll lead you on a magical night safari, and you'll be able to experience the reservation from a trailer affixed to the back of his Majestic Flying Tricycle.[3] If you're lucky you'll see Taszrak and other exciting hybrids, while you're almost guaranteed to spot a Blunderback and endless herds of shitty Gurbos. When the trip's over Bagfists will serve you steaming bowls of his famous spider-claw stew, and regale you with fireside tales until you get sleepy and/or too worried about the alligators.

---

1 It's never good to walk into what you thought was a sweet shop only to find a group of people very suddenly falling silent and looking up at you from a clandestine map.

2 There are twelve of them. They are not in any way tame. They can be very stressful to spend time with.

3 Its name has a comparable relationship with its subject as that of the Nine Tame Alligators.

(DON'T) FAKE IT TILL YOU SNAKE IT: STAYING SAFE IN CRICKLEDALE

Despite the ceasefire, Dark Wizardes won't fraternise with Mundanes and are deeply suspicious of tourists. No matter how tempting it is, however, do not *in any way* pretend to be a Wizarde in order to be accepted here. There was a horrible incident a while back, where a famous offworld illusionist put on a heavily publicised gig in Crickledale, claiming he could bamboozle the Dark Wizardes with his mind-blowing close-up magic. He was fed to a large grey snake.

DAY 5

It's time to say bye to Bagfists on day five, after he tricycles you over the mountains to Crickledale. The territory of the Dark Wizardes was never previously open to tourists, and even now its denizens are frosty to offworlders. Still, in deference to the growing number of visitors, a guest house called the Strangled Stoat has been set up, where you can soak up the gloomy ambience of Crickledale and even share a Dark Repast with the naughty Wizardes themselves. You'll probably be glad to leave in the morning, but you'll be glad to have seen it.

DAY 6

Your trip comes to an end in the blissful Wizarde town of Pranslemead, where you can experience the heights of Wizardely culture. The local theatres are sure to have some incarnation of the Miller Cycle on stage, and these performances are superb fun for families who enjoy audience participation,[1] while the local Grunche stadium is home to the current league champions, the Grozzlers. Before taking your homeward

---

1 There are usually a lot of laughs to be had throwing magically conjured rotten eggs at the pantomime incarnation of the Mundane head of state when she comes in to arrest Miller and Deathwish.

portal to Lundowne at the end of your holiday, do make sure to attend a game – the terrace atmosphere is unbelievable, and you'll find the fans' enthusiasm stays with you all the way home.

 2. YOU'RE A WIZARDE: (57 DAYS, OR LESS IF YOU'RE RUBBISH)

The Full Greeblewhoz

This once-in-a-lifetime experience is extremely expensive, but worth every penny you can scrape together if you truly want to live the Wizardely life.

— TESTIMONIALS —

. . . and another thing, that stoat place was a bloody rip off. Dark Repast?? We queued for two hours just to sit and watch some git in a cape look miserable while drinking soup. Waste of time. Pranslemead was a bit better, but still pricey. Grinning sods saw us coming, I reckon. Five large-farthings for a cup of tea and a sandwich? Unbelievable. And I swear that talking salt shaker gave my change in gilly-farthings, too. And don't talk to me about those fucking alligators. That bloke wants locking up. As for the Grunche, it's a disgrace to call that a family sport, to be frank. Some of the language in the stands was shocking, and I had to cover my youngest's eyes and ears when their lead drangle got done by the Hammer. And all the time the fans were just braying and chucking sweets at each other, as if there weren't people starving in the real world. Honestly, I can see why everyone on the M-side can't stand this lot.

— Extract from testimonial by Jez Blither, father of three[1]

---

1 Eliza, why has this testimonial slipped in during the last edit? Can we take it out – it makes me look like a mug.

DAY 1

It all starts with a bat sent to your boarding house in Lundowne, inviting you to Greeblewhoz through a one-way, single-use portal. When the time comes, just climb into whichever fridge, washing machine or cupboard is emitting an ethereal blue glow, and take the jump. You'll arrive just outside the grounds where, as well as tourists like you, the annual intake of kids will be assembling. This can be a bit awkward if you're in your forties, so find the other 'mature students' (i.e. other tourists) as quickly as you can and begin the process of becoming an inseparable band of chums. Don't get too attached yet, though: at the gates you'll be tested for your magical potential, and if you're found to be a dud, you'll have to say an early goodbye.[1] This can be a bummer, especially as you will have paid the non-refundable tuition fees up front, but it is what it is. Presuming you *do* pass the test, you'll be invited into Greeblewhoz's main hall to enjoy a lavish welcome feast, during which Mr Grinnywithers will determine your house by giving you a horrid bony handshake.

DAYS 2–56

The next eight weeks of education will be some of the most challenging of your life, but also some of the most rewarding. You and your new chums will experience discouraging monologues from haunted paintings, fiascos involving the misuse of devastatingly powerful artefacts, and ritualistic persecution at the hands of the official School Bullies. But you'll also befriend members of staff, to the extent that they'll break the law repeatedly to help you out of a tight spot – so it all balances out. Late in term you'll probably get your first chance to use magic in anger, as the Academy's grounds will no doubt suffer an incursion from some kind of disgruntled monster. Once upon a time these incidents would have been real crises, instigated by malevolent agents of Baron Deathwish. These days they are largely drills with paid monsters, but they're still thrilling to take part in. You'll also probably

---

1 I mean, you can soldier on with canned spells and a positive attitude, but you'd just be embarrassing yourself.

get the chance to go on a field trip to the Mundane world: these tend to involve intense observation of military installations from a distance, without being seen by anyone.

☀ Floyd's Tip

It's worth noting that the war changed more than just the curriculum at Greeblewhoz. The once-jovial ghosts that walked the halls were weaponised into hunter-killer apparitions to guard against Mundane commandos, and still patrol the grounds in shrieking, loping packs. Meanwhile, the castle's main keep remains scarred from blast damage, and the quadrangles are filled with sombre statues of fallen students. Nevertheless, the Greeblewhoz spirit remains undaunted: each night, the students and staff gather for feasts in the Great Hall, which inevitably descend into heated political rallies where magically created food is destroyed in defiant rituals.

DAY 57

At the end of term, as the snow begins, it will be time for the Great Midwinter Banquet, with fun, feasting and brutally uncompromising performance reviews for all students. For many tourist students, this is where the fun has to come to an end. Be warned: if you haven't shown during your first term that you're either a potential Chosen One or at least an exceptionally powerful potential paramilitary asset, you'll be quietly asked to leave the premises by one of the larger members of the faculty.[1] If you're deemed worthy, however, you get to stay and enjoy the party – during which you will probably want to have a long hard think about whether you're ready to abandon your former life and become a Wizarde.

---

1 Despite being the size of a city, Greeblewhoz apparently doesn't have room to carry 'passengers', in their words. If the faculty judges you mediocre, then regardless of how influential or socially prominent you are, your money's no good to them.

📋 3. THE SECRET WAR:

An Elephant in the Room Safari

This tour is forbidden by the Mundane authorities, so be warned: if something goes wrong, you'll be arrested, and no earthly government will be able to help. For the bold, though, it's an eye-opener.

DAY 1

After arrival in Lundowne, transfer by coach to the melancholy northern market town of Skagsbury, where you should head to a defeated-looking pub called the Totally Normal Horse[1] and start asking around for Spooky Joe. Joe is an ageing ex-Greeblewhoz staffer and Whizzbang Lane survivor who went AWOL after the war, unwilling to rejoin Wizardely society but unable to defect to the Mundanes. Now he lives here, in deep cover as a homeless man, on a mission that perhaps only he truly understands. His stories are a good laugh – until you realise he's deadly serious about every word he mutters through his roll-up.[2] If you can win Joe's trust, he'll take you out of town on his decrepit flying bicycle to the nearby Grimblestead War Cemetery.[3] There, at an empty grave, Joe will throw you a shovel and command you to dig while he paces around smoking and ranting.

DAY 2

Somewhere in the early hours, you'll eventually find a limited-use door-key scroll beneath the soil, and Joe will race you to a stretch of desolate

---

1 It used to be called the Unicorn, but the proprietors painted over the sign during the war.

2 In actual fact, I never intended to go on this tour at all. I was just stopping at the Horse to use the toilet and was accosted by Joe. After a half hour of rapid-fire anecdotes, intermingled with rambling theories about prison, I said I would give him a groat if he could prove any of it was real. Joe won his groat. I saw some things.

3 Grimblestead is a tragic place. As part of the Forgettening, none of the Mundanes were permitted to remember their friends and relatives who died in the war, and so every one of the cemetery's graves is forlorn and untended.

pebble beach a few miles away. There, you'll wait, probably wondering what the hell you've gotten yourself into, before a light eventually twinkles on the black ocean. There will be some shouting, some business with rough characters in black hoods bundling you aboard a dinghy, and then a rapid, extremely bumpy ride across the frigid sea. And while it's possibly unwise to make any direct claims about what might happen next on your journey, it's worth considering how you might feel about – say – breaking silently into Blacklox Prison on a tiny boat in the dead of night, with your only promise of safety coming from a tramp you just met in a pub. Or how you might react if you found yourself face to face with the two most dangerous Wizardes in the world, as the aforementioned tramp shows them photos of an atrocity and they nod gravely. If that sounds like a good way to spend your holiday, this is probably the trip for you.[1]

DAY 3?

COPY NOT SUBMITTED BY FLOYD[2]

---

1 It certainly wasn't for me.

2 Eliza – I'm sorry, but I can't finish the chapter. The Grimblestead cemetery visit went badly awry (see copy filed above), and I think I need to stop thinking about Mundania for a bit. I also desperately don't want to make the situation there any worse, so I think it's best if I stay out of it for now. There you go – I admitted it. I fucked up. And it wasn't for the first time, either. I'll come back and tidy up the chapter, I promise. And after that, I think we need to have a bit of a chat. It could be that I've got some things to make right, and some apologies to make. But before all that, I need to get the Wizarde business out of my head: I'm off exploring for a few weeks. In the meantime, you can start editing that copy from Wasteland, maybe? Bye for now – Floyd.

'Who's this?' hissed Deathwish, as I sidled into the cramped room behind Spooky Joe. It seemed to be some kind of laundry area converted into a makeshift parlour complete with armchairs and a small candelabra.

'Just an associate,' said Joe.

'He's clear,' added a gruff voice from the corridor, and the Baron nodded, fangs glinting in the shadow of his prison-issue cowl.

With a clink of silver on ceramic, the figure in the corner finished brewing the tea, and came forward – it was Beatrix Miller herself, unmistakable despite the orange jumpsuit.

'But you're not in separate cells!' I blurted as I looked between the Wizardes, unable to contain my surprise. Miller laughed, sounding every bit the sixteen-year-old Girl Wizarde ever-present in Greeblewhoz archive footage.

'Of course we are, silly! Officially, at least,' she chided, before nodding over our heads at the guards outside. 'Right, boys?' The guards gave a chuckle at this, and even Deathwish joined in with an amused murmur.

'Besides,' he drawled in a cultured baritone when the mirth had subsided. 'We get along rather well, it turns out.'

I looked to Miller, aghast. 'But he drained your power to carry out the Drungsleydale massacre – you begged him not to!'

'Oh, come on, everyone knows it was my idea. Brian here—'

'Don't call me that in front of guests!' barked Deathwish, or rather Brian.

'. . . was all talk and no trousers, wasn't he? Came to rescue me but didn't realise I was planning a blast from the gallows anyway. Said he wouldn't lend his strength at first – said it was all a bit much. But you realised it was the only option, didn't you?'

Brian muttered in assent.

'But . . . it was a bit much, wasn't it?' I offered. 'You know, wiping an entire city off the map.'

'You didn't see the experiments they were conducting in that base they held me in,' snapped Miller, face hardening to make her look twice her age. 'Everything they do – everything they've done, since magic was revealed to them, demonstrates exactly why we kept it from them in the first place. And if we don't fight them as hard as we can now – while they're still weak – it'll be worse later.' Miller paced under the room's sole lightbulb, making the shadows dance. 'They're quick learners, and their advanced physicists were starting to figure out magic on their own, even before the Revelation War. It was always going to come to this. In a way, I'm almost glad that idiot Floyd blundered in and started things early.'

'I think he was quite well meaning,' I added, breaking out in a sweat, 'but go on.' Then Spooky Joe piped up.

'You want to see what the Mundanes are willing to do to get their hands on magic?' he said, gesturing at me with his roll-up. 'Take a look at these photos I took for the masters here.'

At that, Joe shuffled forward with a grimy sheaf of papers, which Brian inspected grimly, before passing them to me with his pale, claw-nailed hand.

The first photo was of the Drungsleydale Memorial Power Facility, viewed from behind security fencing on a rainy night. Several points on the photo were annotated with scribbles. The next shot was blurred, as if taken on the move, but clearly showed the inside of the compound, with a long corridor and a pair of blast doors at its end labelled:

W.A.N.D.
Wizarde-Augmented Nuclear Dynamo

The next photo was presumably taken in the space within those doors, and it took me a moment to parse what I was seeing. It was Wizardes. Dozens of them – prisoners of war, presumably – suspended in glowing fields of green energy, along the length of a cavernous industrial space. Streamers of raw magic were *being drawn out of them through funnel-like devices, and channelled into a massive bank of turbines at the hall's end. The forms of the Wizardes were blurred, as if they had been thrashing when the picture was taken.*

There were more blurred shots from inside – a bank of barred cells, and a lab with its wall plastered in diagrams of bat anatomy and blown-up photos of dissections with 'WHICH ORGAN DOES THE MAGIC?' scrawled over them. There were more photos, but I was still entirely preoccupied with the scene from inside the power plant, and could not process them. Surely all this couldn't be my fault.

'You see now?' said Deathwish, taking the photographs from me and passing them to Miller. 'They're already using us to power their machines. Soon, they'll figure out portals. We'll be done for, and they'll make our world as drab and dirty as theirs.'

'We've got to have this war now, or else it'll never happen at all,' added Miller, thumping a table top. 'It's the death of all Mundanes, or the Death of Magic.'

Needless to say, I got out of that cell, and out of Mundania, as fast as my legs could carry me.

— **FROM THE TRAVEL JOURNAL OF FLOYD WATT**

CHAPTER EIGHT

Wasteland

1. WELCOME TO WASTELAND

Behold, the blasted sands! Witness the mayhem! Feel the roar of the engines, the sting of the grit, and the thrill of the chase in this, the ultimate nihilist adventure destination. High Fantasy's for scrubs: in Wasteland, the world's already over, so you can do what you like. Fuck it, why not just punch a car in the face as soon as you get there? I did. Nobody stops you.[1]

? Why Wasteland?

All things come to an end, and in the mangled psychogeography of the Worlds, Wasteland is the end of all things. While you can head to Wasteland directly, the most common way to get here is by accident: walk out into a desert with an electrically bleak mood, or World-hop while looking at an explosion,[2] and that's it – welcome to the apocalypse. Or rather, the post-apocalypse – because if Wasteland is anything, it's one giant, civilisational afterparty.

Many tourists might baulk at the prospect of such an eschatological getaway. But for those in the know, Wasteland is considered to be one of the best-kept secrets out there. Yes, society may have collapsed, but as any of the locals will tell you (often with a wide-eyed, screaming laugh), it needn't be the end of the world! Indeed, despite all of the radioactive gales, marauding corpses and claustrophobic bunkers, the people of Wasteland are a surprisingly vibrant, carefree bunch.

Since death is always hovering just one minor coincidence away, the locals see no point in worrying about anything besides where the next strip of murkily sourced meat is coming from, or how much fuel is left in

---

1 Hurt my hand, though.

2 It turns out that among the Worlds, there's actually a reason for the cliché of not looking at explosions as you walk away from them.

the murderwagons. You wouldn't call it optimism, but it's a kind of contentment, nonetheless. With the past obliterated and the future teetering on a knife's edge, life in Wasteland is all about living in the moment.

Wasteland is definitely not for novice travellers or all but the mightiest families, and it certainly rewards a robust constitution. Nevertheless, if you're prepared to accept the many horrors of the ruined world as part of everyday life, and you're not afraid to take some fairly extreme cultural norms on board, you're guaranteed many lovely, lovely days, and a holiday to end all holidays.

WHY I WOULD DIE FOR WASTELAND
By Beetle Man, Battle Lad of the Steel Castle

Welcome, traveller! Or as we say at the Steel Castle, *Bloodfight Forever!* You're probably feeling scaredy-bad about visiting the Big Dusty – but don't worry, brother-sister, once you've walked these horizons and stared into the Megaburn, you'll be *burgerfry-good* in no time. I was like you once, ha ha! A seekyman I was, for a firm of *rek-roo-tars*. Came here backing my pack, to find myself, yeah? But I forgot my radgone tabs, didn't I? *Buggerbad! Grot!* I got real sick, I did, but War Mum took me in and cleaned my redpipes right up. Gave me a new name, she did – Beetle Man – and a new job as a Battle Lad. Now I stoke the boilers on Count Truckula, War Mum's big big car, and she takes us out on adventures all the time. We do all kinds of fungoods: sometimes we fight with the bunkerfolk, and sometimes we chase other cars, so the Wrench Ladies can eat 'em up and build new trucks for Mum. I even got a new best mate! He's called Mugnor, and he's a big fella with a microwave for a head. He doesn't say much, granted, but he saved me from the ants once, and he's got this one really cool boot. Together we've found a quiet, trusting love that I wouldn't give up for the world – even if the world wasn't already over.

DIESEL STEPPE

LAND OF THE DEAD

GEIGERLAND

THE ROBOT WARS

BINYARD

PRIMATE KINGDOM

NOT-SO-BADLAND

BADLANDS

CRATER

MUSH

WORSELANDS

1 Stumble upon an ancient, half-buried monument

Nothing says 'post-apocalyptic' more succinctly than a famous landmark protruding grimly from a sand dune, and Wasteland is strewn with them. Still, travellers often don't enjoy the full Ozymandian resonance of these relics, since they aren't familiar with the cultures that built them. Enter the entrepreneurs of the Monkey Zone, who have built copies of multiple earth landmarks in order to give tourists the full 'damn you all to hell!' experience. What better souvenir than a Polaroid of you on your knees, shaking your fist at the ruin of a monument from your hometown, while a gorilla in chainmail gives a thumbs-up in the foreground?[1]

2 Disrupt the order of an oppressive society

There are a dizzying number of survivor cultures in Wasteland, but what they all have in common is a penchant for weird and oppressive social structures, which tend to be so precarious that they can be tipped into chaos by the actions of a single outsider.[2] Indeed, in Hierarchia – the granddaddy of all ludicrously stratified dystopias – there are revolutions on at least an annual basis, giving tourists plenty of opportunities to feel the fuzzy glow that comes with toppling a tyrant.

3 Re-enact a story you barely remember for a crowd of rag-clad yokels

Outside all the fighting, a big part of Wasteland's aesthetic is the veneration and constant retelling of stories from the wayback-times. As such, any traveller with tidbits of pop culture to share will get superb mileage from their rememberings. It really doesn't matter what stories

---

1   Make no mistake, though, it'll cost you a pretty penny. The Apes will be all smiles, gesturing you into frame and waving their cameras, but the second they take the shot there'll be an orangutan right in your face, rattling the tin for an outrageous sum.

2   Sometimes it doesn't even take an outsider. The police state of Magna-City Three became so oppressive the city itself was declared illegal, prompting a grim-faced hypercop to shoot every building into dust with his pistol over the course of twenty relentless years of action.

you recount – it's not like a bunch of irradiated peasants living in a rusty old bus are going to care. With just a carrier bag full of action figures and a dim memory of watching soaps while stoned,[1] you can become a world-renowned bard.

4 Fight to the death in a hellish gameshow environment

Almost every settlement in Wasteland has some form of provision for ritualised combat in order to settle differences:

DON'T MISS: MENTAL DEREK

There's a semi-legendary figure in the Wasteland, and he's called Mental Derek. He's extremely competent with a shotgun, doesn't say much, and has what you might call a habit of getting into trouble. Derek doesn't seek out fights as such – he just wanders around the region in his knackered old police car, seeking redemption or just something to do. Either way, when he travels through a settlement, it tends to either undergo dramatic regime change or disappear from the map altogether. For the right fee, you can travel with him. Strapped into the passenger seat of his car, you can expect truly abysmal conversation, but the most mind-blowing, white-knuckle adventure that Wasteland has to offer. Spend a month with Derek and you will see dictators overthrown, refineries blown sky high, and countless war machines sent careening off the road in explosions of bolts and nails.[1]

---

1 Cynics might say Derek's random wanderings tend to have an astonishing habit of taking him to settlements on the brink of re-establishing organised civilisation. If that seems unfortunate to you, then just consider this – if Wasteland wasn't a constant warzone, where glinting-eyed megalomaniacs spilled endless blood and fuel over conquest and bizarre religious feuds . . . well, it wouldn't be such a great holiday destination, would it? Hooray for Mental Derek, I say.

---

1 I met a woman who'd managed to start a deep animistic tradition based around a selection of faded GI Jim dolls, which her hosts came to call 'the small warriors', so anything's possible.

in Hierarchia it's the national pastime, and even in the most out of the way settlements you won't have to look long before you find two hulks throttling each other in a pit, before an audience with tentacles for eyes and tin openers for hands. And if you want to get involved – go ahead! Just be sure to cheat by bringing an incredibly powerful gun, so you don't die like a dog.

Region by Region

Geography is a bit of a tricky subject in Wasteland.[1] All the world's civilisations are either too rubbish to produce accurate maps or have no interest in doing so, while sandstorms rearrange the landscape constantly. Settlements come and go with such alacrity that there's little point in charting them, but there are some areas and locations permanent enough to be worth noting.

1 The Badlands

Covering a huge swathe of the planet, the Badlands used to be an ocean, until all the water dried up. Now it's a vast, sun-blasted salt flat, soaked with poisonous heavy-metal residues. Thanks to the vast tracts of flat land, this is classic territory for eccentric warlords, who enjoy launching grotesquely inefficient crusades with armadas of cars. Things are just as fun beneath the surface too, as bunkers and vaults of all sizes hold a wealth of claustrophobic nightmare societies.

2 The Worselands

Even grimmer than the Badlands, the Worselands occupy the remains of what was once a continent in Wasteland's Southern Ocean, and which was a notably desolate place even before all the bombs and the madness. For the warlords of the salt flats, it's considered a mark of prestige to be able to trade up for a fortress in the Worselands, and so its inhabitants tend to be an altogether higher class of mad bastard, with a corresponding air of weird snobbery.

---

1   Not least because there are so few colouring pencils available, and so geographers have to make do with bits of bone with poo or blood or engine oil smeared on the ends.

3 The Land of the Dead

During its final days, society on Wasteland was stricken by an outbreak of zombies, which spread like wildfire across its eastern continent. As a result, this landmass is now an eerily silent wilderness, dotted with decaying cities where the dead still roam. Human survivors persist here in fortified shopping malls, where they survive off the wreckage of the old world while having bleak revelations about the empty nature of consumerism.

4 The Monkey Zone

Settled by superintelligent apes who revolted against humanity during the apocalypses, this region comprises a patchwork of feudal states ruled by chimps, gorillas, bonobos and orangutans.[1] Although they have a longstanding habit of breeding captive humans for slave labour, the Apes are relatively affable, and are for the most part fairly accepting of tourists.[2] In fact, the Apes claim they would be open to trade and co-operation with their human neighbours if it wasn't for the tragic 'misunderstandings' that keep kicking off wars between them.[3]

5 The Robot War

The Robot War is many things: it's a conflict, a place and a way of life. Originally kicking off when a network of supercomputers became self-aware and hostile, this conflict still rages long after the rest of the world has fallen into collapse. Its combatants are the Resistance, a band of humans whose scavenged technology would easily empower them to conquer the rest of the planet if they weren't so busy with the Robots, and the Robots, who would be able to crush the Resistance overnight if it wasn't for a set of particularly bizarre programming quirks.[4]

---

1 Since none of these animals are monkeys, the name their region has been given really, really irritates them. Good.

2 Having said that, your mileage may vary. As I have already implied, I found the Apes to be rip-off merchants of the highest order, despite their supposed good manners.

3 I don't think there's much to misunderstand about a man shooting a chimp in the leg for selling him a fake designer watch, and I think they were lucky that's all that happened, but there you go.

4 They . . . well, they think they're cockneys. I'll explain later.

6 Hierarchia

The huge pyramid-city of Hierarchia is seemingly the most civilised place in Wasteland – but it is a society divided. At its gilded apex sits the supreme leader, plotting ever-more Byzantine ways to oppress the masses beneath,[1] while said masses spend their time plotting equally complex schemes to depose the leader. The result is near-constant, usually teenager-led revolution. Indeed, Hierarchia can go through the whole cycle – from initial insurrection through to government overthrow and then the bleak moment when the new rulers realise they are as bad as the people they replaced – in as little as three weeks.

---

1 These strategies usually involve some manner of televised human blood sport, although the specifics vary.

A Brief History

Wasteland doesn't really have a history. If it did, it would arguably lose its charm. Every group of maniacs has their own set of creation myths,[1] which they debate as they cluster round to roast scorpion bums over barrels of burning tar, and that's half the fun of the place. Even so, there are some facts we know for sure:

✳ At some point the region possessed a technologically advanced global society of between six- and eight-billion people. Then it had . . . a real run of bad luck (or hubris – depends who you ask).

✳ It seems the region experienced pretty much every cataclysmic event that can happen to a place, all within the space of a few years. Between an asteroid impact, a nuclear war, a zombie plague, an AI uprising, an ape takeover and a runaway nanotechnology incident, the planet was hammered flatter than shit.

✳ Nevertheless, the apocalypses didn't leave an empty planet. Wasteland's population was reduced to less than a tenth of 1 per cent of what it had been – but that remnant had access to the wreckage of a global society and the vast stockpiles of resources which had sustained it. With close collaboration and careful stewarding, the survivors could have begun the painstakingly slow process of rebuilding.

✳ Instead, they began fighting. Barely had the bombs stopped falling when the first wrench duels were fought over dog food and the first motorcycle gangs were leathering up and hitting the road to find other motorcycle gangs to go to war with. It's been going on ever since.

WASTELAND

---

1 Well, I suppose they're destruction myths really, aren't they?

Wasteland Today

This culture of mandatory violence might seem crazy, given how much the survivors clearly had to benefit from cooperation. But then, cooperation just isn't what you *do* after an apocalypse, is it? And besides, if any psychiatrists had survived the ends of the world,[1] they might have made quiet note of the fact that everyone was a lot less anxious and miserable than they had been when they were *worrying* about the end of the world. And so it goes on. Empires bloom and collapse in the desert, and occasionally some fresh horror of the old world will be unleashed – a cache of nuclear warheads will be set off by some would-be atomic Caesar, or a legion of supersoldiers will awake from cryogenic stasis and go on a rampage. By and large, however, it's never long before life in the Wasteland returns to business as usual, offering a comforting familiarity for travellers.

Climate and Terrain

Wasteland's climate is more varied than one might assume at first. Even so, pretty much all of it could be grouped under the broad heading of 'total dogshit'. Thanks to the evaporation of the seas, the majority of the world's surface is covered in searingly hot salt flats, broken occasionally by the yawning remnants of oceanic trenches, and scoured regularly by ferocious radioactive dust storms. It's all drier than a nine-hour lecture on the history of paperclips – and when there *is* rain it's usually corrosive enough to strip flesh from bone. Some water remains in the highlands, leading to patches of half-arsed savannah, but pools of the stuff rarely last long without being poisoned by gits in trucks with angry faces painted on them. Rumours abound that at the heart of the Wasteland, nature has reclaimed the wilderness, resulting in an oasis of green land unspoiled by human

---

1 And no, we won't count the Brain Queen in her Asylum of Armageddon.
I don't care how many certificates she has nailed to her war mecha: she still isn't a qualified mental health practitioner.

OLDTIMES TELLY

Where better to learn about Wasteland's history than from one of the traditional 'oldtimes telly' sessions in the Badlands? These theatrical extravaganzas are less about preserving facts than they are about creating huge stories full of gods and monsters. Nevertheless, they usually end with two emaciated labourers dressed as legendary corporate mascots fighting over a dog tendon. These storytelling events are often held on the eve of big clashes between warlords, as it gets everyone pumped up on national myth and mitigates the risk of anyone seeing their opponents as human. After all, it's a lot easier to ram a harpoon through someone's neck when you know they don't venerate the same ancient fast-food brands as you.

interference – but this is exactly the sort of 'promised land' bollocks that keeps half of Wasteland's prophets in business, and so should be taken with a pinch of radioactive salt.[1]

 ## Wildlife

After the apocalypses, the number of animal species left in Wasteland wouldn't even have filled one of those depressing zoos where they put wigs on dogs and insist they're lions.[2] Almost the only things to survive were vermin, domestic animals and anything with low enough

---

1 This really can't be understated. Every year, hundreds of tourists fall for the whole 'search for the verdant place' shtick and get taken round the houses on crap package tours, on which every warlord en route gets a share of the ticket price. Don't be taken in.

2 There are many instances of this kind of zoo in Wasteland.

self-esteem to eat rubbish.[1] Even so, Wasteland is a surprisingly good wildlife destination: thanks to the vast quantity of radiation and mutagenic chemicals that flooded the atmosphere in the death throes of the old world, these biological leftovers rapidly mutated into an expansive bestiary of slavering predators.

Zoologists looking over field notes from Wasteland tend to sniff haughtily, proclaiming that 'evolution doesn't work that way' and that substantive change takes millions of years, regardless of how many toxic chemicals you throw at the problem. These know-it-alls also query how a world of barren desert – with no plants to speak of – can support an ecosystem almost entirely comprising apex predators. But they don't ask many questions when they're being chased through a ruined supermarket by a six-foot wasp with muscly arms, do they?[2]

Anyway, here are some of the more exotic types of creature you can expect to spot during a trip to the Wastes:

✳ **Big ol' rats** (*Rattus Magnus*): They say that on Wasteland you're never more than six feet away from a rat. But then again, they also say that a grim messiah called the Burger Lord sleeps at the centre of the planet, waiting to be summoned by the construction of a sky-spanning golden arch. They say a lot of things here. Still, there are a lot of rats, and they've evolved into a bewildering array of different forms, from the dreaded Cheetah Rats that can run down a motorcycle from a standing start, to the Eagle Rats, squeaking majestically as they circle distant mesas.

✳ **Miracle Dogs** (*Canis Mirabilis*): They say that dogs are man's best friend, but they're barely acquaintances when compared with Miracle Dogs. Whether through mutation, pre-crisis genetic engineering, nanotech or some other euphemism for

---

1 And, to everyone's surprise, pandas. Turns out they were a lot more resourceful than anyone gave them credit for.

2 *Floyd, that's no way to talk about Haraldson. He was a good man, and his family miss him. – ES*

DON'T MISS: KANGAROO COURTS

In many Wasteland settlements it's common for those accused of crimes to have to defend themselves from a kangaroo with accusations tattooed on its huge, chest-caving feet. It's a great justice system, and cracking entertainment to boot.

magic,[1] these canines, which resemble delightfully fat golden retrievers, have the ability to consume dust and rocks and excrete pure water. If it wasn't for these incredible living chemical factories, most of Wasteland's survivors would have died of thirst long ago.[2]

✳ **Gribblers** (*Gribbula sp*): If you're easily freaked out by creepy-crawlies, you might want to rethink a visit to Wasteland, as all of its invertebrates have been set definitively to Hard Mode.[3] Known collectively as Gribblers – since accurate taxonomy tends to be the last thing on your mind when you're being beaten to death by a wasp with fists[4] – they swarm in the ruins, caves and tunnels of the Wastes. And while many have stayed conventionally bug-sized, others – such as the **Dire Millipede** (*Myriapoda Caesar*), the **Battlepillar** (*Wrigglius Khan*) and, of course, the **Fight Wasp** (*Vespa Pugilis*) – have swollen to preposterous sizes.

---

1   Important note: unless you're sure of your company, don't use the 'm' word in Wasteland. Despite the blatant necessity for magic in explaining half of what goes on in this world, very few cultures indeed identify as magical, so it's best to handwave with references to ancient technology wherever possible.

2   On the other hand, this means that 90 per cent of the planet drinks dog piss (sorry, 'pet water'), but beggars can't be choosers, right?

3   Except cockroaches, that is. For all that people big up their resilience to nuclear war, they've been notable underachievers here. If anything, they've actually become more rubbish since the apocalypses; although it's hard to verify scientifically, the shamanic bug-talkers of the Badlands claim they have slightly less self-esteem now.

4   Ahem. Sorry. RIP Haraldson.

People

Wasteland has many unique and colourful cultures, and it would be easy to fill an entire guidebook with descriptions of their various habits and practices. Since there are only a few pages in which to do so, here's a quick primer on some of the more common social structures you're likely to encounter during your trip.

Warlord societies

These are the most common communities in Wasteland, and tend to revolve around a single charismatic figure and their bizarre cult of personality. It's hard to say exactly what to expect in any particular settlement, but you can bet your last tin of cat meat it will involve an imposing fortress, ramshackle vehicles crewed by maniacal warriors, and needlessly impractical slave labour. Warlord societies may have a certain degree of self-sufficiency, but where they really shine is in taking things from other people. The elaborate raids, sieges and chases involved will often cost more in resources and human life than they actually earn, but we're talking about warlords here, not accountants, and 'return on investment' is not a phrase that comes up often in addresses to the troops.

Zombies

There are many kinds of zombies in the Land of the Dead: fast ones, slow ones, angry ones, sad ones. Nevertheless, they all have an infectious bite, and are drawn to any sign of life in dizzying numbers. Some wonder how, even with the occasional band of survivors being drawn into their ranks, the zombies can keep coming in such quantities. You'll also likely hear campfire muttering about the implausibility of corpses still being able to walk this long after the apocalypses, or the sheer dismissal of thermodynamics inherent in the idea of a creature that can wander around for decades without food. But you know who doesn't ask any of these questions? That's right: it's zombies.

The Apes[1]

Despite literally keeping humans in cages[2], the various species of Apes who rule the Monkey Zone have welcomed offworld tourism perhaps more openly than any other society in Wasteland. Their castles boast fairly luxurious accommodation options, which you'll certainly enjoy – if you can sit at ease with the fact that they were built by the shaking hands of your fellow hominids, sweltering under an orangutan's lash. It should also be pointed out that the Apes are in no way either damned or dirty, nor do they have particularly stinking paws.

Robots

By far the most exciting Robots in Wasteland are the skull-faced, android prosecutors of the Robot War. Equipped with nightmarishly powerful weapons, a preposterously efficient automated manufacturing base and *the secret of time travel*, many wonder why they haven't yet crushed the human resistance led by the rugged general Jack Banner. It's because the Robots have a fatal flaw: back in the chaos of the apocalypses, a stray EMP blast damaged their controlling AI, leaving it with two minor – but utterly crucial – flaws:

(A) The Robots have a disastrously poor understanding of time travel. While they have mastered the technology involved in sending war machines back in time, they fail to recognise that *the fact the present remains exactly the same* means their attempts to nip Banner's resistance in the bud aren't working. Pitying resistance soldiers have even tried to explain this to the Robots, but they never seem to get it. They just keep wellying mechanical assassins into the past, who inevitably become part of the young Banner's increasingly vast cadre of android father figures, rather than assassinating him.

---

1 Frankly, I would have put this bit in the 'wildlife' section, but Eliza says this is exactly the kind of thinking that leads to so many extremely bloody 'misunderstandings' between the people of Wasteland and their simian cousins.

2 Floyd, you've been there and you know full well they don't keep anyone in cages. Those humans are contractors who get paid a fair wage – unlike the thralls of every warlord on the planet. Is this really all because a chimp overcharged you for a photo opportunity? You need to get over it, mate: you're making a prick of yourself. – ES

(B) They all think they're cock-neys. They speak in ridiculous accents, mix their core code with rhyming slang, and have regular knees-ups around big robot pianos. Worse yet, thanks to a broken logic mechanism, the Robots believe that because all Robots are cockneys, anyone who speaks in a cockney accent *must necessarily be a Robot*. This, of course, means that their empire is incredibly easy to infiltrate and sabotage, offering superb opportunities for tourists with a knack for comedy voices.

ROBOT RHYMING SLANG

01100001 01110000 01110000 01101100 01100101 01110011 00100000 01100001 01101110 01100100 00100000 01110000 01100101 01100001 01110010 01110011 – 'stairs'

01110111 01101000 01101001 01110011 01110100 01101100 01100101 00100000 01100001 01101110 01100100 00100000 01100110 01101100 01110101 01110100 01100101 – 'suit'

01110100 01110010 01101111 01110101 01100010 01101100 01100101 00100000 01100001 01101110 01100100 00100000 01110011 01110100 01110010 01101001 01100110 01100101 – 'wife'[1]

---

1 Robots don't even have wives, or gender, but they certainly love their rhyming slang.

3. PLANNING YOUR TRIP

When to Visit

Good luck choosing a pleasant time to visit the apocalypse.

Getting Around

It shouldn't come as a surprise that the best way to get around in Wasteland is in an outrageous, gas-guzzling motor vehicle – ideally one that has been modified into a sort of moving fortress. Wherever possible, it's good to book passage as part of a warlord's armada, if only to avoid being chased by one. Otherwise, consider either muscle power (peasants in rags can be hired from many fortresses for a reasonable day rate, along with manky donkeys with too many eyes) or vehicles with renewable energy sources.[1]

Eating and Drinking

Food is a weak spot for Wasteland, if we're being honest. For the most part, your best non-radioactive options are ancient tinned foods or hydroponic crops, both of which are pretty bland. If you're willing to enjoy a few isotopes with your food, however, there are plenty of game options available. Cowrat meat has been a staple for some time, with its taste of beef and pet-shop straw, but enterprising cooks are now turning their hands to some of the desert's more nightmarish wildlife. This new 'Gribbler Cuisine' is a bit hit and miss, but definitely worth a go for those with adventurous stomachs.

WASTELAND

---

1 If you do this, the Wastelanders will hate you for it. In a culture where the tragic hubris of the carbon economy is the nearest thing there is to a global religion, the idea of a solar-powered car is a blasphemous insult.

WASTELAND'S
BEST BARS and RESTAURANTS

Valhalla: *Worselands roadhouse run by a retired road warrior; rough as a badger's arse and most of the liquors double up as fuels, but the battledome out back is a thrill.*

Aunt Betsy's Cannibal Buffet: *Charming rustic buffet with folksy decor and welcoming atmosphere. Only problem is the revolting buckets of lukewarm human flesh.*

Doctor Bozzler's: *This bonobo-run cafe is the only vegan food establishment in Wasteland.[1] The food is great even if it's been prepped by chimps, but prices are – predictably – a complete rip-off.*

Big Hongo's Taste of the Beforetimes: *Luxury restaurant serving delicacies from the old world for elite warlord clientele. Worth it if you've got 500 barrels of oil to spend on a tiny tin of caviar.*

The Dog & Neural Net Processor: *Traditional cockney-style robot boozer. Drinks are shit because the Robots can't taste, but the piano-side singsongs are rollicking.*

Airbar Hierarchia: *Swanky joint for Hierarchian socialites, where you can pay dizzying sums to take gulps of fragrant air then blow them in the faces of passing scum while shrieking with laughter.*

Burgerfry Godpalace: *Part temple, part fast-food restaurant devoted to the worship of the terrifying chthonic deity known as the Burger Lord. The chips are superb if you can forget the fact that the deep fryer[2] is also used for human sacrifices.*

---

1 Trust the bloody Apes to take the moral high ground.

2 Not to be confused with the Deep Friar, a chilling subterranean monk who lives beneath the establishment.

Currency

While some communities have their own simple currencies, such as human ears, VHS tapes or remembered dialogue from pre-apocalyptic sitcoms, for the most part Wasteland runs on the barter system. And when the inhabitants of the Wastes aren't stealing from each other, do they *ever* love to trade. If you come with enough technological trinkets, canned food and bullets, you can get whatever you might need for your onward journey.

DAILY SAMPLE COSTS

Costs given in Barter Units (BU), where 1 BU is equivalent to:
* Half a string of creepy plastic dolls' heads
* Three big bullets
* 1 square foot of rat pelt
* A mouthful of petrol

BUDGET: less than 10 Bu

Overnight stay in a one-person dog-leather tent, shared with a dying cyborg: **1 BU**

Transport on the bonnet of a marauder's buggy: **2 BU**

Sundried tunnel fungus, sautéed with cat-cheese curds: **2 BU**

Groundling's ticket for a re-enactment of an ancient soft-drink advert: **3 BU**

MIDRANGE: 10–25 Bu

Bunk in the barracks of a mid-sized death cult (weapon rental included): **3 BU**

Transport on the back seat of a souped-up motorbike with a skull on the front: **5 BU**

1 lb nameless meat, grilled over burning plastic: **5 BU**

A night at the battledome (comes with a strimmer to hand to a combatant): **7 BU**

TOP END: More than 25 Bu

High Priest's quarters in a towering citadel, including mutant butler service: **20 BU**

Transport on the gloating dais atop a warlord's tank-tracked
    slaughter yacht: **15 BU**
Ancient tin of hamburgers in brine, with human milk cheese and
    hydroponic lettuce: **10 BU**
Hire of twenty berserkers and two armoured buses to conduct
    your own raid: **50 BU** (plus fuel costs)

Don't Forget to Pack . . .

A chainsaw: If you can't see how this would come in handy in
Wasteland, I don't know what I can say to help you.

Drugs: Either to guzzle for your own entertainment, or to exchange in
an ancient oil refinery full of nihilists for tinned meat and/or your life.

That's it.

Manners and Etiquette

Don't try to save the world
After arriving in Wasteland, you'll probably make it half an hour before you see an act of such appalling injustice that you feel you simply must intervene. Don't bother. Wasteland's whole thing is that it's *broken*; it doesn't want to be fixed. Even if you get swept up in binning a dictator, don't make the mistake of thinking you can stick around to implement lasting social change. The brutal truth is, the Wastelanders *like things the way they are*, and will always wrestle things back into bleakness.

Feel free to litter
I mean, you can't make the situation any worse, can you? In fact, you'll probably start a devotional sect if you drop something with a good enough logo on it. Wasteland is altogether no place for neat freaks,[1] and tourists should – if anything – make an effort to be more generally wasteful, boorish and

---

1 Except for the order of drag-racing germaphobes who call themselves The Fast
& the Fastidious. There are always exceptions.

DRESS TO AGGRESS – WASTELAND FASHION

More than in any other World, Wasteland is a place where you need to dress to fit in. Show up looking like a tourist and you'll instantly be singled out for a battering with a length of rusty chain. But fear not! Considering almost everything here is made from literal rubbish, it's really not difficult to get together an outfit that'll be the height of fashion.

✳ When considering your overall aesthetic, try to aim for something in between 'medieval infantry' and 'motorcyclist with heavily implied erotic appetites'.

✳ New clothes will stick out like a sore thumb in the Wastes, so distress anything by putting it in a tumble drier with a handful of charcoal and some old meat for an hour.

✳ A rummage in a hospital skip should provide you with all the padding, used bandages and support braces you need to properly accessorise.

✳ Rags are your friend. By ripping up old sacks and bin bags, you can make an outfit for casual nights out or a comfy underlayer to mitigate tetanus risk from rusty armour.

✳ Think automotive! Tyres cut in half make superb (if unwieldy) shoulder pads, while hubcaps and licence plates can be hammered into spiffing improvised armour.

✳ If trying to infiltrate the Robots, you won't need much of a disguise – just a bit of silver spray paint on the face[1] or some cutlery taped to your hands.

While tourists are exempt from Hierarchian law, it's still best to know the visual signifiers of class during the current dystopia. If in doubt, dress like an extremely camp Roman.

---

1 Silver spray paint is definitely worth bringing to Wasteland, even if you've got no plans to visit the Robots.

untidy than they are at home. Throw things away half-finished. Set fire to things for a laugh. If you liked a meal, belch in the server's face. Hell, take a shit right there on the floor, nobody cares.

Talk complete shite

Patterns of speech in Wasteland are eccentric to say the least, so you'd do well to pepper your speech with mangled slogans from the past, archaic words in weird contexts, and slang you've made up on the spot.

Be discreet about medicine

The locals might make it look easy to swan around in the fallout all day and only get a couple of weird lumps to show for it, but they are adapted to this environment – try it yourself and you'll be shedding hair in hamster-sized clumps within hours. You'll need to bring a battery of medications, and you'll need to keep their use hidden, or else you risk a sweating giant with a hockey mask asking if you brought enough for everyone.

Be careful about pretending to be a god

Weird desert cargo cults eat fewer tourists than they used to, but it's still worth exercising caution. If you're a guest of one, don't pretend to be their god in order to swindle your way into swankier digs – it's a classic schoolboy error. Everyone thinks they're the first to try it, but they always regret it when they end up locked in an industrial microwave as a sacrifice after two weeks of luxury.

4. SUGGESTED ITINERARIES

 1. GHOUL RUNNINGS: (10 DAYS)

Zombie Hunting in the Land of the Dead

For some reason, one of the most common shared fantasies among human beings is surviving the mass resurrection of the hostile dead. If that sounds like fun to you, so will this itinerary.

DAY 1

The trip starts out with a serious jolt of adrenaline, as you're dropped by parachute in the middle of zombie territory with only your wits and a rifle to protect you.[1] From there, it's up to you to navigate your way through the eerie, deserted landscape to the nearest shelter, with plenty of great jump-scare opportunities along the way.[2]

DAY 2

Unless you've seriously fucked it, evening of the second day should see you arrive at the fortified Sunnyville Megamall, where you're bound to find a band of survivors. Many of them will be former tourists who've decided to live the lifestyle full time, so it should be fairly easy to beg your way in through the barricades. After a simple campfire meal in a trashed sporting goods store – a great point to start developing alliances for the mayhem to come – it'll be time for a whimsical dance with flickering jury-rigged Christmas lights before a trip to the mall's

---

1 Plus a truck full of hired marauders watching from a safe distance, if you've got any sense. It'll cost you a fair few tins of dog food, but it's a safety net that's worth springing for.

2 For maximum fun, wander slowly through an abandoned petrol station, cautiously shouting, 'Hello?' until a living corpse inevitably bursts from a wall.

roof. There, you can drink old whiskey and look down on the hordes of corpses outside, while enjoying sobering reflections on how the zombies 'aren't that different to us'.[1]

DAYS 3–5

On day three, you'll get your chance to exercise what definitely aren't buried homicidal urges, as you're issued one of the mall's sniper rifles and posted in a water tower to chip away at the horde, bullet by bullet. When you're done shooting, you can join the other survivors in scavenging the mall, picking up some great pop-culture souvenirs in the process. At night, it'll be time for more dancing and whiskey. This schedule of murderous monotony might go on for several days, but it's usually around day five that the survivors pick up a faint radio signal asking for help, and have to send a group of volunteers on a desperate mission into the Z-Zone. Pack your bags!

DAYS 6–9

You'll hit the road at dawn – perhaps in a car, but more likely on foot. Combat will be light at first, so it's worth building a strong rapport with the ragtag band you're travelling with. After all, if you let yourself slip into the role of 'abrasive twat who nobody trusts' you'll be thrown to the dead at the first twitch of a cadaver. As the road trip progresses, your encounters with the living dead will get more and more intense, as will the contrived ethical dilemmas the party faces. Inevitably, a situation will arise where the gentlest soul in the group turns out to be hiding a zombie bite, and everyone will spend a miserable afternoon deciding to shoot them.[2] That's generally the low point of the trip.

1 I never got that, frankly. I mean, they're dead, for a start.

2 Take my advice: just commit murder ASAP. Everyone will think it's a bit much, but it'll save time.

The dust storm abated around midday, leaving a silence so profound that we could hear the trickle of individual sand grains down the pitted faces of the skyscrapers around us. This was it: the fabled Business Place. And although our guide assured us this city was dead rather than Dead, to us it seemed the very definition of 'too quiet', and we kept our hands close to our carbines.

Still, the silence persisted – until I trod on the bloody bone. It was a rib or something, and I barely had time to register the bitemarks along its length before it had snapped in two, echoing through the bleached streets like a gunshot. We froze as the first howl drifted up from some distant rooftop, before being answered from right across the street. Then the noise was everywhere, a dreadful moan that harrowed our nerves, loosened our bladders and rattled the cracked windows in their panes.

The zombies emerged from the darkened lobbies in their thousands, dragging mangled limbs as they lurched beneath the faded logos of ancient firms. Their skin was wrinkled and papery over yellowed bone, torn and flapping like the rags of their suits. Desiccated tongues hung from their mouths like the threadbare ties that still adorned their necks.

We fired clip after clip into the mass, but it was like trying to stop an incoming tide with a teaspoon – in no time at all they had us surrounded in a ring of outstretched, grasping arms, and still more poured from the shattered offices. We were just considering whether to save the last bullets for ourselves when I noticed something. The zombies were not reaching to grab us. They were reaching out, yes, but they were holding things out to us. As a sultana-eyed wretch staggered up to me,

I heard words in its moan. They were barely there at all, like whistles in the wind, but once I noticed them, they were clear as the noon sun. It was saying it wanted to add me to its professional network. I looked again at the withered claw of its hand, and there it was: a business card. Torn and filth-encrusted, but unmistakable.

When our guide clocked this, her orders were clear. 'Take the cards,' she hissed. 'Take the cards, shake their hands, say you'll give them a call – and then run.' And so we did. We shook every one of those horrible hands, we said we'd call to arrange a meeting, and we ran until we threw up. Reader, I don't mind telling you that I never followed up on a single introduction.

— FROM THE TRAVEL JOURNAL OF FLOYD WATT

DAY 10

After a number of episodic encounters with the living dead,[1] you will finally reach your destination. Just be aware that nine times out of ten, the settlement you've set out to save will either turn out to be entirely overrun – making the whole endeavour pointless – or run by a local madman whose draconian social-control mechanisms prove that mankind was worse than the zombies all along. That's just the way of things in the Land of the Dead.

---

1   If it doesn't arise naturally, be sure to engineer a situation where one companion accidentally awakens a horde while sneaking through supposedly deserted ruins; it's a riot every time.

2. PLANET OF THE JAPES: (1 WEEK)

The Lighter Side of the Wasteland

Want a taste of the Wastes without the full-on nihilism of the warlord lifestyle? Got a desperate urge to be grifted by a chimp?[1] This short break is the one for you.

DAYS 1–2

After entering the Monkey Zone, you'll meet with Gubbles, your host for a two-day homestay. Gubbles is a laid-back, middle-class orangutan whose well-appointed treehouse boasts a fountain of actual clean water, a gallery of curiosities from the old world and a retinue of human 'helpers'.[2] Accompanied by Gubbles, you'll be able to join the Apes on horseback tours of their feudal realm, and pay a small fortune to be photographed alongside a poor-quality replica of a smashed-up Big Ben.

DAYS 3–4

On day three, your wallet will groan with relief as your time in the tourist trap of the Monkey Zone comes to an end. Guided by Gubbles, you'll head south to the Ultradome, a huge arena constructed by the Apes and one of the few large buildings in the wasteland that isn't in ruins. It's the venue for the famous Megalympics, where weapons are banned and teams from all over the Wasteland come to compete under the hospitality of the Apes. Ordinary sportspeople are banned: Megalympians need either crude cybernetic upgrades, wild mutations or vast amounts of sports drugs to compete, and preferably all three. Events include Throwing an Engine Block at the Sun, Fighting Huge Scorpions, and Running Through a Giant Microwave, as well as the classic Everyone Gets Locked in a Shipping Container and Fights to the Death. It's superb fun, but do make sure to get a seat further from the ring than you expect *anyone* could throw an engine block.

WASTELAND

---

1 *Oh, come on, Floyd. – ES*

2 They're definitely slaves.

APOC-CON

When there are no sports on due to Flying Rat Season, the Ultra-dome doubles up as an exhibition space and hosts Apoc-con, the annual trade show for marauding despots. This massive exhibition and conference, operating under a blanket ceasefire, gives petrol-headed maniacs the chance to network with peers, share best practice and listen to talks by thought leaders in the field of running histrionic death cults. Here's last year's agenda:

08.00

Chairman's introduction, followed by distribution of water to assembled scum from the gloating balcony

Duke Gorethumb, *conference chair and Lord of Bonesaw Gulch*

08.30

Keynote speech – Fire and Blood: Navigating an increasingly competitive Badlands environment

Jimmy Fiveirons, *Prince of the Dog Men*

09.30

Debate – Pig gas or slave treadmills? Choosing the right power source for your citadel

Commodore Smokebelch, *the Tycoon of Smog Valley*
Judi Piston, *the Gasolina Tsarina*

10.30

Morning break (speed networking available; speed provided, please bring your own motorcycle)

11.00

Sponsored presentation – Choosing the right ornaments for your battlewagon

Three-eyed Joe, proprietor of the Biletown Motor Dungeon

Panel Discussion – Spikes, rivets . . . sensible shoes? Is fetish gear going out of fashion?

Lord Gigantus, the Kaiser of Beefcake City
Strix Nebulosa, Archbitch of Gunsmoke Canyon
Good Times Gordon, Chief of the Lounge Boyz

12.00

Presentation – Is spray paint really enough? How to avoid mediocrity in motivating your death cult

'Eternal' Mike Japes, the Bodhisattva of Beastmode

12.30

Buffet lunch (tiger-meat trough sponsored by Trixie Switchblade's Circus of Suffering)

14.00

Masterclass – Frugal fury: running a landbound death armada on a tight budget

Legatus Tyrannica, Chief War Officer of the Pain Valley Ruffians

15.00

Debate: What must we do to hasten the coming of the Burger Lord?

Culminating in a live sacrifice, and chaired by the **Pickles Tasty**, High Priestess of the Burger People

16.00

Conference close, followed by Battle Golf – delegates may reconvene at 19.00 for the Warlord of the Year award ceremony.

DAY 5

After all the excitement of the arena, it's time to bid Gubbles farewell and enter the Badlands' gloomy underworld of bunkers and fallout shelters. After decontamination, you'll pass through the steel blast doors of Contingency 6, one of a series of identical bunkers, each housing more than 300,000 former government workers, and thus the largest settlements on the planet beside Hierarchia. Contingency 6 is a relatively peaceful place but exists in a constant state of cold war with Contingency 7, the next bunker along, over a difference in spelling between their versions of a particular administrative form. This disagreement might seem minor, but when life is as monotonous as it can get in a cramped steel cylinder full of civil servants, people will do anything for a bit of excitement.[1] Once you're settled in, why not take in one of the three propaganda films on rotation in the bunker's cinema, or watch wheat slowly grow in one of the hydroponics chambers?

DAY 6

After a breakfast sampling of Contingency cuisine – they grow three different crops and two types of artificial meat, so it won't take long – it's time to head to the surface again, aiming for the trenches of the Robot Wars.[2] To get there, you'll need to head through a semi-abandoned subway rail network, where a society of stoic nihilists have carved out their Stygian fiefdom. They're unpleasant sorts, acting as middlemen and spivs between the C-series bunkers and the Resistance fighters above, but they brew legendary vodka from the mushrooms that grow in their tunnels. Do hang around to try some, but be sure to make a brisk exit when it looks like everyone's drunk enough to start shooting each other.

---

1 What happened to Contingencies 1 through 5, you ask? Their inhabitants wore the wrong-coloured jumpsuits. There was nothing else for it – C6 and C7 had to put aside their differences and break out the emergency nukes.

2 You could head to Contingency 8, but I wouldn't recommend it – the only thing alive there is a mad Robot who sets physics-based teleportation puzzles for visitors, and it can be a real time sink.

As you escape the tunnels, you'll emerge into a pitched struggle between the humans of Jack Banner's heroic Resistance and their skull-faced adversaries. Feel free to watch the laser show for as long as you like, then take five minutes to spray your face silver, put on a cockney accent and do a cheeky walk right behind Robot lines. Greeted like an old mucker by the skeletal combatants, you'll be ushered to a chrono-warfare facility to watch an M-200 assassin get sent back in time, before being dragged to a Robot pub to celebrate with a good old-fashioned knees-up. You'll drink warm beer from dirty glasses,[1] dance like an urchin and sing riotous songs around a big Robot piano (which also has a skull face, and plays itself). It's a joyous conclusion to the trip – just don't bother getting into a pub debate about the mechanics of time travel. The Robots may have the godlike technology required to achieve it on an industrial scale, but they *just don't get it*.

 ## 3. HUNGER FOR GAMES: (1 WEEK)

Revolting Times in Hierarchia

Separated from the rest of the Wastes by an impassable wall, the city state of Hierarchia is truly a destination apart, and this trip is tailored specifically for teenage visitors to live the magic.

DAY 1

Thanks to its ever-growing number of would-be revolutionaries, Hierarchia now runs a timeshare system whereby if a dictatorship survives a hundred days without being overthrown, it's uninstalled and returned to the queue, giving another set of tyrants and rebels a chance to play. You'll arrive right after a scheduled changeover, as the new government works out what mad rules to split society by. Orient yourself by working out which bleedingly obvious visual signifiers of caste are currently in

---

1 Well, the Robots will just pour it all over their chrome skull-faces, but it's the thought that counts.

HIERARCHIA: FACTS AND STATS

❗ Population..18,000,000

❗ Average wealth per capita ....10,000 Leaderbucks

❗ Average wealth per capita (excluding Supreme Leader):
Eliza, I can't work this out but it's bugger all. Can you please insert a cartoonish image of some moths fluttering out of a purse?

❗ Average age of revolutionary leaders 17

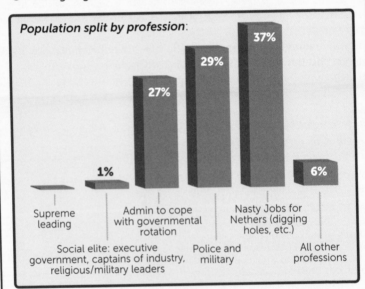

Population split by profession:

- Supreme leading
- Social elite: executive government, captains of industry, religious/military leaders — 1%
- Admin to cope with governmental rotation — 27%
- Police and military — 29%
- Nasty Jobs for Nethers (digging holes, etc.) — 37%
- All other professions — 6%

❗ Current Supreme Leader: The Steel Viper (formerly Kay Brittlestar of Sector 43-b, shaft H)

❗ Regime Gimmicks: Coloured visors denote class. Also something complicated where families send their oldest children to fight against robots in a maze or something.

❗ Statistical likelihood of a revolution occurring during the span of any given three-week holiday: around 15%

vogue: sometimes it's 'the lower your social rank, the more thumbs you have,'[1] sometimes it's the shape of the scarf people wear or whether they can roll their tongues or not.

You'll spend your first evening enjoying the hospitality at the Leader's Palace, sitting like an incredibly fancy gold hat at the very top of the city. Its appearance and layout changes depending on who's at home, but you can count on extravagant throne rooms, huge open-air party spaces, and plenty of spires and rooftops for climactic duels.[2] Enjoy the decadence, as it's the only time you'll see it outside the context of the violent revolution to come.

DAY 2

As you begin your journey down the city, enjoy the statue garden set up around the structure's core, where the huge monuments favoured by off-rotation regimes are stored while they wait for their turn to come round again.[3] Statues from fallen regimes are kept here too, defaced with graffiti, and some may even acquire garlands of vat-grown flowers, as nostalgic citizens sneak in at night to pay homage to classic dictatorships of years past.[4] Further down, you'll pass the Gloat-o-scopes, where massive screens display the luxuries being wasted above by

---

1 Regimes often fall apart under the weight of a gimmick. In this instance, by the time everyone had undergone surgery to get the appropriate number of thumbs, the government had been overthrown by a boy who declared himself Chief Citizen and banned the Culture of Thumbs that the people hated so. Within six months, it was decreed that on a temporary basis (it's always on a temporary basis), people's jobs would be denoted by the colour of a third eye on their foreheads. The people groaned.

2 While leaders make best efforts to prevent any insurrection during their reign, it's considered bad manners not to tailor your architecture at least slightly to accommodate good drama. For the same reason, prisons are often located very near refuse chutes leading into dangerous areas of the undercity.

3 With that said, much of the city's more gargantuan statuary, too big to be moved, is now modular, so heads, insignia and the like can be swapped out for new kit with the speed of a motorsports pit stop.

4 At the very back of the garden I saw the most peculiar statue. It seemed far more ancient than any of the others, and while I'm sure it was just a trick of the ivy growing over it, I could have sworn it had antlers. I didn't like that statue much at all.

CYCLE OF VIOLENCE

Since the relentless, awful action of the Titanaeum is the single biggest spark for rebellion in Hierarchia, it's no surprise that successful revolutionaries always set out with the sworn intention of ending the games for good. Nevertheless, after each revolution, the blood sports always quietly come back. Every rebel leader comes to realise, in the end, that the people would riot just as hard if they *didn't* have their games.[1]

1 On one classic occasion a particularly hated regime was collapsed by four rebellions simultaneously. Their leaders, equally charismatic, and all seemingly fated for power, couldn't work out what to do. After hours of arguments, they agreed – somewhat sheepishly – to fight each other in the very format of televised deathmatch they had all set out to abolish.

the social elite, in order to needlessly enrage the downtrodden lower classes. Finally, you'll reach the sprawling Titanaeum, where Hierarchia's famous teenager deathmatches are held. No matter what regime is in power, it will – for some reason – rely upon mass-broadcast young-adult blood sports to function, and this is where the magic happens. Whether it's the sons and daughters of the aristocracy duelling for the right to join the ranks of their parents, a fight between teams of different castes in a grim labyrinth, or just a load of random kids unleashed into a room full of hammers, you can be sure of a banging show.

DAY 3

Your third day will see you visit the Nethercity, where the lowest social class – known as the Nethers – live in teeming millions. While the aesthetics of the upper city may transform dramatically in the wake of a new regime, barely anything changes down here: the Nethers work in factories and mines, they drink, they dream of a better tomorrow. They're universally beautiful, but in a very slightly grubbier way than

— TESTIMONIALS —

I took my girlfriend to Hierarchia to propose to her, and wanted to pop the question on the barricades as the old regime fell. Sadly, she got a bit involved in the uprising. Now she's their prophesied hero and just accepted a marriage proposal from the woman who forged her sword. Shit holiday.

— Ben Fist, 19, Car Dealer

Even as an offworlder, I've been a keen fan of the Hierarchian political cycle for years, and it was amazing to actually make it to an overthrow. And that last season — what an upset! Can't believe there was a second band of rebels waiting to snatch the state from the first set when they were just a week into government! I mean, they're a bunch of jokers and opportunists, and I guarantee they'll be off the throne by winter, but still — what a play.

— Sasha Bees, 32, Civil Engineer

Outstanding break. We'd been working hard all year and had been promising ourselves a holiday for a while, and Hierarchia was just the ticket. Cocktails on a balcony a mile in the air, and great sports on the TV every night — bliss. There was a revolution halfway through our stay, but aside from a brief hostage situation (where the rebels were frankly charming), it barely disrupted things at all.

— Spencer Work, 44, Solicitor

I came here to admire the architecture of the megastructure itself, but I have to say I've ended up wondering about other structures altogether. This whole mechanic with new governments every three months and constant rebellions . . . isn't that . . . a system in itself, which ensures nothing ever changes? I'm not a conspiracy theorist or anything, but it does seem nobody here's even curious about that, let alone keen to rebel against it. Odd.

—Evelyn Bread, 64, Architect

DON'T MISS: DUNUPRISING

'Not everyone can be the hero' reads the sign above the doors to this quiet community, just outside Hierarchia. It's a bitter-sweet, quiet place – a retirement home for failed rebels. After all, even with the sheer number of opportunities offered by the timeshare system, not every aspiring champion can end up burning the world down. Some just never make it, despite years of trying, and this is where they end up. Burnt out in their early twenties, these poor souls realise they just can't face another year of trying to be the unlikely central figure of a revolution, and retire to Dunuprising for the start of their rehabilitation. It's worth a look before you leave.

the elites. And they tend to take over the city every few months, led by a teenage visionary whose parents died in tragic circumstances. The Nethercity is a gloomy industrial catacomb dotted with shabby markets and shanty towns that encrust the city's support girders like barnacles. In this cacophonous warren you can visit the humble childhood homes of famed revolutionaries of the past, and enjoy an evening of tweedly-deedly fiddle music and homebrewed spirits.

DAY 4

You'll have the chance to meet and greet the various hotheads vying to lead the next overthrow of the government, and you are almost certain to become romantically entangled with at least a handful of them, if you're of a certain age. Life in an insurrectionist fighting force entirely comprising beautiful people in their late teens is a tornado of hormones waiting to happen, and it will be an unusual day indeed if it doesn't end with you bogged down in at least three love triangles.

DAY 5

Your trip will be timed so that day five coincides with some kind of highly spiritual coming-of-age ceremony for the Nethers, in which the potential revolutionaries get to jostle with their rivals in a test of courage and skill. Whatever the set-up, these events almost always end up escalating into riots and then full-scale revolution, and it's a joy to watch: one minute things are just a bit rowdy, then you clock someone giving a speech and kicking the head off a statue, and suddenly every-one's chanting and bashing in windows. One of your love interests might have a bit of a die in the carnage, but don't worry: you'll get over it in the long run, and in the short term you'll be too busy assaulting the Leader's Palace to care much.

DAY 7

After a wild night overthrowing the tyrannical regime of the former leader, your trip will finish where it began: in the golden splendour of the Apex, as the new leader ponders how to set up the society that has fallen into their hands. Take a little time to enjoy the electric sense of optimism washing over the newly liberated Nethers, but don't dally too long – it'll be a day at most before the new leader faces their first dark dilemma and starts Hierarchia back on the slippery slope to dystopia.

EPILOGUE

West

PUBLISHER'S NOTE

Floyd's footnote to Eliza following his trip to Mundania was the last copy he ever filed. Until we began to assemble this manuscript, nobody knew where he had gone, and it was presumed his final destination would remain a mystery for ever. That was until we found a recording of a voice-mail addressed to Eliza in the archive we purchased, dated two weeks after Floyd's last footnote was penned. Going by other records, we know that Eliza Salt left her office just an hour after she received this message - and was never seen again. The next day, access to the Worlds appeared to be closed for good. While this message doesn't do much to explain the disappearances or the vanishing of the Worlds, we have decided to include a full transcript below, for the sake of completeness.

Hi, Eliza, it's Floyd. Listen, my battery's nearly gone, and I've got to go back inside in a second anyway. What I'm saying is, I've got to be quick. So if I start rambling, which I probably will because I'm quite pissed, just go ahead and stop me, yeah? Oh, this is a voicemail, isn't it, so you can't. Well, I'll just do my best not to ramble, then.

OK, so first things first. Do you remember all those rumours we kept hearing about . . . West? You know, the Cowboy World those backpackers swore they'd visited, but we could never find?

Well . . . I found it. And you won't believe it, but they were right. You *do* just have to keep walking west, from anywhere, and you get there. It's really hard to explain – it's not like *normal* west, you see – but it makes sense when you're doing it.

Unfortunately, I seem to be in a spot of bother here. And I promise you, I really do, that it's not my fault this time. Or rather it is my fault, but it's not anything I've done since I got here. Stop, Floyd, you're rambling!

Right. Well. The problem is, while the backpackers had it right on one front – this place certainly *is* West – they were talking complete shit about the cowboys part. I was hoping it would be, you know, ten-gallon hats and gold mines and things, right? But it's not. This isn't Cowboy West at all. I think it's— *[inaudible]*

Oh fuck, Eliza. I think this is the Bad West. Like, where I nearly ended up at the end of the Mittelvelde trip. The *Elven* West.

The big giveaway, I suppose, was the Elves. Antlered gits. I saw them on the sixth day, to the west of course, and I tried to walk away from them. I kept trying, but whatever I did, I just found myself walking west, right towards them. And now they're here. Or I'm there.

Either way, there's a whole shitload of Elves here, in a cave, and they want a word with me.

I know I always used to scoff at what you said, Eliza, about this whole Worlds business being an experiment of some kind. Well, I'm sorry for that. As it happens, I'm afraid you might have been absolutely right.

I think it has been an experiment. Or rather, a test – wasn't that what you called it? – and they've been watching the whole time. And now, Eliza, I believe the Elves have drawn their conclusions.

And if that's the case, then I strongly suspect this is good-bye. I'm not going to ask you to come and bail me out, because you've done that enough. And besides, for once, I'm not sure I deserve the help. So just . . . finish the book, and if you are inclined to be kind, try to make me sound like a bit less of an arsehole.

Oh, and since I won't have to deal with the consequences now, you can tell the Bison King I always thought he was a total c—

[end of message]

AFTERWORD,
by Nate Crowley

When it comes to metaphors for fiction, one of the oldest of all old chestnuts is the idea that books are like gateways to other worlds; that reading is, in fact, a kind of travel. It figures, therefore, that with a bit of jiggling to make the edges fit, it should be possible to write a book that lays into both the conventions of fantasy world-building and the conventions of travel writing at the same time. *Notes from Small Planets* is my attempt to do just that.

The connecting factor that most stands out to me is cognitive dissonance. In both travel and reading genre fiction, we (and when I say we, understand that this is with an awkward glance towards all the other white men reading this) tend to celebrate the worlds we love without thinking too hard about some of their less pleasant details or implications. Just as a British tourist can enjoy a wildlife trip to southern Africa and decide not to think too hard about the profound, spiteful damage of colonial imperialism, it's all too easy to read Tolkien and brush aside the fact that the concept of Orcs might in fact be pretty racist, or that women don't really get to *do* very much in his work.

If this was an article online, there would already be comments springing up beneath it, angrily defending Tolkien and saying that if I looked closely enough or knew enough context, I'd find it's not racist or sexist at all. But this isn't the point: it should be possible to enjoy a work while still recognising the assumptions and conventions – some of them fairly grim – that it sits amidst.

As such, this book isn't an attempt to cancel anything – I love every genre tackled as much as I love travelling. Indeed, as well as pointing out dodgy foundational issues in genre, this book spends a lot of time just looking at what's straightforwardly, harmlessly *silly* about the archetypes we're familiar with and the clichés we wouldn't change for the world.

And Floyd? Floyd is the guy I try my hardest not to be, both as a reader and as a traveller. He's an extremely comfortable white bloke who likes the sound of his own voice and sees the world as something put there for his consumption. Floyd most definitely thinks he's an enlightened, progressive fellow who enriches the places he visits by his very presence, and he doesn't stop to think too long about anything that benefits him. While I've tried throughout to laugh at Floyd rather than with him, if I've ended up tripping over my own ignorance at any point and emulated him myself, I apologise without reservation.

Eliza, meanwhile, is the sort of reader I'd like to be. She loves these worlds as much as Floyd does (even if she's having to look at them over his authorial shoulder), but she can spot bullshit a mile off and isn't afraid to point it out. I hope that, between them, they've taken you on a good trip.

ACKNOWLEDGEMENTS

I've certainly had something of an odyssey. At various points in its life, this book was a first-person travel narrative, a first-person travel narrative with a *ludicrously* overcomplex SF metanarrative, and a parody guidebook with way too long a section about Barbarians. Now, at last, it's the book it always wanted to be, and for that I can thank Vicky Leech and Natasha Bardon, my endlessly patient and extremely wise editors at Harper Voyager.

Sincere thanks to Terence Caven and to Holly MacDonald for the (literally and figuratively) out-of-this-world design work – getting the first proofs was like a surprise extra Christmas

I also owe a huge debt of thanks to my agent, Jamie Cowen. He's been there more than a few times when I've lost the figurative and literal plot during this project, and been a great friend as I've had to deal with deaths, births, illnesses and wild changes in circumstance. Alongside Jamie, I want to thank Chris Farnell for his companionship and bright ideas, Andrew Skinner for being the brother I never knew I had in Joburg, Philip Ellis for soldiering through many a day at 'the office' with me, and Josh Fortune for his endless enthusiasm and confidence in me.

Thalassa, my thanks to you are wasted since you are a baby, but by the time you get round to reading this, I want you to know how many times you made me smile while I was writing. Mum and Dad, you're a bit too dead to appreciate thanks either, but I know you'd have loved this, and that makes me happy.

Last but emphatically most, thanks to Ashleigh for enduring my working habits and for sacrificing endless hours to discuss the most excruciatingly minor details. As ever, love, the Lizardmen are for you.